Sister WITCH

THE LIFE OF MOLL DYER

Legends of the Family Dyer
Book 1

DAVID W. THOMPSON

ALL RIGHTS RESERVED

Publisher's Note:

This is a work of fiction. All names, characters, places, and events are the work of the author's imagination.

Any resemblance to real persons, places, or events is coincidental.

Solstice Publishing - www.solsticepublishing.com

Sister Witch: The Life of Moll Dyer

David W. Thompson

Dedication

For Ter, my rock who always has my back. It took me a while, but I finally found a keeper! To Andy, Terri and Christy—I hope my encouragement of you can match what you've always shown me. For my Dad who passed along his love of the written word, and my dear Mom. You instilled in me a belief that anything is possible. I love you all.

Finally to Moll Dyer—perhaps now you will stop whispering in my ear?

Chapter One

My name is Mary Dyer, or Moll to my family and friends. If you are either, you are among the few. It is for my child's sake alone that I press my quill to paper. I am not proficient in the keeping of secrets, unlike my family, and as my disgrace is the foundation of my woes, I shall confess all for the integrity of my account. My child will know I was truthful in all things, save one. For five generations, our family called Kinsale in County Cork, Ireland home. Kinsale is a sleepy little fishing village on the River Bandon. For the years I lived there, it was a safe, quiet, familiar place. The men fished the channel, built fishing vessels and farmed the land. The womenfolk cared for their families, prepared meals, mended clothes, and of course kept the ever present peat fires burning. Mother loved the smell of a peat fire, saying it reminded her of leaves burning in the autumn. I found the scent to be sticky sweet, like rotten apples.

I had thought all was well until one day I was eavesdropping on my parents after the bantlings were abed, and my breath caught in my chest!

"The work here is gone, Cathleen, and our savings are all but spent. There's money to be made on the Isle of Wight, ship building and working the docks. There's nothing holding us here now."

"Are we starting this again, Killian? This is our home! Are you not happy here?" Mother asked.

"Happy? I'm as happy as a pig in shit living on scraps! It is my duty as a man to provide for my family! I won't be depending on any man's charity! Every day, there's more and more debt we cannot pay. Indeed, I'm so happy I could dance!" I heard the patter of his shoes dancing to an imaginary tune, and stifled a giggle.

"You needn't curse, or play the fool. There is no lack of food for our table, and the peat fires keep us warm at night." Mother said.

"That's not enough, Cathleen! The Dyers thrived here before the Battle of Kinsale. I swore to my father I'd reclaim our family's glory. It's what you deserve, what our children deserve."

"I know the story, we've all heard it often enough, but you, of all people? You would raise our family among them? You think anything good waits for us among the English?" Mother asked.

"To hell with the English bastards! This is about our family's future. Building their ships is where the money is. I'll go alone if need be to deliver this family. I should be able to return in two or three years with bags full of coin!"

"No, Killian. My place is with you, as is your family's," she answered. "We will follow where you lead, husband."

My mother's swift submissiveness perturbed me, and I snuck back to my bed, unable to swallow the lump in my throat. Mother was right, but she lacked the pluck to argue with my father. We were happy here. Our family called this place home for time immemorial, and I couldn't bear the thought of leaving all I knew. Little of life outside of our village reached us, yet I knew Kinsale to be as fine a land as existed in all of creation. I yearned to see other places, know other lands, but as a visitor, not a permanent resident! Two to three years, my father said!

There were few in our village I called friends, but their family's history entwined with ours for many generations. Their presence in our lives would be missed, but it was being away from the land and the River Bandon that I dreaded.

My little brothers and sisters deserved a better life, it was true. Wealth to ensure their future happiness, a life without want. I suspected if my half-sister Anna had married a lord instead of a farrier, or if she'd settled in County Cork in lieu of Killarney, we'd not be leaving for a foreign land!

If I was ever addle-headed enough to have children, I'd never be so selfish as to force my dreams upon them! Sacrifices had to be made by all, and Da' booked our voyage within a fortnight.

The village of Westcowes, on the Isle of Wight, appeared damp and dirty from the windows of our small cottage. The river Medina was a swollen slothful moat. The small roads were formed of shoe sucking mud, and brown was the predominant color of the town. Mother and I cleaned the floors twice daily and still we felt the constant grit of the land under our feet. We knew no one, and were not allowed outside alone in the rowdy English harbor town, so we seldom felt the sun on our faces. I wanted to stretch my legs and run, experience this new place, but I was a trapped wild hare, forced to wait for the hungry trapper to come end my life. Westcowes was our home now.

Despite my father's grand hopes, England did not prove to be our financial salvation. Every evening, he returned to our tiny cottage with the news that another job fell through. From his whispered conversations with Mother, I knew we were at the end of our meager reserves. The day he finally announced the news of finding work on the docks, my spirits soared. It was not building ships, but it was good money just the same.

Our family was Catholic, pariahs on English soil. It was providential that our church was a short walk away. Sundays were gay outings and presented us with a rare occasion to be outside as a family. I sucked in the air on these jaunts, not that it was sweet and clean like home, but because it was free and unencumbered.

One such day, I tried to be attentive to Father O'Hearn's sermon on the virtues of the missionary service to the New World, and how parents should encourage a renewed calling to the priesthood. The dear man was a fine Christian, I'm sure, but a speaker he was not. Surely there could not be any such callings for a sixteen year old girl.

My attention drifted until I felt my mother's elbow dig into my side. I glanced about to see if there were any witnesses to my lack of devotion, and I spotted the fancy boy James Rogers. Unlike most boys his age, he dressed impeccably with never a hair out of place. I confess his dark good looks drew my notice, but his blatant and hungry stare made my cheeks flush! Why was he even here? From what I knew of his family, they were fervent in their Church of England beliefs. Was he spying on us, on me?

I dropped my eyes to the floor and folded my hands in prayer. The seam that my mother repaired flashed at me from the bodice of my dress, why didn't I wear another? The thickness of the air left my hair in a mess of kinks, and I felt the fresh pimple rising from my forehead like a flagpole! Why couldn't I be more like Anna? I sent a furtive glance back to his pew. James' shirt was soaked through, and I giggled. He probably thought he was hell bound for attending church services among the Papists. My mother rewarded my frivolity with another elbow in the side, and scolded me as we filed from the church.

"Daydreaming and giggling in church? That is no way for a decent woman to behave, Moll!" she whispered, pinching my ear. "What will people think of you, and of our family?"

I stalked away. I was the oldest now with Anna gone, but she spoke to me as if to a child. I entertained no cares about these strangers' thoughts. My eternal judgment was not their sword to wield!

The congregation milled about, engaged in various conversations about the weather, politics and ship building. Mr. Cabot extolled the profits to be made in America, if one was brave enough, but I was not in the mood to listen, even about such grand adventures. I wandered in ever larger circles around the church property. I stopped in front of the apothecary and stood tapping my foot, waiting for my parents to note my impatience.

"Hello Moll." I heard from behind me. "Sleepy were you?"

"No James, I slept quite well last evening, thank you very much."

"The moon didn't keep you awake then?" James laughed.

"What do you - "

"I saw you last night, and you weren't sleeping. The moon was full, and there was no mistaking you!"

My mouth dropped open like a carp's, and I stuttered nonsense like an idiot child.

"What? The full moon…?"

"What would your dear father say if he knew of your wandering the village in the dark of the night, with thieves and scoundrels about? I don't believe he'd be pleased, not at all."

"Nor do I, and I'd ask you not to be running your mouth, but do as you will."

"Moll, you know you've captured my poor heart. Say you'll be my girl and not a word will pass my lips." James' smile looked like a court jester's.

"Your girl is it? When just last week you asked Darcy Quinn about the "skinny red-headed Papish girl"? You didn't even know my name. Now I've captured your heart, have I? Indeed!"

"Ah, your laugh! So endearing, as sweet as a sparrow's trill! Why else would I ask about you then? Surely your beauty captivated me?"

"James, many things I am unsure of, but my beauty, or lack thereof, is not one." A sudden heat washed over my face. What game did he play with me? It was cruel of him to mock me so, but maybe...*could* his compliments be sincere? I thought not, years of young women whispering about my too white skin, and my red kinks of hair did little to reassure me. But *could* it be true? James did not hurt the eyes. If he was only Irish, my father might even be pleased for me to be courting with such a fine young man.

"Moll, but I am speaking truth!"

"Well now, my poor captivated James, perhaps you will pay our family a visit sometime then?"

"I would like nothing better, but maybe until we get to know each other better, you might favor me with your company on one of your moonlight walks? I would act as your protector, your knight in shining armor perhaps?"

"Moll!" My mother yelled.

I knew it was wrong, and part of me tried to snatch back the words even as my flapping tongue set them free. "My walks usually end around eleven, by the old oak tree where the fishermen clean their catch. Perhaps I will see you there."

Chapter Two

The walk home was a blur, my thoughts elsewhere. What was wrong with me? I was sure to be humiliated again. James would forget to come and leave me waiting, or worse, remember and laugh at the folly of my naiveté. I was no child, and knew something of what happens between men and women. My mother made clear her thoughts on the coarseness of the men here, but wasn't James different? He lived in the finest house in the village. He was well liked, and sociable, with many friends in town. His father was prosperous and sought out for advice. Surely he'd do nothing to bring shame to his family?

When we arrived home, Father's younger brother waited at our door. Uncle Sean seemed to know everyone and everywhere, and was the rare adult who spoke to children, even girls, without condescension. Although only a few years older than I, his experiences in life made him mature beyond his years. Father was often fond of saying that Sean's hot temper will put him in the briars one of these days, but I never saw evidence of it. He was my favorite relative.

"Sean, how many years has it been?" Father asked in mid-embrace. "And is that a touch of silver I see in your hair and beard, little brother?"

"Two years I think? But too many for sure, Killian."

Uncle turned to kiss Mother's hand, "Ah Cathleen, you are as lovely as ever." He hugged us each, and turned back to Father.

"Fill us in on your doings, and the happenings in London Town." Father suggested.

"Brother, have you not heard then? I couldn't get out of London fast enough. Tens of thousands dead, several of my friends among them. Open pits filled with bodies foul the air with a stench that brings tears to the eyes. Many Londoners claim it is a Papish plot, if you can believe such ignorance!"

"Moll, come help me prepare the noon meal." My mother said standing, and turned toward the kitchen.

"Times change, but people never do, Brother. But to what do we owe the honor of this grand visit from you?" Father asked.

"Well, I've come to see my beautiful sister-in-law of course!" Uncle said in a voice intended for Mother to hear.

"Ah Sean, how many times must I tell you? She's spoken for, and you'll have to find another!"

"I suppose you could say I've come to say goodbye then. I've gotten up the pluck to seek my fortune in America. It's now or never. I'm not getting any younger as you observed with such sensitivity."

"Surely not? You'd leave all you've worked for?" Father asked. "Where would you go? America is a big land."

"The Maryland colony is growing, and they have enacted religious tolerance laws. Their sot-weed crop is in high demand, bringing top money. It's six weeks until I sail, and I'll stay in the village, but I'll be here for Cathleen's good cooking most every night." Uncle asked.

"No, you'll stay here of course. I look forward to your company, brother, but whatever will all the young women in London do without you?" Father asked.

"Ah yes, the ladies…well…I know it will be difficult for them at first, but they'll forget me by and by."

"Not with your reputation as a beard splitter." Father said.

"I'll not have that black mouth talk in this house!" Mother yelled from the kitchen.

I realized I was staring open mouthed at Uncle, and I pressed my lips together. I hated the thought of him gone from our lives, but envied his adventure. All I knew of this America was that it was very far away. So many things I longed to see and experience for myself, so I dawdled, listening until my mother again called my name.

Cooking, cleaning, and bathing the bantlings: all fell to me as the eldest daughter. While my younger siblings enjoyed lives without care, I knew chores. Perhaps it wasn't due to my being the eldest, as Anna was never encumbered with such things. Her life was once filled with visiting friends and suitors that allowed her little time for the mundane. Her beauty demanded attention.

Father loved us all, but Anna was special to his heart. Perhaps it was because Anna's mother was his first love? He took it hard when Anna married and moved away. I did derive some benefits as the oldest. It is why Mother taught me the healing arts when Anna showed no proclivity or interest. Gathering medicinal herbs in the hills and bogs around home was my favorite, if indeed my only, diversion. It provided me with time alone in the Lord's backyard. Perhaps we fall into the role for which we are suited? For the moment though, being the eldest meant a day of cooking, washing dishes and fetching refreshments to make our guest feel welcome. Any other time, especially for Uncle Sean, I enjoyed doing so, but not so on this day.

***

I looked forward to, and yet dreaded my meeting with James. I questioned the sincerity of his heart. I questioned my own morality. Father would switch me if he found me out. A war raged in my heart, and with the moon full in the sky, at last I made my decision.

I threw on my best dress and slipped from my window like a summer breeze, as I had many nights before. But this night was different! I didn't think of myself as the flirtatious sort, and I knew well the dangers of the night, and of young men. Yet, as I approached the oak, my fingers unfastened the top button of my dress, and I blushed as I pushed up my breasts.

As the giant tree loomed before me, my hopes were dashed. James was not there! I waited, feeling jilted, yet still hesitant to leave in fear of missing his arrival. He might yet come! Moments seemed like hours before I turned my back on the oak and the sickly sweet smell of decaying fish entrails to head for home. James had surely enjoyed a good laugh at my expense, but it was his loss, I thought, deciding he really wasn't that attractive anyway!

"Moll?" James spoke from behind me.

"Well, look who decided to show his face."

"I brought you something, it nearly matches your hair, and the leaves are the color of your eyes." He drew a single red rose from behind his back.

I felt my face blushing, my feelings betrayed. His face ran with sweat on this cool evening. Could it be he was also nervous about meeting me? I felt the skip of my heart, his attentions appeared true. Indeed, such duplicity would be indecent!

"So, will you be my girl?"

"When you begin calling on me, perhaps? It might be that my father and mother would approve of the likes of you."

"And what about you, Moll, would you approve?"

"I'm here."

"Show me, Miss Mary Dyer? Favor your suitor with a small kiss?"

I hesitated, then bent forward, eyes closed, to do as he asked. His lips were hot, like an unhealthy child. It reminded me of biting into a peach, all squishy with tickling fuzz and I couldn't quite stifle a laugh. His lips stiffened, and he pulled away with a jerk.

"Do you think me funny, Moll Dyer?" His face darkened as he wiped the touch of my lips from his mouth.

"Not at all James, I was…"

James pulled me into the shadows of the oak. He was just over eager, I thought, and a bit rough as boys tend to be, but how romantic is a stolen moonlight kiss?

Clumsily, I tripped over his outstretched leg and fell. James jumped on top of me, pulling and yanking at the buttons of my bodice. My hands turned to fists as the fabric gave way! I thought of the many hours Mother spent sewing it, of the fine fabrics saved from better days.

"James, that's enough, stop it!"

I slapped at him, but he ignored me. I pushed him away with my knees, but his weight and strength proved too great. It felt like being pinned under a boulder! I bit his shoulder, and he shoved my head hard into the gravel. I felt his hands on my breasts as he rubbed a warm sticky fluid on me, and I felt myself drifting off, my senses dulled. I tried to focus on something else, anything else, besides what James was doing to me. My vision blurred, I noticed odd shapes and patterns in the fissures of the oak tree's bark. One resembled a raven, intricate in detail as if touched by the chisels of a master woodcarver.

I heard more cloth rip as James pushed himself forward. Can ice burn? I floated back to county Cork, to home, and into the false safety of darkness. My mind wandered far to escape, allowing me little recall, but of what I remember, I will not speak.

When I returned to myself, I was alone. My dress was in ruins, covered in putrid fish blood and entrails, and his filthy seed. I never knew a fish to have so much blood! My hand still clenched a crushed red rose. I threw it at my feet, crushed it beneath my heel and spat on it. I walked home holding my dress together, and keeping to the shadows. I wept until dawn.

By my own folly, I let James hurt me. He was a predator of the weak and foolish, and I was both.

Chapter Three

Mother warned me that men possess uncontrollable desires. Wasn't it a Christian woman's responsibility not to tempt them? Was what happened my fault then? Only a harlot would meet a strange man on those dark streets! I recalled undoing the top buttons of my dress, to lure him to me like a fisherman using bait. I gave James reason to question my virtue!

No, no, no! Was James not himself a Christian? Did the accident of being born masculine relieve him of moral dictates? I wanted him to find me attractive it was true, but I didn't want to be with him! I said no! It was not my fault. James was a bastard from hell! A loving God would not hold me accountable for what happened. He knew the guilty party, although I suspect James had a stronger affinity with the devil. High born blood provided no assurance of nobility.

I kept a watch for him through our cottage window. He was not in church the following Sunday, nor the next. I paused for a moment at the door of our church when first entering, fearful God might turn me to ash, but I proceeded safely, without incident. I didn't know what I might say or do when I next faced him, although I considered a dozen different malicious scenes, and spent hours plotting my revenge.

A woman's reputation shatters easily, and I planned to tell no one what happened. In a matter of weeks, however, I missed my woman's time. I was left with no recourse. I sat with our mother at the kitchen table, rubbing its wooden surface, and tracing my fingertips along its many cracks. I told her everything amid a blubbering of tears.

"Moll, what have you done? What are we to do? Does this James love you? Has he spoken of marriage?"

Mother liked the answers to these questions as little as did I.

After our supper, Mother stood as we cleared the table.

"Children, please excuse yourselves, your father and I have something to discuss."

I watched as they filed from the kitchen whispering to one another.

"You too, Moll." Mother said.

I tried not to listen, but some words I could not help but hear. Everyone in the house heard "rape" and "bastard" shouted over and over again. My sweet little brother Patrick asked me what a whore might be, but I couldn't summon the strength to think up even a small lie, so I said nothing.

"Don't cry Moll, I didn't mean no harm!" He comforted me with a hug, the poor innocent lad.

The slamming of the front door was like a slap in my face as my father stormed from the house. I feared the hinges would not hold! Did his anger burn at me or at James? It was the first time I felt frightened in my own home.

Uncle Sean returned from his evening walk, and Mother engaged him in a whispered conversation. I heard a chair slide across the floor, and Uncle said, "I'll baste the little bastard's arse and teach him a thing or two!"

"Hush now, Sean! The children will hear. We will wait for Killian's return."

From the room I shared with my sisters, I sat with my hands folded until I heard Father stumble at the door, muttering obscenities under his breath.

"Where have you been, husband? We were worried." Mother asked.

"Damn well you know, woman. I paid a visit to the home of this James."

"Have you been drinking as well?"

"Aye, that I have, and who could blame a man?"

The kitchen door thumped closed, and their voices became muffled. I strained to hear as the other children slept the sleep of innocents. There was more talk of whores and bastards, and of money paid. Father's voice got louder.

"Love… indeed, love is it? The lout could care less!" Then, Father spoke of my midnight walks in the streets! Under the circumstances, it should have been of small consequence, but I could only think of James betraying my trust yet again.

"Where did we go wrong?" Father wailed. "What are we to do?"

Uncle spoke in a whisper, perhaps to calm our father. He mentioned a great-aunt Nora, a name I never heard mentioned before. He asked about money, spoke of voyages, and the new life he was to begin. The New World was Uncle's favorite subject, but it puzzled me that he spoke of such things at a time like this?

For a good hour, the three of them argued and plotted about "what was to be done about Moll." Strain as I might, I could hear little, and I fell into a fitful sleep. I dreamt of being lost in a dark wood as evil things chased me. No matter how fast I ran, I could not outdistance them. I still felt them on my trail when a light knocking at my door jerked me awake. Mother spoke my name in a soft voice.

"Moll, please come out now." It seemed I was to be informed of my fate.

We sat at the table with the men. Father stared at the floor as if his head bore too much weight to lift it from his chest. His eyes were swollen, and his face colored the red of a bilberry bloom. He looked so old, so frail, and tears welled up in my eyes.

"Moll, we have discussed this… this situation, and I spoke with Abel Rogers, the father of… that boy. The story

James told us is far different from yours, as you might expect."

"Did he deny what he did to me?" I asked.

"He did, said there was no truth to it at all. He confessed that he agreed to meet you at the fish cleaning tree, but swore he fell asleep and never ventured there. He also says you have been frequenting the docks most every night seeking male companionship! Is this true?" he asked.

"Father, I have taken walks at night, but I didn't..."

My father broke into tears and a sob ripped from his chest. It was a sight and sound unfamiliar to me. All this pain I wrought!

"You are not the first young woman to find yourself in this situation, Moll." Uncle soothed. "Nowadays, there are other avenues to consider however. Ways that will not paint you as a loose woman or bring shame to your family."

"What is your advice, Uncle?"

Uncle Sean glanced at mother and father, and continued when they did not.

"We discussed two possibilities. You have an aunt who lives in Whitegate, County Clare. She found herself in your situation many years ago. We need to ask, but I have every confidence in Aunt Nora taking you on until after..."

"Thank you Uncle, but I do not wish to be beholden to anyone, especially a stranger. I'm a grown woman and..."

"Stranger? She's my father's sister!" Father shouted. "And a grown woman now- is that what you are?" He slammed his fists on the table, and Uncle's clay pipe flew across the room, smashing to pieces on the floor. Mother stood as the babies began to wail.

"What is the second choice, Uncle?" I asked, with no strength in my trembling voice.

"The other choice is to sail with me to the New World on tomorrow's tide."

"There is no third choice then? Can I not return to Kinsale? I can sell herbs, and I'm a fair seamstress as well. The men always rip their clothing on the docks."

"No Moll," our mother answered from the doorway, baby Aiden in her arms. "Think of your reputation and your family's, and consider these wee ones. We decided these are the best choices for you and for everyone. Abel Rogers at least agreed to provide some funds to help you along. You must choose."

My tongue caught in my throat and my mouth was as dry and crusty as week old bread. It was just as well, I didn't know the words to say. I was torn between the anger coloring my face, and my love of family and home.

"I'll decide and be ready in the morning, no matter my decision." I stood and turned to leave. I did not wish to look at, or speak to any of them.

"That's a good idea, Moll." Mother said, rubbing my shoulder. "It is a big decision, and not one to be taken lightly," Mother's tears followed my father's lead, "but before you sleep, we need to have a woman to woman talk."

"More talk?" I asked, but nodded.

"Moll, if you decide to sail with me, and I hope that you do, we need to be off at first light. Think of it as going on an adventure, the two of us. I know how dear County Cork is to your heart, but I also know you long to see more of the world." Uncle Sean said.

Uncle's words made me feel welcome, and I tried to smile, but I knew the look on my mother's face. The left side of her lip curled, as the right side dropped and her brow knitted in distress.

"What of our home, and our family?" I asked.

"I'll not lie to you Moll. The colony of Maryland is far away. It requires nearly a year's wages to make the crossing. I believe they will be all but lost to you." Uncle looked down at his hands.

"I'll decide tonight." I bowed my head and followed my mother to her sewing room, the room forbidden to all of us as children. My mother never taught me anything but the simplest of stitches, although she enjoyed it so much. Anna never spoke of what happened when she and mother shared time there, as if it was some great secret I was unworthy to share. In the old country, when Mrs. Payne passed away, I hoped Mother would invite me to join their weekly sewing circle. Instead, Mother found a new friend, a Mrs. Boyle, to join them. Entry to her sewing room was a rite of passage for me. It meant Mother accepted me as a woman, and all it took was getting raped!

"I have things to show you, Moll. I've been negligent in your education, but you know a lot more than you think. The threads just need to be pulled together."

When the door of the dark room opened, the sweet spicy smell of drying plants massaged my nose. Unrecognizable, yet vaguely familiar symbols were painted on the walls. A world I didn't know inhabited that room, but even more, what I learned opened the door to my Mother, a stranger to me. My family's secrets were revealed. It was many hours before I went to bed, confused and exhausted.

Chapter Four

I tossed about on my bed, like a big codfish flopping on a pier. I wondered which way to throw my body, and was unable to make up my mind. What might the New World hold for me? Uncle seemed genuine in his offer to accompany him. Aunt Nora was a name I did not know. Was she a family outcast? Was Whitegate another prison in waiting?

I peered out the window, and resolved to take one last walk. What was the worst that could happen now? Maybe I'd be ambushed for the change in my dress pockets and left dying in a ditch? It wouldn't matter.

All I loved was being ripped away from me. All that I was, denied me. My family deserted me, did not believe me, and cast me as a whore! They disowned me and tossed me to my fate. At least they'd have one less mouth to feed. Love and family were fleeting and expedient, was either worth the price we must pay?

I walked with no planned destination in mind, other than a cleared head, but habit led me back to where it all started. I was horrified to see where my feet had carried me, but there was no denying the huge oak tree looming before me. I surveyed the area to ensure I was alone. I heard no footsteps, no sound of movement, and no shadows passed near. I rubbed the outline on the oak tree's bark, surprised to see it did indeed look like a raven. I had thought it a welcomed distraction conjured by my tormented mind.

I sat at the base of the old tree and cried. What was I to do? My chest squeezed and tightened until a painful sob burst free, then the tightness built up again, over and over until there were no tears left to shed.

Dawn drew near, and my decision remained unresolved. I felt stupid and indecisive, but I knew nothing of Aunt Nora or Whitegate, and even less of America. Mother was right, the little ones deserved to grow up unblemished by my shame, but how was I to choose? A cold finger ran down my back. Was someone watching me?

"Dearest Moll, you came back for more, did you?"

I cringed against the tree's trunk and turned to see James step from the shadows.

"What do you want, James Rogers? Haven't you done enough already? Get out of my sight, you bastard!"

"Now Moll, name calling after all we've been to each other? How have you been? I heard you are going on a trip soon? You always wanted to travel, didn't you?"

I turned my back on him and began to walk away, not too fast, or he might sense my fear. I'd not have him thinking me frightened by the likes of him, but the thumping of my heart sounded like a fisherman cleaning his anchor against his boat's gunwales, and I was sure he heard it.

"Wait Moll, I won't hurt you."

I didn't answer, and continued my brisk walk. His steps moved faster behind me, and my head was snapped back by the hair as he reached me. I kicked at him and screamed, but again I found myself trapped under the canopy of that fateful tree.

"Stop it, damn it, James!" I slapped at his hands to free my hair.

"The boy has to be sure it took, doesn't he?" James said in a whispered voice, and fumbled at the buttons on the front of my dress. I threw up my leg and kneed him in the groin. "Raamh!" He growled, and hunched over releasing me.

"I'm warning you. Stay away from me. I'll not be your day's catch!"

James recovered, and smiled his most trusting, and loathsome smile. "You win, Moll." He stuck out his hand to make peace, but I turned my face away from him. From the corner of my eye, I saw the swing of his fist. I tried to duck, but the impact caught the side of my head, and bursts of light distorted my vision. I fell to my knees. "Warning me, are you Moll? I know why you came here. Just quit pretending!"

My head whirled as I fought back, and something sharp pricked my hand. Its shape was familiar enough, and I bit my lip to restrain a smile as I slid it under me. James pinned my elbows under his knees and pulled again at the top of my dress. I heard buttons pop and felt myself exposed to the night air.

"Help! You bastard! Someone help!" I looked toward the old oak hoping for a savior to appear beyond its trunk. The moonlight glowed on the raven figure with a peculiar light.

"Relax Moll, and it will be easier for you, but it's fun for me either way."

I bit my lip and forced my muscles to relax. "Do as you will." I reached beneath me and grabbed the hilt.

My spittle landed on his cheek, and James shifted his weight to wipe it away. He drew back to strike me, and I twisted sideways and thrust upwards with the fisherman's knife. The rusty old blade met no resistance as it glided into his flesh, as easy as gutting a fish.

James squealed like a lamb at slaughter, and hot sticky blood filled my hand. I thought it strange, so unlike the cold watery entrails of a cod. A poppy colored stain bloomed between his legs.

I moved as in a dream, but felt good, strong, in control. James' eyes grew large and dim, much like a squid's, unsure of what had happened. He looked down at himself, and understanding dawned.

"You bitch! Look what you did to the boy!" James yelled. He held the crotch of his breeches, stood and took a shaky step backwards.

""The boy"? It's no better than you deserve! I hope you rot in hell." I crawled backwards away from him.

James regained his balance, and stumbled towards me again. "Stay away from me James!" I warned, brandishing the blade.

He lunged and I stepped to the left, but he snagged my collar. I heard another tear as I turned and swung the knife, slashing his face. James screamed and fell to his knees, unsure of which part of himself to hold onto. I turned and ran home… my decision made.

Chapter Five

It was either fate or divine providence that the merchant ship set sail for the Maryland colony that afternoon. The other children would not accompany us to the docks, so I said hasty goodbyes to them, and Father whisked me from our home.

Uncle said our ship was one of the finest vessels in all of England, although I knew little of this new place. Her name was the Mary Regina, and she carried four masts with square rigging. With multiple decks below, she carried 120 tons of cargo. Uncle seemed impressed describing her, but Father said she was just a foreign galleon, and little more than a low riding carrack built for speed.

I glanced hastily at the shoreline, and the ever hungry seagulls while father inspected the ship's lines, making sure the caulking was fresh. A young lad hawking newspapers announced the bloody murder of a young woman nearby. It seemed two lives had ended.

"Always remember where you came from Moll," Father said as he hugged me goodbye. His eyes did not meet mine.

Mother embraced me in turn, and whispered, "you've learned what you need to know for now. Do not forget who and what you are. I know your heart is true, and we will meet again." She held me at arm's length, handed over two leather bound books, and favored me with a wink. "These are my mother's memories and my own. You start your own story, and write it down so you do not forget!" With the goodbyes said, Uncle tugged at my arm to usher me on board.

I opened the hatch to go below to the 'tween deck, and I looked back to shore, found my parents and returned their waves goodbye. For a moment, I thought I saw James standing behind them. He did not wave, but glared at me as if I was cattle dung under his feet. I knew my eyes were playing tricks on me. James would not be in any condition to be there, if indeed fate proved so cruel that he survived at all. When I blinked, he was gone.

"Hurry along then," Uncle said with a poke. "We must claim our spaces and stow our baggage." He led the way to our quarters below deck.

Our sleeping spaces were wooden boxes, perhaps five feet long. They were designed to keep us from falling out during the ship's dips and rolls. I needed to curl up to fit in, and my poor uncle's legs dangled over the end. The other passengers had already claimed most of the spaces, but we were lucky to find a pair of bunks side by side.

Crates of fruits and vegetables, bags of flour, dried beans, salted meat in barrels, and large casks of fresh water and rum stood stacked and secured for everyone's consumption on the trip. There was some minimal bedding, and cobbled together furniture, seeds for planting, and farm animals and guns bound for the colony, along with glass beads and small axes for trade with the wild natives there.

Uncle Sean tugged at my elbow to draw me away from the other cabin occupants, and whispered in my ear.

"If by chance you are asked, only say that your husband perished from the sickness in London while away on business. If anyone asks about me, don't mention that I lived there at all. Someone might fear I carry the disease. Agreed?"

"Uncle, I have great respect for you, and appreciate your help, but you needn't hold my hand. We are partners, and I will pull my weight. I won't be needing help from anyone. " I felt ungrateful, and also stupid that I'd not devised such a simple lie on my own.

He lifted one eyebrow and stared at me for a moment, then nodded his head. "Just be thankful the child will not come during our passage. The voyage will be hard enough for you. It would be far worse if we were bobbing about the ocean when your labors began."

One of the seamen poked his head in the door. "Are all of your parties aboard? Are your belongings secured?"

Our cabin mates confirmed both. I sighed with relief when the floor of the cabin shifted, and knew the ship now floated free of its berth. We climbed to the main deck as the ship slipped away. I exhaled deeply, noticing no sheriff's men waiting to impede the progress of a murderess.

A week passed with fair seas and a following wind. The sails remained full as they spirited us on our way. Nothing was as easy shipboard as on dry land. Trying to sleep with the rolling of the waves, and in the cramped cradles proved challenging. Sometimes the ship swayed beneath our feet and I felt like a young child taking her first steps. I reminded myself the passage was the means to our new life in a fresh unspoiled paradise. I considered it a small price to pay to get a rare second chance at life!

Each family group received braziers to cook their meals, and I did so for us. Uncle apologized, but said his cooking skills left a lot to be desired. Some mornings the tossing of the ship made food the last thing on our minds, and I'd lose my supper of the night before. Other passengers in our cabin noted my distress and assured me that seasickness was not uncommon, though I suspected another cause.

The passengers were pressed together like jarred fish, forced to share even the most private of moments. I met a young woman named Elizabeth Coombs. She was not the sort of girl I would have sought out to befriend. Her wavy hair was the yellow of autumn maple leaves, and a face as you'd see only in a painting. Clear skinned, with a pert little nose and blue eyes that sparkled like a trout stream when she laughed.

Other "fancy girls", far less perfect than Elizabeth, mocked me for too many years. They giggled behind their hands when asking when I would marry, or who was courting me. The friendlier girls made trite suggestions, that I pay more attention to my appearance, or I not be so picky in a suitor. It wasn't as if I chased young men away!

They so admired themselves for what God gave them for free. But, as Father said, "of those to whom God gives much, he expects much in return."

I imagined Elizabeth was different than they were, if for no other reason than the man she married. It wasn't that Gideon was horrible to look at. He was tall and lanky with straight mousy hair, moon pale skin with freckles, and a hatchet nose. He was not the prize Elizabeth could win with no more than a wink of her eye. Except for his hair, he could pass for my brother.

Surprisingly, it was Elizabeth who sought me out to be her friend. Every day, she found me on the deck, or approached me at my bunk to chatter. She won me over with her quick earnest smile, and compassionate nature, as she did everyone on board. I thought it grand to start life in a new land with a new friend.

Elizabeth's maiden name was Bowles, and she was born in Croom, County Limerick. Our families were practically neighbors in Ireland, although she knew little of life near the sea.

Her dowry paid for their passage, and her Uncle William in Maryland owned lands for them to plant. She was with child, although no one, not even Elizabeth, knew I shared her condition.

Her belly was already swollen and I thought of Uncle's admonition about births at sea. Her child was expected within two months, and I prayed the baby would not be early, nor the ship late! Gideon hoped for a boy. Strong sons were important in the New World, he said.

"Girls work as hard as any young lad, husband!" Elizabeth informed him with a laugh.

On day nine, our fortunes changed, and the winds died. The sails went limp and the only movement on board was the sailors shifting and adjusting rigging to catch any existing breeze. Day ten and eleven were much the same. It was hard seeing our position in the great ocean remain unchanged for days at a time.

On the afternoon of the twelfth day, thunderheads appeared in the east and the men prepared for the worst. They checked the tie downs on the cargo, and secured anew. The captain ordered all of the braziers extinguished. We ate our meals cold and raw. Just before dusk, the winds picked up.

"Heave to!" Captain Taylor ordered. "Batten the hatches!"

The crew adjusted the rigging to make the sails work against one another to maintain the ship's position. They turned the rudder to keep the ship pointed into the wind on our new tack, and the passengers huddled below decks to ride out the storm.

A sharp boom of thunder shook the timbers of the ship, and forewarned us of what was to come. When the rocking of the ship increased, I fell over one of the small tables. Uncle suggested we confine ourselves to our cradle boxes for the duration of the storm. The waves tossed us to and fro like a child's leather ball. Nauseous, and unable to walk to the ship's head, I lost my supper, soiling my clothing and bed. I was the first to do so, but not the last, and soon the sounds of vomiting echoed mine. The sour smell in the sealed cabin was unpleasant indeed.

Water splashed in with every downward dip of the ship, and drenched the passenger's beds closest to the hull. In the center of the cabin, Uncle and I were spared the constant dousing.

How long this rolling of the ship continued, I cannot say. Day was as night with nothing to mark the passage of time. Finally, the sound of the crew scurrying above on the main deck, and the stillness of the sea, announced the storm's passing.

I found Elizabeth, who had been among those to be doused sopping wet, and we climbed topside to greet the sun and the new day. The ocean lay smooth as glass, and thin misty clouds danced overhead. If not for the arching rainbow, the storm might not have happened.

Uncle met us and we asked what news there was.

"Nothing promising, my ladies," he bowed his head in jest. "The Captain says the storm pushed us far from our former position. He estimates we lost as much as five days' time!"

I felt the slight breeze moving my hair, and knew it would do little to make up our lost progress.

One of the crew asked us to go below until the sails were set to best advantage. This was disheartening after the length of time we'd already spent in the dark confines below, but we did as we were told.

We cleaned our areas, swept and mopped our portions of the deck, and still the stale sour odor remained. We laughed, breathing through kerchiefs and wrinkled noses while playing a game of draughts (that Elizabeth won). There was little else to entertain us on the ship, but we passed the days in merriment and laughter as bantlings might!

After a day and night of stagnant seas, the ocean and the winds began to favor our progress. The passengers and crew started smiling, joking with each other again, and the ocean air smelled sweet. The fair seas continued for two weeks, and we crossed the mid-point of our voyage. It was day thirty one.

The following morning, Elizabeth met me on the main deck. She seemed distressed, and I asked if she felt ill.

"Moll, I am moving slowly this morning. My young one kept me awake most the night." She rubbed her stomach.

"I have something that might help." I said, as I brewed the mint tea, saying the words Mother taught me.

"What are you mumbling about, Moll?"

"It is how I was taught, what the ancients said to give the tea more potency, but we must use it sparingly," I said. "I brought little along, and much of the passage remains."

Beth (as Elizabeth is addressed by her family) looked at me and frowned. "Moll, you often suffer from this complaint. Is it possible you are…?"

I said nothing and served the tea.

"Perhaps we should share this?" She handed the cup back to me.

I took the first sip, wondering if I dared share my secret with her. I didn't want to tell her Uncle's lie, friends don't lie to one another, but I feared her opinion of me would change if she knew.

"I'm scared," she said, "is it normal to have this sickness so late in one's time? Is my baby all right?"

"I helped my mother with the birthing of a few babies. She says the stomach sickness is usually in the beginning, but sometimes happens later on as well. Your baby will be fine, don't worry!"

Elizabeth began to cry, whether from concern or relief I didn't know, but I drew her head to my chest.

"There now, don't fret. I promise to take good care of you, you'll see."

"It's all been so fast, Moll. One day I was a child, and suddenly I was Gideon's wife. Now I am carrying a child and going to live in a strange far-away land. I may never see my family again. It seems like yesterday my only worry was besting my friends at a game of five stones."

Tears seeped from her eyes.

"Beth, you have a fine husband. Your family obtained headrights for land for you, and promised a small cottage for you before you even land. Your baby will share a new world with you, with you and your new best friend, of course. What more could a woman ask for? I wish my future looked so grand by half. I don't know what we will do, or even where we will stay until we get settled! Consider yourself blessed, dear friend."

She stifled a sob and shook her head. "Gideon will hate the baby if it's a girl. I know he will, and he will hate me too. He wants a boy to help him on the farm, and to carry on his family name."

"That is not the Gideon I know, and you know better as well! He will be proud of his little one, boy or girl." Her face relaxed, as she recognized the truth of my words. "Of course, we can always send the baby back where it came from!"

She laughed, and I thought it wise to keep my secret for now. My friend carried enough worries of her own. The tiniest bump in my belly told me I had plenty of time before any stories needed telling. I ate less to postpone that inevitable day for as long as possible.

Chapter Six

"I spoke to Gideon about you last night." Beth told me a few days later.

"The newlyweds run out of things to chatter about already?"

"Not at all, I told him what you said, about him feeling proud no matter what our child is. He hugged me tight and called me his silly beautiful wife. He said he cherishes our child, and will do anything to make us happy."

"Anyone can see it in Gideon's eyes when he looks at you, but he's right, you are silly."

"I just needed him to say it, but that's not all we talked about. Gideon knows how close we are, and about the special tea you make to quiet my stomach."

"Oh, everyone knows about mint tea, Beth."

"Just let me finish before I lose my pluck, Moll. Gideon and I will have a home, and you and your uncle will not, and I'm sure we would at least have a dry place for you to sleep. We wondered if you, both of you, well…if you would consent to stay with us. Maybe until your house is built? You could help me with the baby and the chores. It would be fun…"

I felt a surge of gratitude to Beth and wrapped both arms around her in a hug. It was such a wonderful feeling, being wanted! Is there a better thing? I wiped my eyes as I held her.

"Beth, what a generous offer, but I did not intend to impose upon you. I should not have spoken of our immediate prospects in the colony!"

"Not at all, Moll, and I am pleased you did. What are friends for if not to help each other? This would be so perfect for all of us!"

"I will speak to Uncle then. As for me, I'd like nothing better, but I won't leave poor Uncle to fend for himself. He would die of starvation on his own cooking. Are you sure we wouldn't be intruding? You are but newly married!"

"Gideon said it would be a matter of great relief to him knowing we'd be together while he worked the tobacco fields. There are wild savages there you know."

I left soon after to seek out Uncle Sean, and I found him surveying the ocean from on deck. I spoke of Beth's offer, but he was less positive about the arrangement.

Holding out his palms to me, he said. "With the work of these hands, I've never been beholden to any man. I built mansions in London, and I can surely build us one small house in short order."

Shamefully, and without thought, my lips bunched up in a pout like a little girl. Uncle smiled and shook his head, "How much does this mean to you, Moll?"

"It would mean a lot to me. Beth and Gideon are the only friends I have in the colony."

Uncle Sean shook his head again and his lips pinched together.

"I'll not be as hard-headed as my brother. It is to be understood that we pull our own weight, and as soon as the house is up, we move on to our own farm. On your honor, can I have your hand on that?" He stuck out his hand, and I pulled it aside and hugged him fiercely.

"Of course! Thank you for understanding, Uncle!"

I danced over to Gideon and Beth's side of the cabin to share the news, but found Beth asleep. Gideon said she was not feeling well and looked worried. I decided my news could wait for morning, not knowing the horror the new day would bring.

Chapter Seven

Day forty-five hadn't yet dawned when a noise woke me. I quickly washed with the provided salt water, and again heard the small cry in the dark cabin. It sounded to be near Beth, and I hurried there. Several men and women clustered around her bunk, including Gideon and the ship's captain.

"How early is she then?" The captain asked.

"Nearly a month," Gideon answered, as Beth gave a painful cry.

"You must do something, Captain," Gideon said.

"I will do what I can with no ship's doctor, but being a midwife is not something I've done before, nor should a man. I'll look in the ship's apothecary to see if we have any powders for pain."

"Moll?" Beth moaned.

The captain and the other men made a space for me, noticing me for the first time.

"I hurt, Moll. I think my baby wants to come now."

"How long has this been happening?" I asked in my calmest voice.

"All night," Gideon replied, "it started right after I saw you, and it's getting worse."

"You should have come for me sooner, Gideon. It's still too early, we need to stop the labor." I took Beth's hand.

"Do you know something of midwifery, girl?" The captain asked.

"My mother was the midwife in our village. I helped, but never did so on my own."

"Set to it then. I will see what supplies we have."

"Beth, don't worry. It will be fine."

"Promise?"

I squeezed her hand in answer, and retreated to my own bunk area. I searched my baggage, and cursed myself for not spending more time organizing my medicinals. At last I found the packet of ground nettle leaves. Uncle lit the brazier and I placed the kettle to boil.

"Tea is all you have Moll?" Gideon said from behind me. "She's in pain and I think the baby is coming!"

"Go back to Beth, Gideon. She needs you. Ask one of the crew to find a cask of wine, red wine if they have it. Citrons! Uncle, are there any citrons aboard? No, no, not citrons, limes, they may have limes for scurvy. Uncle, please go find some limes!"

A crewman came back with the wine just as the tea reached its strongest color. I mixed them together and hurried to Beth.

"Drink this, it will help."

"Not sharing with me…?"

"Not this time. It's all for you and the baby." I gave the men a look, and they scurried off while I pulled aside her bedclothes to check on the baby's progress. I hoped we weren't too late.

Beth looked at me through hooded eyes. Her voice was small and her color poor.

"This will help… my baby?" Beth asked. I nodded.

She tried to sip the fluid, but most of it poured out of the side of her mouth. I told Gideon she didn't get enough, and I ran to make more. As the water for the fresh batch of tea began to simmer, Beth screamed.

"It's coming, the baby is coming."

"Uncle, mix this with the wine." I said, and rushed back to her side. I checked her again. I could feel the baby's head had moved down! The men congregated at the farthest side of the cabin, and stared at the deck, the walls, anything except Beth's bed.

"Gideon, we can't stop it now, the baby is coming."

Beth greeted the announcement with another scream that brought tears to my eyes.

"Moll and I are here, Beth." Gideon brushed the hair from her eyes.

The captain arrived with some powders for the pain and a dried up lime.

Beth's exertions left her soaked, again she screamed. She pushed and the baby's head broke free. Beth screamed and pushed, screamed and pushed, and the shoulders followed the head.

"It's a girl!" Gideon yelled with joy a moment later, and the cabin began to clap, but something wasn't right. The baby did not move, and I tapped her backside. I saw no sign of movement, no change of color. I ran my finger inside of her mouth, but found no obstructions. I blew a strong breath into the baby's mouth, again, and again, and again.

"What's wrong? Shouldn't she be crying?" Gideon asked.

"My baby, what's wrong with my baby?" Beth asked. Her voice was weak, but she squeezed my hand so hard I felt my knuckles crack.

"Stop Beth, wait. I don't know yet." I pulled my hand away, but my voice betrayed my thoughts, and Beth began to sob.

I slapped the baby's behind again, tried more breaths into her mouth, over and over again until my vision blurred… The captain pulled me away.

"Enough, stop." He said. "There's nothing more to be done."

"No, no, no, nonono!" I cried. The captain squeezed my shoulder hard, and I winced.

"Stop, you're upsetting the mother. You've done what you could do." Beth wept, with her face the color of chalk, and pulled the stillborn child to her nipple.

Gideon and I tried to calm her, but nothing we did or said helped. At last, exhaustion and grief overcame her, and she slept with her arms wrapped around her baby. Even in sleep, her tears flowed like a stream.

In the night, they took the baby away. Uncle told me they wrapped her in weighted cloth and tossed her over the side. Such was the custom he said.

Chapter Eight

Many tears were shed during the following days. Beth and Gideon walked hand in hand, lost to everyone as if in a dream. Some days they didn't get up from their cradle bunks at all. I tried to hide my own feelings of pain and guilt, but their world was colored by pain and they saw nothing else.

"Give them time and space." Uncle said. "Only time, and not your teas, can cure their ache."

A week passed with little change until one morning I woke to see Beth sitting by my bed.

"Want to take a walk and talk?" she asked.

I led her topside in the hope the fresh ocean breezes and the sun's warmth would help to heal her heart. I could sense the crew watching her, and I'm sure she also felt their eyes.

We spoke of little things, as children might, of boys we knew at home and games we played. She told me how she met Gideon while hunting for mushrooms, and it was the first thing they discovered they had in common.

"Ask Gideon about the New World, and I'll bet he says something about mushrooms! He heard the forest canopies were so large and shaded that mushrooms grew everywhere."

"Was Gideon your first love, Beth? When did you know you loved him?"

"Moll, I knew right away Gideon was the one for me, and I knew he felt the same. Our parents thought we were too young, but many are married far younger than we were. I think my parents' objection was I knew so few young men, but why would I waste time on them if I wasn't interested? As for my father, he just wasn't ready for his baby girl to become a married woman, no matter who the man was." Here Beth's voice caught in her throat and her eyes misted, but no tears did she shed.

"Did they ever change their minds, Beth?"

She laughed. "One night after we'd been seeing each other for about two months, Gideon showed up and asked to speak to my father alone. I don't know everything they said, except what little Gideon related later. He told my father how much he loved me, and that he would do anything, whatever it took, to make me happy. He said he was a man of limited means, but his love and respect for me would make him a far better husband than any of the foolish, vain, wealthy boys my parents lobbied for. I guess it worked because instead of telling me why we shouldn't wed, they began to talk about grandchildren."

Beth wiped her face with the back of her hand and took a deep breath. "Gideon is a bit overzealous in his faith, but he captured my heart and soul. I know I will never want another. But now you, what brought you the most joy in your life? I've never heard you speak of boyfriends? I'd like nothing more than hearing a story with a happy ending."

I thought hard for something to tell her, something spiritual with a sense of continuity and renewal.

"I have no love story to relate," I said, "but I do have a strange experience. When I was young, my mother told us of a place called the Druid's Altar. She said fine Christians we might be, but much of our knowledge came from those ancient ones. The plants she'd taught me and the words to say are from them. "Do not mock them," she warned me. Father would give her his look of amused impatience, his eyes pointed at the heavens with one eyebrow lifted just so, but he agreed to take us there.

When we crossed the hayfield leading to the altar, we saw a circle of boulders as high as my head, and perhaps 10 yards across. I thought if someone took the time to carve, move and embed them there, it must have great significance to them.

When I stepped into the circle's center, I shivered like the time Connor Donovan dropped an icicle down my dress. My eyesight became strange, and for a moment the very ground appeared to spin. I knelt in fear of falling, and the ground felt like it was not of this world, like I knelt before God instead of rocks.

I wondered who these people were who carved the boulders, and what purpose it served them. Were the old ones honoring their God or their dead? I sensed something important there, something I needed to learn, but the cold sandstone slabs did not give up any secrets, only the feeling of supreme peace."

"Why was it built then? Does anyone know? And tell me more about this Connor lad!" Beth laughed.

"Father said no one knew for sure why it was built or even when. He said they were ancient even in in his Great Grandfather's time, and Connor was a supreme brat."

I couldn't explain to Beth the emotion as I stood in the circle. A graveyard, a very old church or even a deep ancient glade in the woods might come close. It felt sad and heroic at the same moment, and welcoming. It evoked both solitude and community, and as I stood there, I wondered how a spot of ground could be all of those things?

Mother stepped over to me and whispered, "It is all that," as if she knew my thoughts. I didn't dare share that part with Beth. She'd think my mind touched.

Chapter Nine

After our conversation, Beth allowed herself ever fewer such moments, and then she crept back into her dark shell. I prayed for her comfort even as I allowed her time to grieve. During the day I often walked past their side of the cabin in the hope of catching a smile on her face, or at least seeing them consoling each other in their pain, but they seemed shut off even to one another now.

Uncle reassured me I did everything possible for her.

"You were amazing that day, do not sell your efforts short. I was proud of how you took charge, and for the compassion you showed for your friends. The whole ship speaks of your courage and resolve. You should be comforted in that knowledge."

"Her child died! These are my dearest friends and I was powerless to help, both then and now."

"The child was dead when it was born, Moll. You are an amazing woman, but you do not have power over life and death. Give them time, it is the only cure. In but a few days' time, we should land at the Maryland colony. Things will improve then, you'll see. We will have much to do, and little time for remembering."

I tried to do as Uncle suggested, but every day my friends slipped further away from me, and from life. Night overcame another day, but my inner voice would not be silenced.

When at last I slumbered, the old sinister dream filled my head. Once again men chased me through strange unknown woods, gaining on me with every step. The dogs bayed close on my heels. I glanced over my shoulder as I ran, and saw that one of the men in the front of the pack limped as he ran.

A heavy amulet carved from horn or bone flapped at my chest, but it was unlike anything I owned.

I heard Beth's voice in my head. "Run Moll, run!" she said.

On and on my legs pushed me forward until I came upon a familiar small stream crossing. Dashing across, and jumping up the bank from the cold water, I glared behind me. Whirling around to continue my flight, the limping man jumped from behind a large pine. His gun aimed between my eyes. A long jagged scar ran from above his eye to just under his chin. I thought myself rid of him, and had scrubbed all thoughts of him from my conscious mind, but still James haunted my dreams!

In the shadows stood another man whose features I couldn't see. He was tall and thin, but friend or foe?

"There's no place to hide that we can't find you. Where are you now, Moll? I'm coming for you, witch." He said, and squeezed the trigger. The blast from the gun blew me backwards, and out of the dream.

Awake on the floor beside my bed, I shook the cobwebs from my mind. I heard the sound of many booted feet on the deck above me.

"Man overboard!" Was I still dreaming?

"We need ropes, torches, now! Man overboard!"

I raced to the main deck where chaos reigned. Men and women ran in every direction, unsure where to look or what had happened.

"Circle the edge of the main deck, every other man grab a torch. Ropes, we need ropes!" The captain ordered.

"What the hell happened here?" He asked one of the crew.

"I don't know, Sir. I yelled and yelled at her, but I couldn't make her hear me. She climbed up the forecastle with a wrapped bundle cradled in her arms. I ran after her, and she looked at me sort of strange, or looked through me more like. Then she just slipped over the side without a sound! Damnedest thing I ever saw."

The captain shook his head and tugged on his hat, and I strained to hear his whispered words. "Not one chance in hell we'll find her in that sea."

Chapter Ten

Gideon and I never left the top decks that night. We walked from the poop deck, dropped down to the quarter deck, across the main and back up on the forecastle. Then we started over again, torches in hand and calling Beth's name. I walked well behind Gideon, not knowing what to say, and unable to bear the weight of his pain.

Uncle Sean was the last to leave us, and asked me to give it up and come to bed.

"It was a terrible thing that happened, but it's a lost cause now. She's gone, Moll."

"I'll go below shortly, Uncle." As long as I saw Gideon's torch moving around the deck, I'd continue to keep vigil too.

The crew said nothing to either of us, leaving us to go where we would in our futile search. As the sun broke over the horizon, the captain and Uncle Sean approached me.

"Moll, it's past time to give it up. Beth is gone." Uncle said. He placed his hand on my shoulder.

"I know Uncle, but I keep thinking, hoping maybe there's some small chance?"

"There is no chance at all, Miss." The captain said. "Even if she snatched ahold of a rope and somehow managed to keep pace with the ship, she'd not last fifteen minutes in that water. The ocean is a cold and merciless mistress."

I reached the same conclusion long before, but I wouldn't allow myself to accept it. I shook my head in agreement as a sob wrenched my body. I dropped my head to hide my foolish tears.

"Let's find Gideon," Uncle said. "Dear God, this was a voyage of death for him."

"He's curled up under the mizzen mast," the captain said. "He fell asleep in a coil of rope, passed out most likely. I instructed the men to leave him be. Sure you want to wake him?"

"Moll, what do you think?"

"I don't want to Uncle, but that's just cowardice talking because I don't know what to say to him. I basically asked Beth for help when we land, and I know in my heart if I had never spoken of it to her, this would never have happened! Nothing good comes from begging help!"

"You are your father's child, Moll, and that's just not so! We all need help sometimes. As for what to say, it's of no concern. It's not the time for wise words nor platitudes, just be there so he knows you care."

Uncle and I found Gideon tossing about in a troubled sleep, and I touched his cheek.

"Gideon, let us help you to bed." I said.

"What… Beth?"

"It's Moll, Gideon, let's go below now."

"Moll, dear God, is Beth gone, is she really gone? What shall I do?"

"I don't know Gideon, I just don't know." I consoled, caressing his cheek. "Come downstairs with me. I'll make some tea to calm you."

Gideon took a deep calming breath, and wiped tears from his face. He squinted his eyes, and looked at me as if I was a stranger to him. His eyes turned wild and dark, his pupils dilated.

"Tea? Yes, the teas, the seasickness, the baby disappearing in the middle of the night, now I understand. I don't know why I didn't before. Gaining any weight yet, Moll?"

"I don't think so, but maybe? I might be getting fat on my own cooking." I said, confused.

"What did you do, Moll? Beth was your friend!"

"Of course she was, as you are!"

"Beth told me about your potions, and about the spells you cast on her and the baby! She told me you worshipped at some pagan altar as a child!"

"She never said that!"

"No, those were not the words she used, so blind was her love for you. She wanted you to be like real sisters. You envied her life, she told me so. I was a fool not to see it!"

"What are you talking about, Gideon?"

"Besides casting the spell that sent Beth to her death?"

"Gideon, what…? I loved …"

"But that wasn't enough! I know what you've done, just not how."

"I've done nothing, I wouldn't –"

"You stole our baby, and made it your own!"

"What? Sweet Jesus, Gideon, think about what you are saying! That's insane talk!" Uncle said.

"Insane? Crazy am I? Hell yes, it is crazy. Crazy and beyond hateful, but your niece knows it's true nonetheless!"

"Gideon, your grief and lack of sleep are affecting your judgment. You need sleep, son." The fiery heat of Gideon's eyes never left me.

"You and Beth are the best friends I've ever had!" I pleaded and reached out to touch Gideon's face, but he snatched my hand.

"Friends were we? Is that what you call it? Is that how you treat your friends? It's not enough that you've killed her and stolen her baby, now you'd have her husband as well I suppose?"

"No Gideon, my love for you is that for a brother. I just want you to know I'm here for you."

Gideon shook his head and swayed on his feet, and held his hand to his head. Shaking, I reached out my hand to him.

"Gideon, please, let me help you below?"

Gideon looked at me for a moment, and I misread the softening of his features and the tears escaping his eyes. I put out my arms to hug him.

Gideon slapped me hard, and I fell backwards slamming into the mast.

"You God damned witch!" he yelled through tears of sorrow. "You're an ugly, disgusting woman, inside and out. Stay away from me!" Gideon grabbed a pole, and raised it to strike me again.

The narrowed edges of my vision whirled as a shadow leapt between us. Gideon changed the angle of his attack to swing at the shadow figure instead, but Uncle moved too fast. My eyes couldn't follow the two punches he delivered, but I heard something crack in Gideon's face as he dropped in a heap to the deck.

"Land ho!" I heard, and my world went dark.

Chapter Eleven

The crew secured the Mary Regina at the Saint Mary's City dock. Uncle and I gathered up our meager belongings, and awaited the signal to disembark. Gideon was held in restraints below deck, to be escorted off after all of the passengers were ashore.

"Then he'll be the colony's problem to deal with," the captain told us, "but I'd watch him for a spell if I was you... least 'til he gets his sense back, poor lad."

I wondered if Gideon would still settle here after all the suffering this voyage cost him. I thought it probable he'd take the next ship headed back to England. I would consider it myself if it was an option. No good had come of our journey, but nothing good waited for me back in England either.

The men lowered the gangplank to the pier, and I took in the landscape before us. The town was no better nor worse than my imaginings, but just beyond town, the river flowed clean and swift through a vast primordial wilderness as far as the eye could see. The roads we observed were little more than oxen paths, and the dwellings a hodge-podge of hastily constructed shacks amid elaborate brick buildings.

Uncle asked one of the men about lodging, and they provided directions to Smith's Ordinary in the town proper.

"We'll stop there first and get settled in, Moll. Then we're off to the Land Office to apply for our headrights. We are entitled to fifty acres apiece just for importing ourselves!" Uncle laughed.

"Ah yes, a bath with fresh water!"

"Land office first, and then you may soak until your skin wrinkles up like some old hag's."

"When can we see our farm?"

"Listen Moll, about what happened on the ship. That wasn't Gideon, he was just crazy with grief. I don't want you to-"

"It's all right Uncle, but we needn't speak of it, do we? But thank you, for what you did."

"Of course, Moll, but I…oh yes, the land. There's a bit of paperwork to do, but I understand it moves quickly here in the colonies. Sot-Weed is not fetching the price it was, but it is still in high demand in England, and this is the beginning of planting season. So the less time we spend lining the innkeeper's pockets, the faster we can pay our annual land rents to Lord Baltimore. You know- death and taxes, Moll."

The clerk at the Land Office was less confident than Uncle, however.

"There are few patents left in this part of the colony. I suppose that's the price of housing the capital here. What's left is neither land nor water but something in between. You'd make no headway with plow or boat in those swamps." He advised us.

"Where would you recommend, sir? We need land suitable for farming."

"Are you newly arrived on the Mary Regina? Well then, first I must verify your names against the passenger's list. Who are you then?"

"Sean and Mary Dyer."

"Well, Mr. and Mrs. Dyer, I will submit this with a certificate of importation for your warrant application. Once approved, you may select the acreage, and a survey will be done. Then you will be awarded a patent and have full headrights to the land."

"It's Mister and Miss, sir. Moll is my niece, but how long should this take? We want a crop in the ground this season."

"It doesn't take long to process, but surveyors are a scarce commodity, and then it's up to Governor Calvert for approval, of course."

Uncle extended his hand, and the clerk took something from it.

"Is there any way to speed it along?" Uncle asked.

"Well, it is a big colony now, isn't it? There is Newtowne, about fifteen miles north. Not really much of a town yet, but some 50 acre sections are already surveyed. There's some fine farming land, might save you some time."

The clerk provided directions by land, and by boat as well, to the settlement of Newtowne, and to the waters of Britton's Bay. He suggested we find a John Hammond when we arrived there.

"Everyone knows John, they hold county court proceedings at his house. Is there something on your mind, Miss?"

"Indians? Are there any of the wild Indians there? Are they dangerous?"

"I don't reckon we've had anybody killed by Indians for six months or better. Our Indians are right friendly, not like down in Virginia. Bigger worry for new folks is surviving the seasoning. If you live through your first year without catching the ague, slow fever or dysentery, I reckon you'll be fine."

"My niece will keep us healthy," Uncle said, "but I would like to know something of the natives. What can you tell us about them?

"Well Mr. Dyer, you'd be surprised what I hear in this office. News from the mother country, and from the farthest outposts of the colony as well. Up around Newtowne, you're most likely to run into Indians from the Conoy or Chaptico tribes. They may come around looking to trade, or beg, maybe even to share a meal with you, but they won't give you no trouble. They figure we're allies against their enemies, the Susquehannocks. Those ones now, they're bad news."

"How can we tell which ones are Susquehannocks?" I asked.

"Well ma'am, they dress in bear and wolf skins, and you won't ever see one without his bow and arrows at hand, and likely a club too. The men cut a thin strip of hair short on top of their heads and grease it up so it looks like a rooster's comb. Nightmarish looking cannibals they are."

I looked to Uncle for his reaction, but he seemed unconcerned.

"Oh, one other thing, they wear shirts with half-sleeves to the elbows with the dried up skin of some critters head on the cuff. But with the Susquehannocks, chances are they'll see you first, and then it won't matter a lick no ways."

Chapter Twelve

The proprietor at Smith's Ordinary was very accommodating, and provided a warm, if not hot, bath with fresh water! I allowed myself to soak until the water cooled and I began to shiver, reminding me of Beth's death in the cold ocean. While I bathed, Uncle went out to procure a horse and carriage.

Newtowne was a few hours ride, and we started early in the morning to view the land. The road was little more than a woodland trail, but it was well packed from frequent travel at least. As Uncle drove, I admired the unspoiled scenery, identifying some plants I knew from home and we made a game out of spotting the many deer and rabbits along the way.

We came to a nice homestead on the banks of Britton's Bay off of the Potomack River. From the description we'd been given, we knew the large brick house and extensive fields to be John Hammond's. We introduced ourselves, and explained the purpose of our visit.

"You must have a friend in Saint Mary's City, Mr. Dyer, or pay a fair bribe. That land has just been surveyed, and is some of the finest cropland in the whole colony. I'd be glad to show it to you, as a potential neighbor."

"I'd be in your debt, sir. Perhaps you'd be so kind as to show us your holdings as well? We will be new to Sot-Weed farming, and would appreciate any words of wisdom from an established grower such as yourself," Uncle said.

John Hammond laughed. "It's really a new crop to all of us, but we are learning. When I started twenty five years ago, a man could tend perhaps 5000 plants, but with modern techniques, a hard working fellow can handle

10,000. Two headrights? Is that what you are entitled to? You'll want more. Remember, you'll be needing to feed yourself and your niece there as well."

Mr. Hammond saddled a horse and we backtracked south to the surveyed land. His horse trotted beside our carriage, and the two men discussed planting, something called "topping" and different methods of drying the crop. They spoke of the colony's Indians, and how indentured servants provided the best and cheapest labor.

"Isn't indentured servitude just a nicer word for slavery?" I asked.

"That may be one way of looking at it. I see it as a way for the lower class to have their voyage here paid for, and eventually establish themselves as land owners. There's unlimited opportunity in this land for everyone."

"Even the Indians, and woman as well? And I have seen a few black slaves…?"

Uncle cut his eyes in my direction and hushed me with his lips, but Mr. Hammond laughed.

"Well now, another Margaret Brent are you?"

"No sir, I'm a Dyer. My friends and family call me Moll."

Mr. Hammond laughed again, a full, rich and honest laugh.

"I meant no disrespect, ma'am, and I'm showing my age. Miss Brent was a successful planter and a brilliant businesswoman, although many do not share my favorable view of her. She never married, which is strange in a colony with so few women, but that did not stop her. When Governor Calvert died almost twenty years ago, he appointed Miss Brent his executor, high praise from his lordship. What folks remember of her though, occurred a year or so later. She held that as a landowner and Lord Baltimore's attorney, she was entitled to the vote, woman or not, and so she petitioned the general assembly! Can you imagine a woman doing such a thing, and such a curious idea, women voting?"

"So after all she'd done for the colony, the first help she asked for herself became a joke?" I asked

"That is very progressive thinking, Moll," Uncle said.

"Indeed yes, and the family was progressive on other matters as well. When this land was first settled, the Indian tayak, or I reckon you'd say the king of the Conoy was named Chitomachen. Our own Father Andrew White converted this Indian king to Christianity early on. No other colony treats their Indians as well as we have. When the Tayak died, his only daughter Mary became a ward of Margaret Brent, who saw to her education. Miss Brent's older brother married the young girl some years later. How's that for enlightened thinking?"

"What happened to them?" I asked.

"Miss Brent or her ward?"

"Both I guess," I said.

"Mary bore several children for Giles, but she died young, about twenty-two years old. As for Miss Brent, she fell out of favor with the Calverts when she sold some of Lord Baltimore's cattle to pay the desperate soldiers in the colony. Eventually she moved south to Virginia. She had spirit, an independent woman. Much like you I believe, Miss Dyer."

Mr. Hammond didn't know me at all, I thought. I wished I was like the Brent woman, determined and self-sufficient. She stood on her own, for what she believed in, and did not fawn at men's feet, or let them hurt her or make decisions for her. She needed and depended on nobody but herself! I doubted her fall from grace was due to the loss of a few head of cows! Still, even a woman of her resolve and prominence changed little in the world. Twenty years later, her common sense views were still described as "progressive." I simply answered, "Thank you for the compliment, Mr. Hammond."

"Ah, and here we are." We tied the animals to trees and followed his lead into the forest. Some of the trees were of a size that I could not put my arms around them. Uncle asked about water, and clearing of the land.

It was disappointing to discover the river was a fair ride distant, but we walked to a small tannin stained stream that Uncle expressed an interest in. Mr. Hammond said the colonists did not clear the land at all, but rather followed the Indian method of girdling the trees and planting the hills for seed and Sot-Weed plants beneath them.

"Much more efficient," he said. "You're too late to establish plant seedling beds now, but I always have too many. I can supply what you need for this year's crop."

Uncle thanked him, and gazed over the property. "What do you think, Moll? Does this look like home? We could build the house on the rise there and the stream is right here for water."

"It's beautiful, Uncle. What more could a girl want?" Then I remembered saying those same words to Beth, and they sounded sad, ominous and raw to my ears.

As we rode back to the Hammond farm, Mr. Hammond said the land application needed to be concluded in Saint Mary's City, but there was little else we would need from there.

"Do not pay the inflated prices they get for farming tools and animals back in the city." Mr. Hammond said. "I purchased a whole passel of new ones last year directly from Mother England, and I can give you a good price on my old implements, if you'd like? Robert Morgan keeps oxen and cattle, and Richard Duke has a few horses to sell. William Bowles has pigs and chickens he may part with as well."

"Your kindness is appreciated, John," Uncle said.

"Just being neighborly. Some confuse our religious tolerance for lack of devotion, but we are good God fearing Christians here." Mr. Hammond said.

We were given a tour of the plantation. Uncle went with Mr. Hammond, who granted me free run of the estate. While they inspected bedding plants and the implements for sale, I walked the wood's edges, memorizing plants, and observing wildlife.

I saw a young man hacking at weeds, and walked towards him. He paused in his labors, pushed his hair from his eyes, and leaned on the handle of his hoe when he saw me approach.

"Good day, sir, I'm Moll Dyer. My uncle and I are visiting Mr. Hammond."

"I'm Peter, Misses, me and my wife are Hammond's indentures."

"Hard work is it, sot-weed farming?"

"That it is, getting in the seed beds, drawing 'em and planting, weeding, topping, cutting, hanging and curing, it never stops."

"Have you been here long? When do you complete your indenture?"

A smile lit up his face. "This season's crop will be my last. Then, my agreement with Mr. Hammond is done, and he provides what's needed for me to strike out on my own."

"What is it like being owned by another?" I asked.

"No disrespect, Miss, but where were you raised? We're no slaves here. Hammond paid our passage, which would cost me a year's wages, if indeed I found work in England at all. I've learned about planting with room and board provided, but it's the promise of land ownership and independence that brought us here. I made the decision of my own free will, unlike some. After seven years, we'll be square, I'll be a landowner and my own man. That's a fair trade I'd say."

"Are there slaves here as well?"

"No, not on Mr. Hammond's farm anyway. Some of the planters brought in some African men, but Hammond says they're wasting their money. He says no man, no matter his color, will work hard if there's no hope of ever enjoying the fruits of his labor. He says it will never catch on in this colony."

I congratulated the man for reaching the end of his indenture, and wished him well. I walked down the slope to the bay, and sat at its shore considering how much there was to learn in this new colony.

For my dearest friend, Beth, and for my child yet unknown, no matter my cost in sweat or blood, our farmstead would prove a success!

Again I heard Mr. Hammond's words, "William Bowles has a few pigs and chickens he may part with." How many men in the small colony could be named William Bowles? The man had to be Beth's Uncle William. If so, and Gideon stayed in the colony, he would be in Newtowne soon also. I decided not to tell Uncle about it, or of how our stream was eerily familiar to me from a dream.

I thought of home, no, not of Westcowes, nor even of Kinsale, but just wherever my once family rested their heads that night.

Chapter Thirteen

John Hammond insisted we spend the night at his home before returning to Saint Mary's City in the morning. His generosity and hospitality to total strangers was amazing, and most appreciated. Mrs. Hammond proved herself quite a cook, and placed before us a meal such as I'd not seen since departing home. Although John (as he now insisted I call him) teased that she only prepared such repasts when company came to call, his pot belly (that he held whenever he laughed), indicated otherwise.

In the morning, Uncle and I took our leave from the Hammond's with some regret, and looked forward to renewing their acquaintance upon our return to Newtowne.

Driving back toward the capital, Uncle asked my impressions of the land and of our hosts. We chattered about all we'd learned of the land and of farming, and I told him of the bounty of fish I'd observed in the bay, knowing his taste for them when cured with salt.

"What did you think of John's story?" I asked.

"Story? About his wife's cooking?"

I punched Uncle's arm, knowing he was poking fun at my expense.

"The one about the Margaret Brent lady."

"It's a good lesson. Women need to know their place, now don't they?" he asked in a serious tone. I stared at him for a long moment until he burst into laughter.

"Very well, Moll, a brave woman she was. Perhaps too much ahead of her time, but the day she dreamed of is coming."

"Indeed Uncle, you find her brave? A woman? Even though you shed your women as easily as Father does his socks? Have you never thought of marriage, Uncle?"

"Don't believe everything you hear, Moll. Besides, those women your father so loves to tease me about, are not real to me. They are diversions, and I don't allow them enough time in my life to become anything else. I make no promises to them. Do you understand?"

"Yes, I think so, whoever she was, she hurt you badly, Uncle."

"Ah now Moll, you see too well. Many admirable women I have known, my sisters, your mother, and one certain niece who shall remain nameless, but only one I would have shared a life with, and she wanted another. The others were only sharing my… umm, company."

With the sun straight overhead, we came upon a man with a mule and cart turned sideways blocking the muddy road. The mule seemed quite determined not to take another step. His poor owner laughed with us as he pulled and prodded at the mule, but his efforts were in vain. Uncle climbed down from the carriage to assist, but between the two of them they only managed to draw the mule to the side enough that we might pass. The old man took it in stride, and said the mule would move when he got hungry enough, and he had as much time left in the day as did the mule.

As Uncle bid him good day, and grasped the reins, a horse and wagon pulled up short to allow us to pass.

Gideon's nose, wrapped in a white bandage, contrasted with the blackness of his eyes when they met mine. I trembled as a shiver ran down my spine.

"Good day, Gideon, what brings you here?" Uncle asked. He climbed down from our carriage and walked towards him with his hand extended. Gideon slapped the reins, and his horse surged forward, knocking Uncle backwards. He slipped in the wet road and fell face first into a mud puddle. Gideon's dark gaze never wavered from me as he pushed his horse on.

Uncle pulled himself to his feet, and slapped at his muddy clothes, never taking his gaze from the departing wagon.

"Not a very sociable fellow now, is he?" The old man asked with a grin.

"Well, it would appear he holds a grudge for imagined wrongs," Uncle replied.

Driving on toward the city, the heat of the day dried the pasty wet clay on Uncle's clothes, hair and beard. He looked like the mud men we made as children, with only his eyes shining through the mud.

"What might your fancy ladies in London think of you now?" I asked, and he managed a feeble laugh. Once back at Saint Mary's City, it was Uncle's turn to crave a bath.

We entered the Land Office, and identified the parcel we wanted to claim. The clerk promised to submit the documents with haste, and said he thought chances were fair they'd be signed off before week's end. We ate a humble dinner of cornbread and venison, and retired to our beds early.

A week spent waiting is a very long week indeed. Most days, we entertained ourselves by riding around the countryside, observing the people and the farms. One day we sat at the docks and waited for the fisherman to come in, curious about their catch. Many of the vessels were solely devoted to the taking of crabs, a local favorite. The boats carried bushels stacked upon bushels full of them, caught with trotlines and hand nets. Many made their living in this manner in the warm months, and dredged for oysters in the fall of the year. Maryland was a land of plenty.

Whenever at the docks, I observed the large sailing ships and wondered if one arrived to take me back to England for trial. Uncle too, stared at the ships with a look of unease. What drew his gaze there? Could he know what I did to James?

One afternoon as we returned to the Inn, the Land Office clerk met us waving documents.

"Congratulations, Mr. Dyer!" he yelled. "The patent is signed, and the headrights assigned. You are now officially land owners!"

We wasted no time getting to work. The building of a house is no small feat, but we attacked it with vigor. The cabin was small, but we would add to it later, after the crops were in. There were plenty of raw materials at hand. We cut the trees where we intended the house to be, and used the logs for building.

"This clearing will give us a nice spot for our garden, Moll. From here there is a long view of anyone approaching the farm. Hope we don't need it, but helpful if there's a problem with the natives."

Looking down the clearing, a young man come into sight, walking towards us and waving. "Good day," he yelled.

"Welcome Peter," I yelled back.

"Mr. Hammond thought you could use some help, and offers my services for a fortnight. I haven't done much carpentry, but I can girdle trees, and I'll try my hand at most anything."

"Indeed we can, Peter, and you are most welcome."

The second day Peter came, he carried a chicken under each arm.

"These cacklers are laying right good now, and Mr. Hammond said I should bring another pair to you tomorrow. Cracked corn goes in and eggs come out, fair trade, eh? Mostly they fend for themselves, as long as you have a roost where the varmints can't get to 'em," Peter said.

By the end of Peter's first week, half of the trees were girdled, the cabin walls were up, and the log roof rafters were in place. It started to look like a home.

Our ritual at day's end was to sit around the fire discussing the day's progress and the plans for the morrow. As every night, I faced the woods, with Uncle on my right studying the emerging house and plotting the next steps to be taken, and Peter to my left feeding the fire.

"I'd say our headway deserves a celebration," Uncle said, "except there's nothing to celebrate with. I have a few jugs of cider, and rum, but jerky, eggs and dried corn does not make for a feast!"

"I can set a few snares and we could have fresh rabbit tomorrow, if you'd like sir? I've seen plenty in the woods. Some I could hit on the head with a stick," Peter offered.

I gazed into the fire, and to the woods beyond. Some small movement caught my eye and I stared, but heard no sound. Was a man standing in the shadows watching? Just a trick from the flickering light of the fire? Then the shadow moved.

"What are you looking at?" Uncle asked, and turned to see for himself.

A tall, half naked man leapt from the cover, bow in hand. His skin was the color of the leaves on the ground, and animal furs were his only covering. One side of his head was clean shaven, the other side hung to his shoulders. I screamed.

Chapter Fourteen

Dropping into a crouch, the man lifted his bow towards us.

Peter leapt from the fire and rushed him. The man dropped his bow and turned to face Peter's charge with a savage smile on his face. Uncle went for his gun as Peter and the Indian collided and wrestled each other to the ground.

Uncle pointed his gun, but was unable to get a clear shot as they grappled.

"Peter, get out of the way!" Uncle yelled.

First Peter was on top, and then the other, and Peter again. My throat choked tight, as I searched for a stick to use as a weapon, and grabbed a burning brand from the fire.

"Stop it, get away from him!" I said, swinging the branch.

The strange man caught Peter under the arm and flipped him to the ground.

"Ouch, damn it, Two Bears, that's enough!" Peter said with a laugh.

"Don't move Peter, I've got him." Uncle said, aiming the gun.

"No, Sean, stop!" Peter shouted. "Two Bears is a friend!"

Uncle lowered the gun with reluctance, unsure what was happening, and hesitant to drop his guard. The man named Two Bears stood and offered a hand up to Peter. He said something I could not follow, and Peter shook his head no, and they both laughed.

"Two Bears says my fighting has improved, but I still need a woman's help," he said pointing at the still burning stick in my hand. I tossed it back into the fire.

The two men walked over to us. "Easy Sean, everything's fine," he said holding his palms up toward us. "Sean and Moll of the English, meet Two Bears of the Conoy."

"Irish actually," Uncle said, extending his hand to Two Bears, "but we'll not split hairs, which is what I thought was about to happen to you, Peter."

"Two Bears? He's my oldest friend here, and the first native I met. Mr. Hammond trades with the Conoy often, but I think Two Bears is the only one who truly enjoys our company."

"Where do your people live, Two Bears?" Uncle asked.

"He speaks some English, and between what he knows and what I know of Algonquian, we communicate passably well," Peter answered, "but you'll need to speak slowly."

"Near," Two Bears said, "where Potomack make bay you call Britton's."

Two Bears held up his palm, said "Wait," and walked back to the shadows where I'd first seen him.

"Come," he spoke into the brush, and I could see another shadowy figure move to his side. I could hear them dragging something through the leaves. As they entered into the firelight, we watched as he and a young woman flipped a small deer on its back. The woman drew a knife from a sheath on her neck, and began skinning the animal.

"Sean, Moll, looks like we'll be having a feast after all, what a deal!" Peter said.

Two Bears and the woman (introduced as his wife, Bluebird) presented us each with a thick steak impaled on a stick. Following his lead, we roasted them over the fire.

"I suppose we should make this a proper celebration," Uncle said, pulled out a jug, and took a long swallow.

"Ah, nothing like a cup of the beast in the evening." Uncle passed the jug to Peter's friend. Sniffing the contents, Two Bears scrunched up his nose and shook his head.

"No, not thirsty." He turned to Peter and said something else.

"He says strong drink makes him addle headed, but he thanks you."

"It does the same to me," Uncle replied with a laugh. He poured some in a cup and offered it to me, and passed the jug to Peter. "Go ahead, you work like a man. You earned it."

I took a small swallow and felt the spicy hot liquid throughout its journey down my body. My face felt feverish, and my eyes watered.

"This tastes like swamp water, Uncle!" I said spitting out what I could, and taking a bite of the half raw steak to kill the taste.

"It's good for you, Moll," Peter said. "Mr. Hammond says most of the deaths during the seasoning comes from folks drinking the salt fouled waters."

"Thanks Peter, but I'll take my chances with the water," I laughed.

"You shouldn't have problems with the salt tides on your small stream. Just let it sit a day before you drink it." Peter advised as I handed the cup to Uncle.

"Wait Moll, one small toast first?" He tilted the jug toward me and said "To my partner," and then to Peter and the Indian couple, "and to new friends." I only wet my lips with the foul drink, and sat the cup at my feet.

I moved to sit by Bluebird, and soon found her English to be better than her husband's. She was also naked to the waist, save for the knife and an amulet she wore around her neck. Tattoos decorated the skin of both Indians.

Peter and Uncle were staring at the young woman's chest, and diverted their eyes whenever caught in the act of doing so. Bluebird seemed not to notice or care. It was a cool evening, and I placed a blanket over Bluebird's shoulders for her comfort, and to relieve my embarrassment at the men.

"Bluebird knows many plants and what they're good for." Peter informed me. I asked her to follow me, and showed her the dried plants I'd brought from home to see which grew here. Some she knew, and others when I described their use, she would say the name of another plant used by her people.

It was the first of several celebratory nights before our new home was dry against the elements, and secured from animal or human intruders. Bluebird was the first female my age I met in the new colony, and little did I know how fateful this meeting with a wild Indian was.

Chapter Fifteen

The next day, the Indians left before the sun was up. Two fresh gutted rabbits waited for us by the embers of the fire, and I skinned and cooked them for breakfast.

Uncle's head pained him, so I planned to begin chinking the walls of the cabin. I thought of the tricks our father used for caulking boats with plenty of pine pitch, and fibers from the fields mixed together.

"Remember Moll, hemp fibers for the straight portions of the hull, and moss on the curves." I could still hear him say.

We had plenty of moss and fibrous plants, but pitch was labor intensive to make or required a trip to Saint Mary's City to buy. I thought of how the local clay hard cured on Uncle's clothes, and thought it would serve the same purpose.

Before Peter returned to the Hammond farm, the cabin stood completed with the exception of the fireplace. We could cook outside at the fire for now. Heat was the last thing on our minds during the hot, humid days of summer. The house was far from fancy, but at least it was weather tight! No rains would fall on our heads, and that was good enough for now. There were fields to plant.

Once a week or so, Two Bears and Bluebird visited with us. After a few such visits, Bluebird often came alone. I would be engaged in some occupation, and with no warning she stood before me, appearing like a wisp of fog.

In the beginning, it was the native healing plants, and Bluebird's knowledge of them, that interested me, but we soon spoke of things such as I would with a friend back home, if I had any to confide in. Sometimes I forgot she was a heathen savage.

When we were halfway finished planting the Sot-Weed fields (with the young plants from John's farm), I lifted my head to wipe the sweat from my eyes and there at the next seed mound stood Bluebird, smiling without a care in the world.

"Good day, Moll." she said.

I smiled and stood to embrace her, and admired the shirt she'd made from brain tanned leather, though I suspected she only wore it when among us. We found a shady spot to sit.

"Bad storm coming, but plants need rain." She said, looking at the sky while rubbing her amulet.

"What is that you wear?" I asked.

"Okeus?" She took it from her neck and handed it to me. It was a piece of deer antler with the carved figure of a dark skinned man who appeared to be cloaked in pearls.

As I rubbed the face of the ornament, I felt a strange sensation in the pit of my stomach, and I placed my hand there. Bluebird's look formed a question.

"I think I swallowed butterflies, and they beat their wings to escape," I said laughing.

She smiled, touched my stomach, and put her arms together cradling an invisible baby. She rocked back and forth. "Sean is father, yes?" she asked.

"No!" I said, "Sean is my uncle!" I could see she didn't understand.

"Who is father?"

"Who is this Okeus?" I asked.

"Okeus is dark god, causes much suffering to our people."

"He's like the devil?"

"I do not know Devil?"

"You pray to a dark god?" I asked.

Bluebird laughed at me as if I was a dull witted but favored child.

"Ahone is a good god, he loves the people whatever they do. Okeus? Only prayer and sacrifice can make him happy, so that he will not hurt the people. Why pray to good god? He good no matter what. Understand?"

I did not, but shook my head yes. Bluebird leaned forward to touch my belly again, and her shirt slipped open. I noticed a crooked arrow tattoo on her breast.

"What is that marking for?"

Bluebird, in all innocence, pulled open her shirt, and pointed to the marking. "Protection from the dark, from the Manitou. I will make one for Moll and her baby."

I began to shake my head, but thought better of it. Bluebird tried to be helpful in her own way, and it was hard to find fault with that. She left soon after, promising to return soon.

At dusk, a thunderstorm burst upon us with a brilliant display of light and sound, validating Bluebird's prediction. Uncle and I rushed inside, propelled by the powerful rains, and ate a cold dinner of salt fish and boiled eggs.

Planting continued, and as soon as the Sot-Weed was in the ground, the sowing of corn began. Weeding and plucking the horn worms from the Sot-Weed followed that. By late summer, the corn tasseled out as high as my shoulders. The little one kicked me with regularity now, and the swelling of my stomach seemed obvious to me.

When the flower spikes shot up from the Sot-Weed plants, Peter arrived to help us "top out" the crop. He showed us how to snap the flower growth where it emerged from the leaves of the plant.

"Peter, this is nasty work." I said.

"I remember telling you it was no picnic, Moll. Just wait for the time to cut it all down." Peter laughed, and worked down the hills away from us.

"What do you think about getting some help before the cutting season, Moll?" Uncle asked. "Next year Peter will be working on his own land, and won't be around to help us."

"An indentured servant?"

"There's still money left from our nest egg, and headrights to another fifty acres would be most welcome."

I pried my fingers apart from the sap that glued them together. "You want us to be dependent on someone else? We can work our own land."

"That's not dependency, but rather assures our independence. We pay for a service."

I thought about his proposal. I did not like the idea of being master over another. I hated to think of being indebted or dependent on someone, but didn't indenture make that person dependent on us? The reality was I could not work the sot-weed in the last stages of pregnancy, and we could little afford the failure of our first crop.

"Peter says indenture is a "good deal" for everyone, and I suppose we would be fair masters? I hate to spend the money, but I suspect by summer's end, I'll be getting in my own way." I glanced at my belly.

"I think that will happen well before summer's end. We need to talk about the baby, and the future," Uncle replied.

"What do you wish to discuss?"

"Your reputation here, and how the baby will be perceived."

My lips were tight when I replied. "And what do you propose to do about that?"

"Easy Moll, we're partners, remember? My last trip to Saint Mary's City, I stopped to speak with the Land Office clerk, and we came up with a plan."

"You spoke with him about my baby?" I asked.

"Not at all, well, not directly." Uncle said. "Barter is the primary means of exchange here, and that makes silver even more valuable. John Hammond said the clerk might be willing to adjust some records for some hard currency, so I approached him with my plan, and… stop tapping your foot, Moll. I know you do that when you're impatient."

"What records is he willing to "adjust" then Uncle?"

"Importation. He said he could write it up as your baby being my child, or make one small entry in a ship's log and make it your brother or sister. I could be the guardian, and all that is ours will pass to the child."

"No, Uncle. This is MY baby!"

"Think about it. It would solve your problem, and gain us an additional fifty acres! No harm is done to anyone."

"No, I can carry the weight that's been placed upon me for my child. I don't need anyone's help, or more than my share. This is my responsibility." I felt the color of anger flush my cheeks.

"That's exactly it! I am thinking of your baby! Are you so damn prideful you cannot even accept this help from me for your baby? I think it's high time that you thought of the little one too!"

Red filled the edges of my vision, and I slapped his face. "Enough!"

He dropped to one knee.

"How could you?" I screamed and ran from the cabin.

Chapter Sixteen

After a suitable cry, and a lot of soul searching, I regretted my actions. My uncle was concerned with the future, as I should be. I wasn't the only one I needed to think about any more. Perhaps I was enamored with the idea of personal martyrdom, the purest display of a mother's love, for too long? I knew that foremost was the maternal pride I felt with every stirring of life within my womb. What manner of woman denies their own child, unless in exigent circumstance? No woman worthy of the name would, not for the mere sake of her reputation, and certainly not for greed or convenience.

Still, my mind tortured my heart until one or both would surely perish. Every crisp spark of reason conjured up to guide me, drowned in the quagmire of "what ifs." What if Uncle was right? My child could come into this new world unblemished by the sins of its father. No man would ever need to know of my child's foul conception. A family's reputation is a sacred trust, and as the child's mother is perceived, so too is the child. Then too, the fifty acres of land would be my child's birthright.

My uncle's offer of a guardianship made me uncomfortable. He owed me nothing- my baby nothing. Altering records to gain property rights? What good could come of this?

So much richer my child's life could be! I recalled my father's stories, passed from his father before him. Our father regaled us with tales of family glory, and bitter defeats. Stories of how (after the Battle of Kinsale), the English robbed us of our title, holdings, and soon thereafter, our honor as well … but that was long ago. This might be the chance to return the family Dyer to our status of old, at least in this new world? Every night I prayed that my child never know poverty or want.

Hours passed, and well after the sun set, Uncle had yet to return to the house. I looked outside and spotted him sitting alone by the fire, staring at the flickering flames.

"Uncle?" I yelled, but no response, so I hastened towards him.

"Uncle, please come inside."

"Moll, it was not my intent to hurt you, but there are things, well there's our future here that must be considered." Uncle replied, but did not take his eyes from the fire.

I sat beside him, lifted his face to mine and noticed remnants of the marks my hand left behind, and kissed him on that fevered cheek. I embraced him.

"I know Uncle, I know. Can you forgive me?"

"Forgive you, Moll? I'd not forgive you if you were anything other than passionate about your child. There's nothing to forgive, but you must remember, one of my many vices is I say what I think."

"It is not a vice to speak your heart, although you might refine your method of delivery."

Uncle laughed. "There are decisions to be made, and they are yours to make."

"I have been thinking of nothing else, but I would like to think on it some more. How would we accomplish such a thing? People will see that my belly has grown, if they are so blind that they have not noticed already?"

"Ah, you are indeed a woman. Only a woman notices so small of a change in her body. I don't know how you've stayed so thin until now. Although Peter did just ask me if you've been eating too much seasoning meat. I don't believe your secret is known by anyone, not yet. We need to ensure it stays that way for the next month or so, and that means sacrifice."

"If I eat much less, I become light headed, and it could hurt my baby. What sacrifice would you have me make, Uncle?"

"You need to eat, but you can't be seen by any of our visitors, rare though they might be, except perhaps Bluebird or Two Bears. Their customs are so unlike ours, and they are not much given to gossip, especially about the doings of the whites."

"There is much to be done on the farm, Uncle. The barn for curing the Sot-Weed is not finished, and the plants soon need cutting, the corn harvesting, how would you manage it all alone if I remained as a prisoner in my own home?"

"Not a prisoner, but in truth, I could not manage it. We need to make the trip to Saint Mary's City soon, to inquire about an indentured servant. I don't know how long it takes, but I am informed that some folks come here with their passage unpaid. In that case, anyone with the silver or sufficient pounds of Sot-Weed can pay it off, and own the indenture contract."

"And if it takes some time to get an indenture here?"

"We'll do the best we can. For a while yet, you can work near the house and go inside at the sight of any visitors. You could always drape a blanket over yourself, and tell the curious you have a case of ague. Would that work for as long as you keep up your strength?"

"I can see that you've given this some thought. When did you become so smart?" I giggled.

"There's that laugh of yours! I have missed that. Hearing it, I often thought you were touched by the fairies, dear niece!"

"Thank you, Uncle...I think? Still, it is good to have a clever uncle about!"

"Devious is the word you're looking for," he laughed, "but I'm only thinking of you. I may not always be here." He answered.

Chapter Seventeen

The following Saturday, we harnessed the horse and carriage and made the journey to the city. I hoped it would not be a waste of the whole day's labor for the thin promise of future help. Still, it was a pleasant day for August, a fine day to be out in the Creator's paradise, and indeed, this new land was that! Black-eyed Susans danced in the soft breeze near the road in the shade of majestic oaks and hickories- as old as time itself. Arriving in town, many of the store bound workers mulled about outside, also enjoying the day.

We tied the horse near the Inn and walked toward the town center. Uncle yelled "Good day, Christopher," to the clerk from the Land Office.

"Good day to you, Sean. What brings you and the young lady to the city on this blessed day?"

"I'd thought to stop to ask your advice on a matter. Moll and I are considering bringing an indentured servant here, but maybe you can tell us how to purchase the contract of one already in the colony? We need to speak with someone knowledgeable about such matters."

"More headrights?"

"Indeed, though our farm is already enough work for Moll and I to handle, but we cannot be beholden to John Hammond's generosity forever."

"This may be a doubly blessed day for you then. A small merchant ship is due in dock any time now from the southern islands. Normally, she'd carry sugar cane and molasses, and some spices to trade, but as you'll see from that poster, she carries additional cargo today."

The clerk pointed to a paper nailed to the wall behind us. It began "Just Imported in the Ship Wren, Capt.

Davis from the isles of the Caribbean, a cargo of choice healthy slaves…"

"We aren't looking for a slave, sir," I said.

"It may be in your interests to attend, Sean. There are often indentured servants on board as well, if the idea of a slave offends the delicate sensibilities of the young Miss."

Uncle thanked him and bid him good day. We turned to walk to the docks, and Uncle turned back and asked, "Has there been anyone new in town asking about me, Christopher?"

"Only that young man of whom we spoke, Gideon I believe? That one has nothing good to say about the two of you. Are you expecting someone, Sean?"

"Oh, no one, but perhaps some news from home."

There were no merchant vessels within view at the docks, so we took our meal at the Inn. It was my first taste of the local crabs, and it would not be my last! The innkeeper was kind enough to show us the proper method of picking them, and once I got past the arms and the fins sticking out, I savored the salty sweet and moist meat inside. Juices from the crabs ran down Uncle's chin, and he needed to mop his face with regularity. He played with the claws discovering when he pushed and pulled on the thin membrane inside, the claw opened and closed as if alive.

We took our time with the feast, scraping off those parts the innkeeper said make people sick, but after eating a half dozen of the succulent creatures, my stomach rebelled. I excused myself and hurried to the bog-house.

Upon my return, a man stuck his head inside the doorway. "The ship's in dock. Auction's about to start."

Uncle finished the last sip of what he said was sour wine, settled up with the innkeeper and we made our way to the auction block.

The population of the town doubled in size this day, and all surrounded the town square. Women wore their fanciest dresses, and likewise the men sported their Sunday best attire. The children danced, sang and played tag in the streets. The articles for sale were on prominent display, hogsheads of goods encircled the auction block, and a temporary pen held the dozen or so black men and women.

I still felt nauseous after our meal, and hoped it would be over quickly. Uncle wormed his way through the packed crowd, and slipped up to the auctioneer.

"My niece and I are in need of an indenture. Did the ship bring any unspoken for?" He yelled over the clamor of the mob.

"Only a very young boy. I suspect the spirits may have lured the lad away with candy and promises, and snatched him up. He's not stout enough for the work in the islands, nor here. I believe the captain plans to take him on as a cabin boy, and he wasn't brought ashore."

I tugged at Uncle's sleeve. "What manner of spirit does he speak of?"

"It's what they call the unscrupulous men who nab young people near the docks and ship them here against their will."

"What? How horrible, the poor babes! At least the captain will care for him."

"I'm sure he'll earn his keep," Uncle said.

"If there are no servants aboard, we might as well leave. Who do we need to speak to about the next ship bringing indentured servants?"

"We'll need to ask the harbormaster when he's done his chores here. He knows everything about the docks, and will certainly know when the next ship is due to arrive."

The auctioneer stepped up to the block, and stated the auction values would be stated in pounds of tobacco, or Sot-Weed.

"But we're not adverse to pounds sterling, mind you!" He quipped, and announced the trade goods to be auctioned first. Most such trade ships brought manufactured goods from England, but raw goods, and foods that were not available here, were much sought after. In short order, these goods were sold. The major attraction was the sale of the men and women, so of course they were saved for last.

By the time the human chain was led to the auctioneer, the crowd grew half again as large. As each man or woman reached the steps, a helper unshackled them, and draw their shirts down to their waists.

"Why are they doing that, Uncle? It's disgusting."

"Be still, Moll," Uncle whispered, as I noticed several sets of disapproving eyes turned in my direction.

"They check them for their health, and more importantly, for the marks of the whip."

"A whip?"

"Yes, when a master requires punishment to maintain control over a slave, some resort to the whip. A man of reasonable intelligence would not do so by choice, and ruin the productivity of his servant for several days, so it is assumed that only the laziest or unruly bear such marks. Things are not so different here as in old England."

"I gather they don't consider those with black hearted masters?" I asked.

The first two men were the biggest, and strongest, and were brought forward to be inspected. The bidders looked over their skin, and were allowed to pull open their mouths to see the black men's teeth. One sold for 250 and the other 300 pounds of Sot-Weed. The next several men were described as "past their prime, but with many years of fieldwork left in them." They brought between 125 to 200 pounds of Sot-Weed each. The assistants led an old and very heavy woman to the block next, and she slapped at her captors when they tried to pull down her shirt. Some of the young men in the crowd were most uncivilized, and made the hooting noises of a barred owl. They left the woman's shirt and chains on, and advertised her cooking and cleaning skills, but she still only brought a pittance of 75 pounds.

I noticed a young woman, perhaps twenty five years old, standing next in line. As I watched her, she lifted her head and returned my gaze. She stepped ahead of her captors to the block, unchained but still clothed. The auctioneer began to describe her value.

"This young woman has excellent potential, gentlemen. She is a strong, hard worker who can handle field work, and she's not unseemly to look at for the fine gents among you who can afford house help, or who lack companionship. Let's start the auction at 250 pounds?"

"Is she sickly?" Came a call from the crowd.

"Healthy as an ox with plenty of years left in her!" came the reply. "Can I hear 250 pounds?

"What's wrong with her? Smallpox scars? Whippings?"

"Let's see her!"

The auctioneer, with apparent reluctance, finally submitted to their demands. When he pulled down her shirt, she threw back her shoulders making her exposed breasts prominent, the left one branded with the number 3.

There were "Oohs, and Ahhs" from the crowd, but not from the vulgar young men and their appreciation for her figure, but rather because of the crisscross pattern of scars on her back, sides and breasts.

"Can I hear 250 pounds?" Silence.

"200, can I hear 200 pounds of tobacco for this woman?"

"What's going on, Uncle?" I asked.

"No one will spend that much on a rebellious servant," Uncle replied.

"Bring up the next one," someone yelled.

"One hundred pounds even. Do I hear one hundred pounds?"

I saw movement beside me, and turned to see a young man toss a handful of rotten fruit at the woman. Some hit her face, and she wiped it off with a swipe of her hand.

"Stop it!" I yelled. The young man ignored me and threw more.

"Seventy-five! Seventy-five! Seventy five! Can I hear sixty-five pounds?"

"Buy her, Uncle."

"What? But you don't want a slave-"

"Buy her."

"She's a trouble maker."

"Sixty five pounds!" I yelled, and the eyes of the entire gathering turned to me.

"Seventy, do I hear seventy? Going once…Sold for sixty five pounds to the young woman with the discerning eye."

Chapter Eighteen

"What in hell did you think you were doing, Moll?" Uncle asked. "That woman will be nothing but trouble, mark my words. You saw the scars on her back! She will run off before the week's done. We don't have enough funds to save the world, we need someone who will work for us!"

"She will, Uncle. She has pride, but she'll work."

"And how is it that you know this? How will you get any work out of her when the harsh slave masters of the south islands could not?"

"When she learns she will be a freed after a term of labor, she will have the incentive to work."

"Moll, Moll, Moll," Uncle said shaking his head at me. "I hope you know what you are doing. I'm not very happy with you. This was an irrational and emotional decision, and as partners, it is something we should have discussed! Don't you agree?"

"Yes, Uncle, I do, and I won't act so rashly again. I admit I would be perturbed if you did such a thing. I don't even know why I did it. There was something about her, and that evil boy throwing things at her…I, well I knew how she felt!"

"Well, pray she doesn't become a liability to us, or a runner." Uncle said.

Uncle signed some papers, and there was some haggling over the real and current value of a pound of Sot-Weed, but the exchange went smoothly enough, and all were well satisfied in thinking they'd gotten the better of the other.

The auctioneer's assistant led us to the holding pen, and handed me the chain lead holding the woman shackled.

"Would you please remove these?" I asked.

"Can't ma'am, but I'll give you the key. We can't have her running before you can get her shed of the auction now, can we?"

"I suppose not," I took the key, unlocked the chains and let them drop to the ground. "Please come." I said to the woman, turned and walked back toward Uncle Sean. It was difficult not looking back to see if she followed. At the carriage, I introduced myself and Uncle Sean to our servant, and asked her name.

"Nema, Misses."

I held out my hand and after staring at it for a moment, she grasped it and shook it firmly.

"Nema, this is how it's going to be. We expect you to be honest and hard-working and loyal to us in all things. The work is hard, and the hours are long. We do not have a dwelling for you yet, and you will help us to build one. You will not run away! You will hoe, cut, plant, weed, or build, and work as needed on our farm."

"Yes'm, Nema work hard, make no trouble for Master or Misses." She said with her head down and eyes hidden from our view.

"Nema, our names are Sean and Moll. In exchange for your labors, Sean and I will draw up a contract for your term of indenture. You will work for us for seven years. At the end of that time, if you have fulfilled your contract, we agree to sign the papers to make you free, and provide you with what is needed to start out on your own, or to return to your island if that is your wish."

Nema glanced up in surprise, and dropped her head again. "Free, no slave?"

"You are not a slave now, Nema, you are our indentured servant. We will treat you well, I promise. But yes, after seven years, your contract is fulfilled."

Nema raised her head and smiled, revealing a dimple in one cheek. "I will work very hard for you, Miss

Moll. I will be the best worker this colony has ever seen, and I promise I will not disappoint you or Mister Sean."

I smiled to myself, startled by Nema's sudden command of English.

"Where are you from Nema, which island?" Uncle asked.

"I hail from the British colony of St. Kitts. My mother was from Africa."

"And what of your father? Your skin is…?" Uncle asked at loss for words.

Nema paused for a moment. "My mother was African, a young girl when captured and taken to the island. Master bred her with a captured Carib slave, but she died in birth. My father died trying to escape the cane fields when I was but a small child."

"That's terrible, Nema. Who raised you then?"

"A slave woman in Master's house, but that was long ago."

"What is a Carib?" Uncle asked.

"They are the native people of my island, Indians."

I looked Nema over, noticing her skin was colored more like Bluebird's and Two Bears' than the other men and women sold that day. Her hair was not like either one. It was also black as a bear's fur, but wavy in nature.

"Why were you whipped, Nema?" Uncle asked.

Nema dropped her eyes. "Master want Nema, I fight, Master whip. Nema run, Master catch and whip. Nema pray to keep Jumbie away, Master whip. Nema work in field, fall down and Master's man whip."

"That's also in the past, Nema," I said, "have you ever helped build a cabin?"

Chapter Nineteen

We rode on in silence until nearing the small wooden bridge spanning St. Mary's river (it was but a small creek there). Our horse, Blaze, acted skittish and began a sideways trot. Uncle pulled back on the reins to slow him to a stop. We got down from the carriage while Uncle inspected his hooves. The horse's eyes were large as saucers, and he tried to rear, but Nema held him and spoke in his ear while Uncle lifted each front hoof in turn.

"I see nothing." Uncle said shrugging his shoulders. "Ah, here we go," he said, grabbing a stick. The copperhead snake appeared dead, crushed by the horse's hooves, but Uncle took no chances, and used the stick to hold its head while he picked it up and twisted its neck. He tossed the snake into the bushes at the side of the road.

"That takes care of that." Uncle smiled, and brushed his hands off on his trousers.

I saw Uncle's eyes focus behind me, and as I turned, the man jumped onto Nema's back, wrapping one arm around her throat. A knife appeared in his other hand, and he pressed it against her chest! Nema lost her grip on the horse's reins as he reared up, and off it ran.

"Now that's just a damn shame." The man said. "I figured on riding today."

"Easy Mister, I don't know what you've done, or what you want, and I don't care. Just let us go in peace." Uncle said.

The man laughed showing a mouth lacking most of its teeth. His clothes hung in rags, and he smelled of the unbathed.

"Just pass along any valuables you might have, sir, and then I'll be on my way. Maybe I'll take this fine young slave to keep me warm at night too."

Nema twisted her head to look at the man. "You! Master, this man is no good. He was an English convict on the ship that brought me here. His sentence was transportation, and was to be sold as a slave in the city, but he escaped and jumped in the river."

"That will be enough out of you," the man said tightening his grip on her throat, and running the knife blade through the front of her shirt. "Understood? But the black bitch is right about one thing, I'm not a man to be trifled with!"

"Easy now. You can take anything you want, the slave girl too, just don't hurt us," Uncle said.

"There's a smart fellow. The New World is the land of opportunity, and I'm getting my piece! So let's start with your money. Empty your pockets, and put it at your feet."

Uncle pulled the coins from his pockets and dropped them. The man turned to me. "And you Miss? You ain't much to look at, but I reckon you have something to add to that pile?"

I turned the pockets of my dress inside out. "I have no money."

He lost interest in me and turned back to Uncle. "Regular paupers now, aren't you? That's all the chink you have?" he sneered.

"Yes sir, we're just poor farmers is all. Please don't hurt us."

"Quit sniveling, and maybe you'll come out of this in one piece, just a bit lighter for your journey home."

"Yes of course, whatever you want," Uncle sniffed. I stared at Uncle in surprise until his eyes caught mine.

I took a few steps to the side.

"You'll be staying right where you are now, Miss," he ordered and slid the knife along Nema's shirt for emphasis. Nema flinched and I knew his knife touched her flesh.

"What's that shiny little chain you have there?" he asked, pointing with the knife at Uncle's pocket watch.

"That's my father's watch, and it's all I have left from him," Uncle said. "Please let me keep it?"

The man rolled his eyes. "Hand it over."

Uncle drew the watch from his pocket, and tossed it toward the man. He reached to catch it with the hand holding the knife, and Uncle snatched it back by the chain. Nema let her legs go out from under her, and dropped from the man's grip. Uncle was on him like an avenging angel.

He twisted the man's arm to the sharp crack of the bone snapping. He snatched away the knife, and hit the man in the face with his forehead. Several sharp blows from Uncle's fists followed. He continued the attack, landing punch after punch until the man fell to the road in a heap.

The fight left the man. He tried in vain to cover his face with his hands. Uncle continued to pummel him in the face and guts.

"Uncle, stop," I said.

The man's head jerked left to right like a pendulum as Uncle's fists connected with their target. Splatters of blood flew with the blows, covering Uncle's face and arms.

"Uncle, stop it, that's enough!" I said, pulling back on his shoulders.

Uncle drew his arm over his head, and smashed the man in the face. His body went limp.

Uncle drew back his fist for another go, and I grabbed his hand.

"Uncle, stop, he's done. You'll kill him!"

Uncle yanked his arm away from me. "Some men need killing, Moll. You of all people should know that! He's a filthy thief!"

Blaze did not run far, and Nema and I retrieved him and the carriage with haste. Uncle had the man tied up by then, and Nema added a noose around his neck, tying the end of the rope to the carriage.

"In case he tries to leap to his freedom again." She said.

We then retraced our journey back to Saint Mary's City. Uncle turned the still unconscious man over to the High Sheriff, and received the three pound reward just posted by the ship's captain for the convict's apprehension.

"He goes by the name of Oliver Hodges," Sheriff Lowe told us. "Convicted of inciting a riot in London, he was. The sentence was transportation to the colonies for 10 years."

"Isn't that excessive?" I asked.

"You can ask that after your experience, Miss?"

"Well, yes, I suppose he is quite violent."

"That he is, Miss," and he turned to Uncle. "Mr. Dyer, you did a good thing in bringing this man to justice, even though he's half dead. You seem to be a man with a temper and plenty handy with your fists?"

"Only when I have to be, Sheriff. The man had a knife!"

"Indeed, so you said. Just remember, we're a peaceable colony here. If you'd beaten a free man this way, I'd put you in the stocks until your arms rotted off."

"Understood, but as you said, Sheriff, he's a violent criminal."

"That he is. He'll be jailed until the next auction and should cause no further distress to you and yours. Good day then, Mr. Dyer, ma'am." The sheriff nodded.

Uncle later said the convict fetched a mere 4 pounds at auction, partly due to his scarred face, I'm sure.

Chapter Twenty

The Sot-Weed cutting began in earnest. Although the walls for Nema's small cabin were built, the roof would have to wait until the crop was in the barn. Nema slept on a bedroll on the cabin's floor, but never complained.

One morning we took a break from the sun, and sat down between the rows. The height of the plants easily shaded the hot sun. Nema spoke little, and I felt she had something on her mind.

"So, are you going to tell me about it?" I asked.

"About what, Miss Moll?"

"Whatever it is on your mind that has you so subdued. I'm nearly keeping up with you cutting the plants."

"I lied to you, Miss Moll, about when I was younger, and about the whip marks too."

"Nema, I told you, that was a long time ago. It doesn't matter."

"It does, and I need to tell you." I gestured for her to continue.

"Misses, you know a lot about plants and healing, but I know you believe in Jumbie too, because of the words you say when helping someone. Well, not the words you say, but how you say them."

"I don't know what Jumbie is, but I think I know what you are talking about. The other world? The world of spirit?" I answered.

"Yes, the beings of the spirit world then, what do you know of them?"

I looked away from her, not sure how strongly she held her beliefs, or how crazy she might think me.

"I know some, what my mother taught me. I know the plants, and some words to help. What is it that you want to tell me, Nema? Do you know something of these dark spirits?"

"No Miss, not much, but the woman who raised me knew much of them. Miss Grace told me many stories, but she would not teach me about these dark spirits, except for one. She was African, and learned much from the Caribs. Her former master was of your old country, and he told her of a legend of that land. She was afraid of what I was, or what it was I might become."

"What do you mean she was afraid of you? You were a child." I said.

"She thought me the child of a demon, Moll, and she told a different story of my birth, and of my parents."

"That is nonsense, Nema! You were a perfectly innocent child!"

"Perhaps, but please let me tell you her tale, Moll. She said my father did not take well to slavery. He screamed at night, suffering from all manner of strange dreams. The field slaves said he spoke of visions of a woman coming to him at night, promising him freedom. He even told them he had relations with this woman. The other slaves thought him touched in the head. This went on for some time until the master mated him with my mother in the hope it would settle him down, but it didn't work."

"What happened to him?"

"He slept one night with my mother, and once was enough to plant his seed to make me. The next morning, the overseer found him dead. He was covered with blood, as if he'd bathed in it they said. He still had the knife in his hand that he used to slice open his neck. The same afternoon, the master searched for a missing cow, and spotted circling vultures. He investigated, and found a young slave woman, not much more than a girl. She had been dead for several days, her throat slit just like my father's."

"Nema, that is horrid! Did they think your father killed her too?"

"They had enough certainty to convict a slave anyway, and he could not tell his side of the story. My mother swelled with child, with me, and Miss Grace remembered the demon story her old master told her years before."

I shook my head, and started to speak…

"Please do not poke fun at me, Miss?"

"I promise I will not. There is much I do not know," I said.

"Miss Grace said the female of these demons is called a Succubus, and the male form is an Incubus. They appear more beautiful than any human, and never show their true appearance. This beauty makes it easy for them to mate with human men and women, but they are not averse to raping their intended victim if need be."

"I am not familiar with this tale," I said, but my body stiffened, and the hairs raised on the back of my neck. "How or why would a demon create a human child?"

"The children are called Cambions, and they are often very pleasing to the eye, but they are also very vulnerable to the psychic whims of the succubus, being readily possessed by them."

"How then? How can a demon create life?" I asked, but feared the answer.

"The succubus, the female form of the demon, mates with a human man, and draws forth his seed where it becomes tainted, corrupted as demon seed, but it remains dormant within her."

"How then is the seed passed? Do they wait for the full moon or something?" I laughed weakly.

"Please Moll? There is some confusion as to the next step because the demon may present itself as either male or female. There are two schools of thought. Miss Grace maintained that the original demon takes possession of a male human, most often a Cambion, then seduces or rapes a human female impregnating her with the demonic seed. The other theory is that two such demons are involved. The act of copulating somehow passes the seed to the male and at the same time corrupts it. Both theories involve a ritual involving the sacrificial blood of a virgin, and the possession of a human male."

"The young girl they found murdered?" I asked.

"Yes, or so Miss Grace thought."

"Then why you? Why did your Miss Grace say these demons picked your family for their evil?"

"Families with the gift or the knowledge to touch the other world, are always in danger from these demons. They are the ones the demons most desire to impregnate, and my mother was a healer, called a sangoma in her own land. When a family comes to their attention, they target its weakest member to seduce."

"Dear Lord, and this is the story your guardian told you as a child?" I asked. "Aren't devils and demons supposed to hate humans? Why would any mother, even a demonic mother, leave her child to be raised by someone she hates?" I asked.

"Perhaps they trust the evilness of their seed to turn the child to them? Demons are known to be self-serving I guess? I don't know, but Miss Grace was convinced this happened to my parents, and to me. She said she would drive it out of me, make me wholly human."

"You believe this, Nema?" I asked.

Nema shrugged. "Would you take the chance? Do you believe in God, the angels and the saints, Miss Moll? I do, and I believe for every good thing there is a bad thing. Every coin has two sides."

"Why would this woman tell you such a story?"

"To prepare me to watch for the signs when my first woman's time came, for any changes in me, physically or otherwise. Miss Grace said children like me, like she thought I was, a Cambion, were the biggest prize of all for the demons."

"So they can corrupt them and use them in our world?"

"Yes, and they can possess them at will, and use them to create more Cambion children. They conspire to mate these children together to create a new, more powerful being. One who can walk in either world at will. To what end I fear to imagine."

"So, assuming such a crazy story to be true, how would anyone know? How could they discover if they were the offspring of such a union?" I asked.

"They are marked somewhere with the sign of the demon."

"Do you think you have such a mark?"

"Miss Grace said three scratches are hidden on the body. Streaks on my breast were the mark, but they are gone now. I guess I was lucky the brand burned them off when they sold me to the slave merchants." Nema answered.

"You think that drove out the demon? You cannot believe being branded by those animals was a good thing?" I asked.

"No, destroying the mark doesn't change anything, but I don't have the reminder every time I bathe. You were the only good thing that came of it, Miss Moll."

I gave Nema a hug, as dirty and sweaty as we both were.

"If Cambions exist, is there no hope for them? You said she was going to drive the demon out of you? How did she plan to do that?" I asked.

Nema dropped her eyes. "Deals can be made with demons, Moll. That's where the whip marks came from, but I believe Miss Grace also paid with her life."

Chapter Twenty-One

With my belly stretched as tight as Two Bears' drum, we cut and hung the tobacco to cure. Sticky brown tobacco gum coated our blistered hands, but the pride I felt at getting in our first crop dispelled any inconvenience! I limited my hours in the field, and ran to the cabin at any sign of company. In my entire life I'd not read as much as I now did sitting by the light of the window that summer, and I learned many things. Bluebird was our most frequent guest that season, as Peter had plenty to do in his last year with John Hammond.

Bluebird and Nema became quick friends, and I confess to some degree of jealousy. Sometimes at night when Bluebird visited, the two of them spoke in whispers I could not hear, or Nema would take her to see her cabin, although it was unchanged since Bluebird's previous visit. It felt like the old days, and I was being shunned by the fancy girls again. Mother often said that women often have silly thoughts while carrying a wee one.

One hot day, Nema and I whacked away at the plants on the streamside of the cabin when Bluebird appeared with a tobacco knife in hand.

"Good day Nema, good day, Moll," she said, "I help some, and brought groundhog to eat. Feel bad today, Moll?"

At that moment, I was. I felt sharp pain like that at a woman's time, and I hoped my baby was healthy.

"Yes, I'm fine, it's just the heat," I answered and made a show of wiping the sweat from my eyes.

"Go sit on the porch in the shade," Nema directed. "We will draw some cool water from the stream."

"Yes, I'd love some of Adam's ale," I said and smiled.

Bluebird said something to Nema I could not hear, and pointed towards the woods. Nema nodded, and they appeared to exchange a few heated remarks before they returned and sat with me.

Bluebird reached into her buckskin pouch, pulled something out, and handed it to me from her closed hand. "To protect you and your baby," she said.

I admired the antler amulet that was similar to Bluebird's. I touched the crooked arrow carved in the antler, and felt something on the other side. Turning it over, I saw the carving of a raven. I was neither surprised nor upset to see it there, and I was pleased the awful memory had dampened with time.

"Raven is a trickster, but he also helps the people. Raven is your protector," she said and pointed overhead at the dozen black birds perched in the trees around us.

"Many ravens here, Moll. Arrow good medicine too."

"Thank you, Bluebird," I said, and pulled the leather thong over my neck. "My ancestors also believed in the raven's spirit. They said people touched by the raven have many personal demons to fight, and often devote their lives to a larger cause. They are also said to walk the world alone, yet I have two of the best friends a woman could hope for."

I hugged her in appreciation.

"Tell Moll now, Nema," Bluebird said.

"Misses, is there another friend I have not met who might come to visit with you and Mister Sean?" Nema asked.

"I believe you met all of our friends? Peter, Two Bears and Bluebird are about it, perhaps John Hammond on a rare occasion."

"And this Mr. Hammond, what does he look like?"

"He's an elderly gentleman. Short, with gray hair…, but what is this about, Nema?"

"There is another who watches you," Bluebird blurted out.

"Yes, and we've both seen him. He is never here in the full light of day. He comes just before and after," Nema added.

"What does this man look like?"

"He's tall and bony thin, a very white man, as white as the full moon, but a young man, not like you describe Mr. Hammond."

"Gideon," I said and shook my head. "What does he do here?"

"He only watches," Bluebird said.

What could Gideon want of me, of us?

"Is he coming here often? How long has he been spying on us?"

"I saw him the first morning I was with you," Nema said. "I took a bath in the stream at sunrise, and saw him watching. I hurriedly dressed then, and did not let him know I saw, but twice more I have seen him. He hides in the bushes hoping to see you I think."

I winced as another sharp cramp twisted through my womb.

"And you have seen this man also, Bluebird?"

She nodded, "I saw this man two times. I watch him while he watches Moll's house."

I felt a surge of confusion, anger and of fear. "Why are you only now telling me this, Nema? Why didn't you tell me before?"

"I am sorry, Miss Moll. At first, I thought I was being watched as I bathed, and I didn't want to speak ill of a white man to you. Then later, I didn't want to scare you…"

"Hello ladies." Uncle shouted as he stalked toward the cabin. "Got enough water that you might share a taste?"

"Uncle," I said standing. "Come here, you won't believe…" I stopped, realizing what Uncle's reaction to this information might be.

I felt a strange wetness, and a sudden gushing flow drenched my legs. I glanced down and saw the porch floorboards soaked at my feet.

"Her water's broken!" Nema cried.

The women helped me inside, and led me to my bed as another cramp twisted my insides. The muscles in my lower back tightened without warning.

"What can I do?" Uncle asked from the doorway.

"Go away, Mister Sean," Nema ordered. "Boil some water, bring some clean cloth from the clothesline, and tap at the door when it's prepared."

"I know that you've helped to midwife before, Nema, and my baby is early. It should be two more weeks!" I said.

"The baby is ready, Misses. It knows when it's time."

The muscles inside of me twisted, and kinked even tighter when I felt a downward pull. I felt I was being gutted. Then with mercy, it would slow, only to begin again, over and over, the pain racked me.

"How bad is it now, Miss Moll?" Nema asked.

"The pain attacks in waves, like the ocean's ebb and flow. Ebbing at the moment."

Nema laughed. "You must relax, Miss Moll. Pretend the pain is a wave then. When it comes, do not fight it like you are drowning, but let yourself go and float to the surface when it passes. It won't be long now."

"I'll try Nema. Oh, my back hurts," and then Bluebird's hands were there pressing, rubbing to ease my discomfort.

"What good friends I have," I thought, and realized I'd spoken the words aloud.

"We are here for you, Misses. Just get ready to push now. Do you want to push?"

I heard a knock at the door, and sat up. "It's just Mister Sean, relax."

"Yes," I said as a surge hit me again, and screamed.

"Push, Miss Moll, I see your baby's head."

I felt a fire burning in me there as I pushed, and pushed again, then a sudden movement.

"The head is out, Misses. Push again when you are ready."

I was as tired and weak as after a full day in the Sot-Weed fields. I wondered if another push was in me! Then the next wave swept over me, and the urge to push became impossible to resist.

"One more should do it, Miss Moll." Nema assured me, and when the next wave crested, I pushed with every fiber of my being. A sudden voiding, an emptiness, then:

"Congratulations, Misses. You have a big strong healthy boy!" A great relief washed over me when I heard his first small cries.

"Nema, please let me see my baby."

Bluebird went to retrieve the water and the cloths from the porch.

"What's happening? Is everything going well?" I heard Uncle yell.

"Yes Sean, you father to strong baby boy." Bluebird answered.

"No Bluebird, Sean's not …oh, never mind," and Nema and I burst into laughter.

As they bathed my little one, I noticed three graze marks just below his belly. Bluebird applied a salve to help them heal, and to keep them clean.

"I must cut his little nails, they are as sharp as eagle talons." I said, watching for Nema's reaction.

"Yes, they do appear sharp." Nema said. She nibbled her upper lip with her teeth, wrapped Zachary so he'd not get a chill, and placed him on my chest. So beautiful was my little boy! As I admired him, a feeling of deep calm and peace filled me. As Zachary drew at my breast, we both drifted off to sleep.

I dreamt of running through the fields of Kinsale with a young Zachary at my side. We hunted for herbs, skipped stones across the River Bandon, and lay on our backs soaking up the sun and imagining figures formed from the clouds. I woke covered with a blanket, and my baby still slept on my chest. Sweat poured over my body.

Nema stared at me, and I sat up. "Is Zachary all right?"

"Zachary is fine, and we are all here. Congratulations, Moll," Uncle said, and kissed my forehead. "A fine looking boy he is too. You'd never know his conception was…" Uncle stopped, reining in the rest of his remark before it passed his lips.

"Umm, you'd never know his considering coming so early. You sure wouldn't, he's a big boy." He tried again, with blushing cheeks. Even my uncle could not keep my child's origin from clouding his thoughts.

I sat up in the bed, and noticed a powdery substance sprinkled around me, both white and red in color.

"What is this?" I asked, brushing it off of the bedclothes.

"Don't ask me," Uncle answered. "Nema and Bluebird insisted. I don't know much about babies and such. Good medicine I guess."

Nema put a finger to her lips to shush me. I took a few deep calming breaths, and looked back to my uncle. "Uncle Sean, meet the newest member of the Dyer family … my brother, Zachary." My eyes misted over and I gritted my teeth, but did not allow any tears to fall. Nema squinted, and pulled her mouth into a straight line, confused.

"Zachary Dyer, meet your Uncle Sean. He really is my favorite relative, but don't tell him so. It will be our secret."

Chapter Twenty-Two

I tried my best to ensure my son did not want for anything, but such an intense focus often drives a wedge between friends. Bluebird's visits now centered on Nema's cabin, unless she'd come to conduct a trade with me. Uncle spoke about farm matters with Nema more so than he did with me. Overnight, I became a non-entity, an afterthought in my own home, and I didn't like it. Zachary and I had a major stake in the prosperity of our farm, and I would not be ignored.

One evening as I fed Zachary, Uncle and Nema discussed sowing the Sot-weed plants for next year's season, and going over the farm accounts. Bluebird knocked at our door.

"Nema?" she asked, sticking her head in the door.

"We can finish up tomorrow," Uncle said. "It promises to be a wet morning. I see a halo around the moon."

Nema walked to the door, and the two of them departed for Nema's cabin without as much as a word to me.

"Uncle, have you forgotten we have a partnership?" I asked.

"Ahh, so that's why you've been so moody with everyone? You think we are leaving you out of things?"

"I'm not moody at all, but I do wonder why it is you seek our servant's council instead of your own partner's?"

"Did you really just call her that?" Uncle asked.

"Who? What?"

"Moll, you do more than your fair share around here, there's no need to feel guilty about caring for your…brother."

"This isn't about that. Yes I work hard, we all do, but I'm your partner."

"We are trying to give you the time you need with the little one, not exclude you."

"Well, you are excluding me! You all are!"

"Fine Moll, I understand. We will make sure we include you from now on," Uncle said.

"This is my future and my son's future too!" I shouted, still not ready to let go of my anger. I left the cabin, and walked down to the stream. I bent down, and took a sip of fresh water, unsure why I was so upset. As the water seeped down to my stomach, I realized how chill the night air was, dressed as I was. I shivered, and heard Bluebird and Nema laughing in the other cabin. I was not ready for Uncle's companionship after my tantrum, and decided to pay them a visit. Knocking at Nema's door, I heard the whispered voices of my two friends.

"Hello? Nema, Bluebird?"

"Nema be right there, Misses."

"Hurry up, it's cold out here." I rubbed my hands over my arms.

The door opened a crack, and Nema peered out. "Yes, Moll?"

"Aren't you going to ask me in?" I asked.

"Miss Moll no wanna come in Nema's poor house." Nema answered.

I wasn't sure if it was her awkward reluctance to let me in, or her resorting back to broken English that agitated me more. I pushed hard against the door, and Nema half stumbled backwards into Bluebird.

"What are you two up to?" I asked, and strolled into the cabin uninvited.

They did not answer, but stood aside as I swept into the dark room.

"Nema and Bluebird pray." Nema said.

While my eyes adjusted to the dark, they didn't speak a word. A small flat topped chest sat atop a crude table, and the candles placed there provided the room's only light. I walked over to get a better look, and saw engraved black and white candles that shed minimal light on the surrounding items. Between the candles stood two small figures, in front of which was a stone bowl containing smoldering charcoal. To the right of the bowl was a clear jar of water. The open area of the table held a mound of salt, and a bowl of dirt. A knife lay atop a cluster of fresh roots.

"What is all this?"

"Nema and Bluebird pray, Misses," Nema said.

"Stop talking like that Nema. What are you praying for? Who are you praying to?"

"Yes ma'am," Nema answered ducking her head. "We are calling on the powers of protection, Misses."

"What is this?" I asked, and picked up one of the rough carved figures from the top of the chest. It was dressed in the manner of Bluebird's people, but painted black. Its hair was as long as its body on one side, and shaved bald on the other.

"This is the devil god Okeus, isn't it, Bluebird?" I asked again.

Bluebird nodded, "Yes, this Okeus." I sat the figure back in place, and turned to face my friends.

"Nema, you are a Christian woman, what do you know of such things?" I asked.

She shrugged her shoulders. "I am a good Christian, Misses, but as you know, the woman who raised me remembered the old ways, and taught me some. Bluebird is teaching me what she knows too, the magic of her people. We do not ask for any harm to come to anyone. We are doing no wrong."

I smiled recalling my mother saying much the same thing at the Druid's Altar. "Why then did you hide this from me? What is it you pray for?"

Nema looked out of her lone window, and crossed her arms when she answered.

"We pray for good crops, and a mild winter," she answered.

Bluebird scrunched up her eyebrows. "No Nema, we pray to protect Moll and baby from crazy man," she corrected.

"The crazy man?"

"He is still coming here, Misses, that man. Not like before, but he still watches you and Zachary," Nema said.

"Gideon? Oh for the love of God, and I never told Uncle about him." I doubted Gideon posed any real threat, but I couldn't believe I'd forgotten about his spying.

"Yesterday you left Zachary in the shade of the barn while you checked the curing of the plants, and this man crawled through the grass towards him. He looked like a cat stalking its prey. I grabbed Zachary without this Gideon knowing I saw him."

My legs felt weak as Nema described the scene.

"Nema, thank you. I must tell my uncle about Gideon, we can't guard Zachary every second of every day."

Nema shook her head. "If Mister Sean knows, he will kill the bastard. Come see what we are doing, Misses. If the protection spell does not work, we will take care of whatever needs to be done."

Nema led us through the ritual. We cast a spell to protect Zachary from harm, from Gideon. I wept at the thought that the husband of one of my closest friends now considered me an enemy, an evil thing, and my child as well! How did it come to this?

The very idea of Gideon crawling on all fours towards my baby "like a cat stalking its prey" sent shivers up my back. Perhaps I placed too much trust in the man he used to be. If I was lost in some idyllic dream for the first few months of Zachary's life, I needed to wake up if I was to protect him.

Chapter Twenty-Three

Since Zachary's birth, my dreams were full of joy and images of beauty, but that night my dreams were the foulest of nightmares. I huddled behind my bedroom door in Westcowes, a scene I recalled often, even in my waking life: sitting, waiting for my mother to call me to the kitchen.

The tap came at my door, and Mother asked me to follow, but as I entered the kitchen, it was not my uncle and father sitting at the table, but James Rogers! He smiled and the scar across his cheek raised up from his skin.

"Please join us." He pulled out a chair for me. I turned to my mother for guidance, but she was gone. Closing the door behind me stood a beautiful young woman. Her coppery hair flowed over her shoulders in gentle waves, not tortured into woolly curls like mine. Her skin saw little sun, its only color was the slight blush of her cheeks. A forest green gown matched her eyes, and unhidden by her plunging neckline hung an emerald necklace formed in the shape of an owl. If James was not standing at my back, I might have stared at her for hours.

"I am called Laris, and my lovely friend here is Ladonna," James said.

"I know who you are James. Do you think me a fool to forget you, and what you did to me?" I asked.

"Ahh, yes, James, given the attraction you have for males of this appearance, he's the Cambion of choice for my visits with you. A little ragged and unsophisticated for my taste, and a trifle boring I suppose, until I engage him of course." He touched the scar on his face. "You did him no favors with this unsightly blemish, and he is of no further use to the females of your species- without my help that is!

How convenient for you that some dullard fisherman left his gutting knife for you to find!"

"I wish the knife's bite was deeper, James or Laris or whatever you want to call yourself," I said.

"That's no way to be, Moll. Poor James knows little to nothing of what he did to you, the poor lad. Although he remembers the cutting part well enough. Nor was there any call for what your dear old Da' did to him. Fine Christian that he is."

"What did… what do you want? Why do you torment me?" I asked.

"Torment? Dear girl, we are here out of concern for you. We were unable to find you or protect you for so long. Why did it take so long for you to use your knowledge and powers I wonder? No matter, we are here now, your guardian spirits!"

"My guardian spirits? No thanks, I do fine on my own. Why do you haunt me at all? Why not go make some other girl feel special?"

"Your dearest mother opened the door for us, the door to you, but do sit and be sociable, Moll," the woman said, revealing glowing teeth as white as a hens' eggs.

"Yes, do sit and relax," Laris said. "It won't be long now."

"Long? Long for what?" I asked.

"Darling child," the woman said, "until it begins for the two of you." She smiled her beautiful smile.

"The two of us?"

"Well, you and our boy, Zachary of course. Do take good care of him until then, Moll," the James creature said.

"You stay away from my son, you damn demons!"

"Damned we are. Demons? Must we debase ourselves with name calling, you filthy whore! There, I feel better now, how about you? We are the Lilin, if you must give us a name. We are the children of Lilith, and on a mission for our dear mother. Have you forgotten that

Zachary is my progeny too? He is already ours by birthright, ours to claim at will. Still, fear not. He will be allowed to live out his years, and we will be gentle with him, but his child we will claim with your help. We will come when you call."

"I'd never call on the likes of you for help!" I said.

"Well of course you will, dear. Soon you will beg for our aid, not once but twice more, and unlike your mortal family, when you call, we will be there!" Ladonna said.

"Your first innocent casting helped us to find you again, but your power will grow. Your family has one strike against it, your mother's. Twice more, you will use maleficium in your pride and arrogance. The price of our last intervention will be high, but you will live long enough to fulfill your destiny and conclude your service to us. If you do well, we may allow you to keep your precious soul for your troubles, a reward if you will." Laris added.

"Three strikes then, you Christians like things in threes I believe? Our labors do not come cheap, I fear, but we're worth it of course." Ladonna's high pitched, cruel laugh reminded me of the voice of a screech owl.

"I have nothing of value, what do you want from me?"

"I think you know, or was your dear departed mother so negligent in your training?" James-Laris asked.

My eyes flew wide open, but I knew demons were liars.

"Oh my, it seems she didn't know, Ladonna. How special for us, thank you for sharing this extraordinary moment! In answer to your question, our needs are simple. Our children are Cambions, like James, and Zachary, your slave Nema, and many others. They become our vessels for entry into the mortal world, and except for the short periods of time they lose of themselves, they are seldom even aware. We reward them with power in return for this service, more if they do as they are told when we whisper in their ears. If not, they die. Lilith granted us the span of three human generations to accomplish her task." Laris said.

"How wonderful for you, but I grow weary of your prittle-prattle. What is it then that this Queen Mother Lilith of yours wants of me?" I asked.

"When two Cambions mate and produce a child, our task is complete. The child, your grandchild, will be very powerful, and immortal. He will reside in either world at will, a new mate for our Queen Mother, our new king. Alas, Lilith's mate Samael was not forged of the same red clay as was Lilith and Adam, but of some fragile ethereal stuff. He, shall we say, burned out."

"Why tell me this?"

"Concessions must be made."

"I'll not let you to hurt my son, or my son's son. I'd die to protect them."

"Is death the worst fate that dying little ape brain of yours can conjure, Moll?" Laris smiled. "Perhaps that's it, Ladonna, the mortality thing. This is the only existence they recall, so death is the worst outcome they can imagine. What do you think?"

"She is pathetic. Her family, her greed and her pride are among her many weaknesses. Is there anything you wouldn't do to justify your hubris, Moll? Our incentive is great, we will not fail. Those who incur Lilith's wrath condemn themselves to an eternity of darkness and pain, and the tortures of hell are beyond your understanding," Ladonna said.

"You are damn fools. Knowing your intent, you think I'd call on you? I'll watch, and I'll not allow Zachary to be with another Cambion! I'll send you straight back to hell!" I shouted.

Laris flashed a smile revealing sharp pointed teeth, his face seemed to melt like candle wax, and his breath reeked of rotted flesh. Translucent black wings fluttered behind him, then he was as before- James.

"Oh, but you will call, or your family's mortal suffering will be sweet. You might add a few years to your own miserable existence if you betray them, but the darkness will draw you in. If not, we'll still find a way to make you ours. Ours with an eternity to play with you. Bound in the foulest pit of hell; chain raped by every vile, filthy beast of the abyss. Every one of us will know you, and delight in your screams of torment. Ah, the thought is so sublime, it has me all aquiver! I can already taste you."

He leaned across the table, and the forked tongue of a snake flickered from his mouth, forcing its way into mine, exploring. I gagged and tried to bite it off, but my jaw locked. An oily secretion filled my mouth, tasting of rancid fish oil and ashes. Laris withdrew the vile appendage and winked at me. I spat out the taste of him.

"Zachary will mate with a Cambion, and he will do so out of love. That part is important for some reason. What more fitting mockery than the corruption of love, such a fickle human emotion?" Laris asked.

I stared at him, and then into Ladonna's glowing green eyes.

"You are a woman, or what passes for one. How could you want this for any child?"

She stood and walked around the table and knelt beside me, looking at me with caring eyes, a gentle smile and placed her hand on my cheek, and spoke to me as if to a child.

"Moll, he will be a king, a ruler over our world and yours. Isn't that what every mother wants for her children and grandchildren? Happiness, acceptance, and every wish fulfilled? You seek strength, and independence? We will allow Zachary to live his life, but his child will be ours, and we will treasure your descendants. As a bonus, yummy yum, you might be with us too!"

Her snake-like tongue slid down the front of my dress and explored.

I awoke screaming Zachary's name, and I vomited until my stomach convulsed on nothing but stale air. It took some time to fight down the terror. I got up and looked behind every door, out of the windows, under my bed. The dream felt so real.

Chapter Twenty-Four

For weeks after, I spent little time with my friends, and never spoke to them of my dream. I made no mention of our session in Nema's cabin, and feigned ignorance whenever they broached the subject.

As a result, my friends grew more and more distant, and I questioned my resolve and the reality of my dream. Mother always told me I needed to be true to myself and to never forget who and what I was. Surely I was being a fool? My superstitious fear may well cost me my best friends. I'd never cast for harm against another, and I'd surely never allow Zachary to be with another Cambion, if such a creature truly existed. No, my family's trials and tribulations were of this world, and some of my training could help ease those. I suspected, if indeed my dream was real, the lying demons hoped I would not put my humble powers to use.

The three of us "sisters" began enjoying a night together once a week, our version of Mother's sewing circle from many years before. I can't say how effective any of our spells were, the protection one against Gideon clearly was not, but we also cast a protection spell on our stream during the drought. We tossed pyrite, brick and eggshell dust into the waters as we prayed to the universal God. Our stream never stopped flowing. To appease my fears, I was careful to never call upon the aid of anything dark, and we never cast for harm to come to anyone.

Love spells were fun, and we were good at them. Bluebird and I cast one for Nema, as she wanted nothing to do with it. She had her eye on a young freeman from Delaware who settled in the area. Nema laughed at us, and said the spell didn't work when the man took up with someone else. Then, after all these years, we discovered Bluebird had a widowed brother who took a serious interest in Nema. That is the way of spells. What you hope for, and anticipate happening does not. You must keep your eyes open for how your prayer will be answered. Discovering my two friends' secret reopened the door to our friendship

When Uncle Sean delivered a letter from home, his face was dark, and unnatural in its lack of expression. When I saw an open envelope jutting from his pants, I knew the message was not good news. The first page contained a note from my father. He apologized for writing so seldom (this being my second letter from home), and said he had sad news. Mother caught the ague, and met her savior the week before the date of his writing. He thought she came down with it while picking stinging nettle root by the river for his gout. My brothers and sisters were fine, as was he, with the exception of the hole Mother left in their lives that could never be filled.

They appointed my father the overseer on the docks, and he said the money fell like rain. He hoped, in four or five years, to return the family to Kinsale. There was a bit more about the family, and about the neighbors in Westcowes, people I did not know. Mother too, had written a letter to me on her deathbed, and he hoped it wouldn't upset me too greatly, but he enclosed it also for me to read. He signed off "Your Loving Father."

I flipped over to the second page and paused with my eyes closed before I looked at the writing of her delicate hand, unsure if I could read it with the tears blurring my sight, but somehow I did. It read:

Dearest Moll,

A serious illness has befallen me, the gravity of which I keep hidden from your father, but whatever comes to be, do not grieve for me. I am shamed by many mistakes in life, and I cannot claim to be without regrets, but I always tried to do what I felt right for my family and those I love. I am unafraid of death. There are far worse things we must face.

I ask for your indulgence toward an old woman, as I write what I need to say. I want you to know that your birth changed my life forever. I was a young girl, what did I know of love, and what could anyone know of the love for a child, save a parent? You opened my eyes to many things, to a love as fierce as a lion the moment you grasped my hand, and strengthened anew at your first smile. You showed me a pride as tall as the mountains when you took your first wobbly steps, and continued as you grew into a strong woman (yes, do not doubt this about yourself!). You revealed sorrows as deep as the sea whenever you hurt. I will never be free of the guilt and pain of that horrible day when we said our goodbyes. Even then, your only thought was of family and how you could make right for us the horror that was done to you. When I speak your name, Moll (and I do so often), I speak it with pride, and with a crack in my voice.

I pray this finds you well, and that the birth of your child will go easy, as easy as it can be at least. I feel it will be a boy, and he will grow into a strong man, but he will still need your protection and love. I hope you find all of your heart desires, and that you continue to see the beauty in all of God's creation. I pray for your happiness.

Do not take the troubles of the world upon your shoulders! You will face enough with keeping your family safe in the days ahead. You are strong, but remember any strength that stands alone, will be broken. Do not stand alone! Please take care of my precious little girl, you, while you battle the dragons you will face in life!

I want to know everything about your circumstances, and there is much I want to tell you! Are you reading the books I gave you? In the one that was my mother's, there is a story about three angels I must share with you. Their names were Senoi, Sasenoi, and Semangloph, and I believe you will find their story of interest, but I grow weak, and will write more of them later.

Now I must make a confession. Some doors once opened, can forfeit your life, and bring suffering to all you love. I fear I opened such a door when your father could not find work in Westcowes. I called upon powers I didn't understand! The dock foreman hated the Irish almost as much as your father does the English. He poisoned the masters against your father, and they'd not give him a chance to show his mettle. I cast a spell to soften this man's heart, but instead, the poor man's heart burst in his chest! Father was employed within a week, and then my horrid dreams began. Dreams too real to ignore. I wished to bring our family happiness. Instead, I fear I brought a blight upon us all! I tried to keep the darkness from your life, and so I neglected your training since you were a child. I hoped sending you away would put distance between you and this curse of my making, and I pray this was not in vain!

I wanted so for you to know of your heritage, and only taught you enough to protect yourself. It was safe to teach Anna as she was not of my blood, but as I told you then, if you work no magic, you will be hidden from those who would harm you. Whatever happens to me, be wary of your dreams, dearest child, for that too is part of our family's curse. Know that whenever you think of me or call my name, I will be with you.

Do no harm, my beloved,
Mother

With my heart pinched in my chest, I read both pages a second time, folded them neatly and returned them to the envelope as a treasure to savor. Before I slept that night, the pages were already worn, and wet in many places. It was some time before the tears stopped flowing.

Were Mother's slumbers haunted by the same dreams that plagued my resting hours? Was she suggesting these foul imaginings were more than illusions of a tired, restless or guilty mind? Did they somehow portend a future event? Or did the ague that took her life, first take her rational mind? Her warning to do no magic came too late, but if this doorway of which she wrote truly existed, could it come here to harm my family from across the ocean?

Mother was right about one thing, having a baby to love and care for changes your life, your priorities. I rattled on and on to Nema and Uncle about every detail, every new thing my son learned. Whether he smiled at the angels, made sounds that might have been words (with just a little imagination), or the first time he sat up in his cradle, they heard about it all. I'm sure it was a bit tiresome for them, although they had the good grace not to tell me so.

My life and Zachary's were one now. We were joined in the spirit, and physically as well. I worked the fields with him in tow, making sure he had adequate shade to protect him from the sun, and I took him with me to gather herbs for cooking and healing.

Bluebird knew the plants I used the most, and often brought them to me to barter, although she made sure I received the better end of any trade. One such trade (not a trade but a gift for a friend she insisted) was a soft doe-skin leather cradleboard. With it, I could carry Zachary everywhere with my hands free.

The late summer and early fall seasons passed in the blink of an eye. The Sot-weed hung in the barn, and we completed the finishing touches on Nema's cabin. We had sufficient corn and vegetables saved (along with salt cured hams purchased against the sale of our tobacco) to last out the winter.

One evening while Uncle Sean visited John Hammond, Bluebird came to visit just before darkness fell.

Nema and I were sitting in the shade of the porch taking a well-earned rest.

"That bad man, Gideon, he sit now in blackberries by stream," Bluebird said.

I had enough of Gideon's foolishness, and without thought, I grabbed a stick and rushed toward the stream.

"Wait, Miss Moll, you don't know what he'll do! He's not right in the head," Nema said.

"Three women, only one man." I heard Bluebird answer, and I smiled.

"Not enough if he has a gun!" Nema replied.

That wiped the smile from my face. The thought of a gun, or of Gideon shooting at any of us, hadn't even crossed my mind, and for the briefest moment, I almost turned back. Run and hide in the cabin with your friends, my inner voice screamed, but then came the thought of Zachary, and I knew I couldn't allow Gideon to know my fear!

"Gideon Coombs, come out here this instant!" I yelled into the bushes. He did not move, but I saw a flash of blue where none should be.

"I see you Gideon, you may as well come out!" I yelled. Nema and Bluebird ran up behind me.

"I see you, Moll Dyer, and I see you for what you are." He grunted as he pushed his way through the canes. He pulled the thorns from his clothes before deigning to look at me. He appeared many years older than the last time we'd met. His clothes needed mending, his hair was greasy, unwashed, and his face unshaven. The biggest change was his eyes, dark, empty black hollows displaying the burning hatred smoldering within him.

"Get off of our property, Gideon, or you will have my uncle to deal with."

He flinched, and I knew he well remembered his encounter with Uncle Sean. I suspected he heard of our adventure with the English criminal as well; it seemed that everyone in the colony knew the story.

"I'm not afraid of Sean Dyer, witch, and he won't blindside me again, but I have no quarrel with him. I'm breaking no laws, and I'm doing no harm to anyone. I only watch, and wait."

"Wait? What do you wait for? There's nothing for you here."

"Your "brother" is here," he sneered. "I believe you've named him Zachary?"

"I did, although the doings of my family are of no concern to you!"

"I'll wait and see who the child favors, then we will see… if it's all the same to you."

"Well, it isn't, and you are trespassing! Leave now, Gideon!" I shouted, and slapped the stick on the ground and heard it snap.

He laughed. "As you wish, but I'll be watching. When I know for sure if the boy is of my blood, then you, Sean, and your two witch whores won't stop me from taking back what is mine. You can count on that!"

"Gideon, stop it. Do you know how foolish you sound? This is not what Beth would have wanted for you."

At the mention of Beth's name, he glared at me.

"Don't even speak her name out of your disgusting mouth, you witch!" He spat at my feet. I felt the flush of blood heating my face.

"Beth! Beth! Beth! Just leave already! You are not welcome here!"

He made a great show of brushing off his pants, then turned his back, pushed back his shoulders, puffed out his chest and walked away through the woods. We watched until he was well out of view in the waning light.

"It is as I feared, Misses. Gideon is touched in the head. He might do anything, but he's not going to just go away," Nema said.

"Two Bears fix him?" Bluebird asked.

"No, if Two Bears did anything to him, the whites would come after your people, Bluebird. Do not tell him of this, and I'll think of something. Maybe Uncle can talk some sense to him."

"Miss Moll, remember what the Sheriff said. Gideon is a free man, and your uncle has a reputation now. With his temper, if he knew about-"

"I know, I know, Nema! But I can't have him lurking around the farm like a crazed buzzard either now, can I?"

"Look there," Bluebird said, and pointed at a soft green glow among the leaves. I bent over to take a closer look, and saw that it came from some mushrooms at the water's edge.

"We need to take care of him ourselves, Misses, and I know how, I promise you," Nema said.

Try as I might, I couldn't get Nema or Bluebird to reveal their plan, but I did manage to gain their promise they would do no serious harm to Gideon, or do anything that reflected back on us.

A week passed, and then another with no reports of Gideon. It was as if he never existed. We made no mention of his name. I feared to ask Nema what she did, but finally got up the pluck, or perhaps my conscience got the better of me.

"I just did what needed doing, Miss Moll," she answered.

"Tell me, Nema. I won't be mad, and the good Lord knows I shouldn't feel any empathy for the man."

"I did nothing to him, Miss Moll. What was done, he did to himself. I merely bathed in the stream as I always do. I may have lingered at the water's edge a bit longer than usual, but it was such a beautiful morning, and the cool air felt so wonderful on my bare skin."

Nema punctuated her description by rubbing her hands down her body as if reliving that moment at the water's edge. Bluebird giggled at her display.

"And your stunning beauty struck him down, or made him see the foolishness of his ways?" I asked smiling.

"Not at all, misses. I wanted to give him a pleasant memory, for when the sickness overtook him."

"Sickness? Oh Nema, what did you do?"

"I did nothing. When I finished bathing, I stepped from the water, but fool that I am, I forgot my towel! I didn't want to dress while still wet, so I grabbed my basket and gathered some mushrooms for our breakfast."

"Naked? You picked mushrooms naked in the moonlight?"

"Well, I couldn't bath with my clothes on, could I? That would rather defeat the purpose. Anyway, I recalled you saying this Gideon loved fresh picked mushrooms? I made sure he watched to see where I picked the nicest puffballs."

"That's all you did? Showed him our puffball patch?"

"Yes, I thought it the neighborly thing to do, and oh yes, I picked some of the pretty orange ones too. You know, the ones that glow in the darkness? I thought how beautiful they'd be as a decoration in my cabin, so I put a good amount of those in my basket as well. I took a couple of nibbles off one too, but I spit it out where he couldn't see of course."

"Oh dear God, Nema, are they poison? Is he all right?"

"Not so bad, orange mushrooms," Bluebird said. "Make bad sick belly," which she demonstrated by rolling on the floor of the cabin making vomiting sounds and rubbing her stomach.

"They are bad enough he won't be bothering you for a while though, I think," Nema laughed.

I tried my hardest not to, but their laughter was contagious, and I rolled on the floor with the two of them making disgusting vomiting sounds and laughing so hard that tears rolled down my face. Our laughter was like a boat in full sail with a stiff tail wind, and it seemed it would take a force of nature to stop it. The growing din from the three of us eventually woke poor Zachary (and probably half the colony), and with much regret, I bid my friends good night.

Chapter Twenty-Five

Many years of hard work followed that evening, years filled with the joy and excitement of watching Zachary grow. The farm grew prosperous under our nurturing hands, and we faced few trials beyond the routine struggles on any farm. It is tempting to fill this narrative with the sights and sounds of those between years, and reminisce about that short, sweet lull before the storm. The good times I remember as if in a vision, but the coming bad times never dimmed. They will stay with me always. Contentment isn't what drives our fates though, life's challenges do, forcing our hands and providing the impetus to propel ourselves forward. Moments of soul wakening horror either ends us or makes us grow, and my time for the telling of tales grows shorter.

Zachary grew at an alarming rate, looking more like his uncle every day. I hadn't reached a time of life to appreciate the fact that as he aged, so did I. Zachary spent a lot of his time at the village of Two Bears and Bluebird. He shot a bow as well as any Indian child, and his knowledge of plants surpassed my own. I know he enjoyed the freedom of the people, but I feared the attraction also involved Bluebird's daughter. I recalled my dream of demons, and I was embarrassed when I asked her, but Bluebird assured me she'd known no other man besides Two Bears. This knowledge eased my fears, and I may even have encouraged their developing friendship. If Bluebird knew no other man, surely her daughter Chenoa couldn't be a Cambion?

In Saint Mary's City, they completed construction of a huge new state house. Assembled from bricks fired in the colony, it was the first real symbol of permanence here.

When I heard of it, I thought of the potential for this colony, and how unlimited Zachary's future might be.

The three of us "sisters," and we were as close as that, continued our gatherings in Nema's cabin with some regularity. Some nights, Zachary sat with us, but I think our slow paced activities bored him. Uncle was still unaware of what we did on our girls' nights, as he called them.

He made frequent trips to Mr. Hammond's farm that fall. He always took a fresh bath, and wore his finest clothes for these occasions. I teased him that fine feathers make for fine birds, but he was not amused.

If Uncle was suspicious of the amount of the time I spent in Nema's cabin, he said nothing. In turn, I made no mention of knowing that Peter's unwed sister Sarah arrived in the colony and was in Mr. Hammond's employ.

We thought Uncle would wed with Sarah at the end of her indenture, but that day came and went. Sarah still remained with the Hammonds, much as Nema stayed on with us.

"I'm in no hurry, Moll, and neither is Sarah." Uncle said often.

"You're not getting any younger, Uncle."

"I've some unfinished business, and I'm not sure I should take on a wife just yet."

"What business, Uncle? Our farm is doing well enough. I can't imagine a woman as thin as Sarah eating us out of house and home? What else concerns you?"

"I'll tell you all about it someday, Moll. No need to worry, but I'm off to the Hammond's now."

A month after we cast the love spell, Uncle announced the betrothal and their plan to wed when the crop was in. Nema said even the most innocent spells come at some price, but what harm could come of setting the cornerstone for someone's happiness?

Perhaps my friends cast such a spell on me too, but if so, it went unanswered. I had little time for such things anyway with the farm and a house to attend to. Zachary's love and my extended family were enough in my life.

As is often the case when caught in a deep sleep, it took a jolt to pull me from the dream. The jolt came in the form of the cabin door slamming.

"Moll, I caught someone sneaking around by the hog pen. I yelled at him, and he ran off, but I think I shot him!"

"What Zachary? You shot a man?"

"With an arrow, but it just had a blunt point. He'll have a good bruise on his backside though. I think he was trying to steal one of the shoats!"

"I can't tolerate a thief! What did this man look like?"

"I didn't get a very good look at him, but he was a white man, tall and thin."

"Never shoot at people unless your life is threatened. Uncle is in town picking up supplies, and I need to speak with Aunt Nema about this."

It was ten years gone since the mushroom incident with Gideon, but it now appeared he forgot what he learned. The number of times our paths crossed could be counted on the fingers of one hand, and I couldn't fathom what might have reignited his insanity.

I saddled two of our horses, and with Nema at my side, rode the mile to Gideon's cabin, arriving before the morning dew dried on the leaves. William Bowles purchased the property when the former owner returned to England. The farm adjoined William's, a good place for his niece and nephew-in-law to settle. Despite Beth's death, Mr. Bowles honored his commitment to her husband.

I saw few improvements to the place. The farm looked to be maintained for sustainment, not growth. No new land stood cleared or trees girdled, and the livestock fences were in desperate need of repair. The late summer garden wilted, choked with weeds, and the door of the cabin hung loose on one hinge.

"Gideon, open up!" I said, knocking on the door with the butt of my rifle. "Hey, we need to talk!"

"Misses, he's behind us," Nema whispered.

I turned to see Gideon approaching from the barn with a sickle in his hand.

"Good day, Moll, and it is Nema I believe? I heard you are a free woman now. Congratulations!"

"Why after all of these years are you again darkening our lives?"

Gideon scrunched up his eyebrows. "You came here to my farm, but I have thought of paying you a visit."

"Is that what were you doing there this morning? Paying me a visit?"

"Moll, I'm not sure what this is all about, but I haven't been near your farm for a very long time. I had a … well, a sudden change of heart, you might say."

"A sudden change of stomach is more like it." Nema said.

Gideon smiled. "That's true, Nema, you certainly fooled me with those mushrooms, and I thank you for that."

"Thank me?"

"Yes, if it wasn't for that, well… look, I don't expect either of you to believe this, and you'll think me a dolt, but when I ate those damn mushrooms I got sick as a dog, sure. I swear I lost every meal I'd taken in for the prior two weeks, but Beth appeared to me that night. Now I'm a bit of a skeptic about such things, but it was real enough, Moll. It was as real as you standing there. When I woke the next morning, I cried for hours when I discovered she wasn't still there at my side."

"Beth was a special woman, we were lucky to have known her." I said.

"Beth told me I was a silly man. I used to call her that, "my silly wife." Do you remember that, Moll? She said our baby was gone, and she was with her, and some day we'd all be together again. I want that every day, but she said it wasn't yet my time, and we'd have forever together. She said I should go to you, tell you I was sorry, but after what I'd done, and the horrible things I said to you? I didn't have the pluck, but I'll say it now. I know you can't forget what I did, but I beg your forgiveness if it's in your heart."

I gave him a brief hug. It was all I could give and still maintain my composure. Not even Nema was unaffected by his words, and a tear moistened her cheek.

"Gideon, I knew it wasn't really you. Grief and pain became a madness that carried you along. I doubt I would do any better. Is this why you planned to visit? To say you were sorry?"

"It is, but there is something else I need to tell you. An Englishman was here asking about Sean, and not only here, but at several of the other farms as well."

"What does he want with my uncle?"

"He asked where your farm is located, who lives with him, has he engaged in any altercations in the colony? I didn't tell him anything. I said I heard the name Sean Dyer before, but that I knew nothing of him personally."

"Did he say why he asked about my uncle?" I asked.

"I can't say for sure, but it has to do with a crime he thinks your uncle committed in England. A serious crime is my guess, for him to travel all this way."

Chapter Twenty-Six

Nema and I rode home after Gideon's revelation, hoping to find Uncle still there. We sped down the road, leaving our horses in a lather, but upon our arrival discovered the note Uncle left. He and Sarah took a carriage ride to Britton's Bay to catch crabs and picnic for the day. I placed the paper in my dress pocket.

I was too overwrought to be productive, and paced the floor. Nema tried to distract me in every way she could. She even consented to learn the game of draughts which she had long resisted.

"Do you think Gideon spoke the truth?" she asked.

"About Beth, or about Uncle?"

"Both, and about you, do you think he will cause you any problems?"

"I thought him sincere in his apology, and truthful in his report about the Englishman. I don't know if Beth appeared to him, or if he just had strange dreams from the mushroom, but he believes it, and his perception is his reality."

"What will you and Mister Sean do, Misses? What do you think he's done?"

"It's what this man thinks he's done that matters I guess. I hope Uncle has some understanding of it."

Nema and I waited with little patience at my cabin for Uncle's return, and when we at last heard the sound of his horse's hooves at dusk, she departed for her own home.

"Uncle, we must talk," I said, as he cleared the threshold.

"Moll, goodness, what's so important to discuss that you're skulking around the cabin waiting for me? Give a man a chance to take off his boots first will you?" He made several unsuccessful attempts to do just that, then lit his pipe instead.

"Uncle, have you been in the rum this afternoon?"

"A few nips is all, Moll, on the way home. What's this all about now?"

"Nema and I went to see Gideon today-"

"Indeed, isn't that grand, Moll? I didn't know you were on friendly terms again."

"We aren't... weren't, but this was about you. Gideon says a man is roaming around the country asking about you. It has something to do with a crime he thinks you committed in England, but that's all Gideon knew."

Uncle shook his head and rubbed his eyes. "I guess I knew it would catch up with me sooner or later. I was beginning to think that chapter of my life finally closed."

"What's it about, Uncle? What does the fool think you guilty of?"

"I am guilty, Moll. Do you remember when I showed up at your family's cottage in Westcowes? I was in a hurry, on the run. I needed to get out of England fast."

"From what?"

"From murdering a man, or what passed for one. I met a woman in the city, of course it boils down to a woman! Her name was Leila, and we got along rather well. She lived off of Cheapside in the market district. You're a grown woman now, so I won't mince words. Leila was tall, and slender, a redheaded goddess child of Brigid with full firm heavers. She was a very adventurous lass, in a manner I was unaccustomed to. Your father and I were raised as strict Catholics remember. When we had ..., well relations, even her skin heated up, like a warm pudding just pulled from the oven, even though other parts were as cool as the first frost."

"Uncle, I appreciate your rum addled confidences, but I have no need of the gory details," I said.

Uncle laughed, giggled in fact, and his eyes took on a faraway glaze. "Of course, forgive my black mouthed candor, the rum… So, every evening, this lady would ask me to leave her house precisely at the stroke of midnight, and I surmised she was a woman with concern for her reputation. I was foolish to not consider other possibilities!"

Uncle looked at me for either approval or scorn, but I waited to hear more.

"This particular evening, Leila was even more affectionate than usual. I know, Moll, no details, but I think this part is important. Anyway, affectionate is not the word, she was demanding, nearly ripping the clothes from my body. I left afterwards, and walking down Milk Street, I realized I'd forgotten my pocket watch on her bedside table, and walked back to retrieve it. When I reached her door, I heard a commotion, and Leila screaming. I charged in, a knight in shining armor and all that I suppose. A man was beating her, because of me or some other offense, I didn't know, but I saw one of her eyes swollen shut and blood running from her nose, so I didn't ask any questions. From the look of him, I wasn't sure who was getting the worse of it, but I charged in anyway with fists flying. I gave him a taste of his own medicine. At one point, I struck him hard, he fell backwards, and his head slammed against the rocks of the hearth. I knew right off that his neck was broken from the unnatural angle of his head.

Leila screamed, "Oh my God, you've killed my husband!" and that's when I first learned she was married."

"Then it was an accident, Uncle! That's not murder, more like self-defense," I said, remembering James.

"Well, Moll, murder was in my heart, and if he was just some ordinary fellow, it might have been looked at as you say, but this particular husband was cousin to the Lord Mayor of London, Sir William Lawrence. It would not go well for me, a common carpenter, and as it turns out, an adulterer."

"So you fled?"

"As fast as my legs and the sails of the Mary Regina would carry me. Luckily, well for me at least, there was another murder in London that night, in St. Paul's churchyard no less. A young woman was viciously attacked, her throat slit from ear to ear. A friend of a friend who is with the constabulary said there were two suspects in the crime, a man and a woman. He said from the evidence recovered, this couple rolled around naked in the pool of the young woman's blood, sick bastards. A sensational murder like that took the attention away from my misadventure, but I knew I needed to flee to the colonies. I hoped to be safe here, a world away, and I was at least for a while. Long enough for us to get the farm up and running at least. I think you'll be able to get by fine without me."

"It will blow over. What proof can they have after all of these years?"

"Faithfulness was not one of Leila's strongest virtues. My guess is she pressed the issue, perhaps falsely claiming rape to protect her reputation. I'm sorry, Moll, I didn't mean to imply you were of that ilk." He said, noticing my frown.

Zachary entered the cabin just then, and sensing the weight of our discussion, excused himself to his small bedroom.

"Don't make any rash decisions yet, Uncle. Let's wait and see what tomorrow brings before we decide what to do. I'll pray with Nema and Bluebird that this tribulation will pass us by."

"Prayers certainly can't hurt," Uncle shook his head in agreement, but I saw no optimism written on his face.

"Well Moll, now that you know all of my secrets, care to share yours? What keeps you up at nights? When we are at the shore, what draws your gaze across the ocean and causes you distress?" Uncle asked.

"I didn't realize I was so transparent, Uncle, but that's surely a story for another time. We have enough to weigh upon our minds this night."

I gave Uncle a hug goodnight, and suggested things would look better in the morning, not knowing what we would face before that new dawn.

Chapter Twenty-Seven

I tossed about in my bed, unable to find a comfortable position. The bed ropes needed tightening, or my inner voice needed silencing. I felt certain Uncle found sleep no easier to obtain than I did.

Sleep did come, but with little mental relief. Again, I dreamt the dream of being chased through the woods. I ran along our now familiar stream, and came to an opening in the forest. Peering through the trees, I spotted our cabin sitting in the reddish glow of the moonlight.

For a moment, I forgot the baying of the hounds, and relaxed my eyes soaking in the familiar scene. I focused on the reflection of the moon in our window when a figure darted from the back of the cabin, too fast to identify.

The clearing filled with many running men, some with leashed dogs, and all with guns and torches. Two of the men ran up to the door and beat on it. The knocking was so real, and so forceful, it jarred me awake.

I sat up, and surveyed my room, but saw no cause for concern. Then I again heard the pounding at the door, and jumped from my bed. I saw the lights of the torches outside, and heard the murmuring of many voices. I pulled on a dress, and ran from my room.

"Open up, Sean Dyer, it's High Sheriff Vincent Lowe. Don't make us break the door down now. Come on out peaceably!"

I looked to Uncle's bedroom door and saw no light, and heard no movement as I stepped towards the door. "Uncle?" I whispered.

The men slammed against the door, and it rocked on its hinges.

"I'm coming, Sheriff!" I yelled. "What's all this fuss about?" As I reached to open the bolt, the second assault struck, bringing down the door. Three men holding a log ram fell forward with the momentum, and landed on the floor at my feet. A half dozen men rushed into the house. As they brushed past, I lost my balance, tripped over a chest, landing draped over a man on the floor. He was bleeding from a cut on his eyebrow.

"Sheriff! What is the meaning of this invasion?" I shouted above the din.

"We're here for Sean Dyer, Miss. Where is he?"

"I have no idea, Sheriff. If he's not in his room, I suspect he's answering the call of nature. This couldn't wait until morning? He's out among you every day, yet you need to assault his home in the middle of the night? Look, your men are bleeding all over my rug."

"I'm sorry about the blood, ma'am. Are you all right Robert?" He handed me a handkerchief for the blood.

The man shook his head yes, and went back outside.

"This is a murder charge," the sheriff said. "We wouldn't want a murderer knowing our intent in advance now, would we? Though that appears to be the case here. Miss Dyer, if you see your uncle, he needs to give himself up."

"Turn himself into this mob, Sheriff? Who would protect him? Are you responsible for them? Can you guarantee his safety?"

"These are duly sworn men, Miss. I'm sorry about the door, and the spot of blood. The men are a bit on edge, and eager to be done with this. I'll send an undersheriff out tomorrow to fix the door, if there's one to spare. Come on men, nobody here but the woman. Turn the dogs loose, let's get after him! He can't have gotten far."

The dogs seemed to understand his words, and their howls became frantic. It was easy to follow their advance through the farm by the dark music of the hound's pursuit.

I walked around the cabin in circles, numb to my surroundings. Uncle was free for now, but Zachary's whereabouts too were a mystery. Did he follow Uncle Sean into the woods? Would he be safe, or another target for the mindless mob?

I heard a sound at the door, and when I turned, my heart jumped in my chest, until I realized it was Nema standing there. I smiled to see Bluebird's' brother, Grey Deer, standing just behind her in the shadows.

"Mister Sean?" she asked.

"Gone, Zachary too."

"Shall we follow them? We might stop those idiots from shooting Mister Sean in the back."

"I'm not sure if we would help, or if he'd see us and think we needed protecting. Uncle knows his way around the woods, and Zachary even more so, and some of those men would love an excuse to shoot a free black woman, Nema, so you stay."

Grey Deer stepped out of the shadows, and placed a hand on Nema's shoulder.

"I will follow the men, but not let them see. Brother Zachary is with Two Bears, he too follows. Bluebird come here now. You wait for her?"

We nodded our assent, and Grey Deer turned to go.

"Zachary is only fifteen years old, Grey Deer," I said. "Watch out for my little brother."

Grey Deer laughed. "No harm come to Zachary, he is achak kitchi."

I looked at Nema for an explanation, and she shrugged.

"Zachary is spirit brave," Grey Deer pointed at the heavens, and then spread his arms to encompass everything around us. He smiled, and trotted into the woods at an angle to the path taken by the men.

"What do we do now?" Nema asked.

"I don't know, sit and cry? Sew a quilt? Pray for a miracle?"

"Misses, I heard one of the men talking. He said Mister Sean murdered a man in your old country. I don't believe it, but if he did, I know that man needed killing. Sean is a good man."

"I know he is, and I'm worthless to help him. What can I do? Nothing! I feel like a feeble, helpless old woman! It's like the night my son was conceived, and when I couldn't save Beth or her child! I hate it!"

"You are neither feeble nor helpless, Misses. You are a woman, yes. I helped birth your son. No man can do that, but you cannot lay claim to the rest." Nema said with a half-smile. "Let's wait, Miss Moll. Everything might work out."

"I'm tired of waiting, Nema." I thought of waiting for James at the oak tree, waiting huddled in my bed for my parents' summons, waiting through our voyage here, waiting for our land, waiting for Zachary's birth. I was done with waiting. I was done with life being done to me.

Bluebird appeared where my door stood only moments before. She wasted little time.

"Bad men are in the woods. Ready, Nema?"

"Ready for what?" I asked.

"Tonight is the Full Red Moon, Misses. It will give our spells power over others, and we will call upon all of the forces in play tonight."

"Power? Forces? Nema, do you know what you are talking about? Some of the spells we cast bore fruit, it's true, especially the love spells, but this is real life, real life and death!"

"There are other things we know a little of, Miss Moll, but feared trying. We can-"

"No, Nema."

"We have to try and do something, he's your uncle. Besides, do you have something else you need to do? Sew a quilt, perhaps?"

I thought of Uncle welcoming me into his life with open arms, and how he treated me as an equal, how he defended me against Gideon and the highwayman, how he worked to better our lives. Any sin of his was no greater than mine. I loved my uncle, he was my family.

"No quilts Nema, but I will go to my sewing room. I hid things from you too, perhaps even from myself, but now they must be revealed. Love potions and weak protective spells are not enough tonight! But you are right, I will conjure forces, any forces who will heed my call. I swore to my Mother I'd only do so in matters of life or death, desperate times, and these are that."

"We will do so together then. Mister Sean is our friend," Nema said, "so this is our fight too, but he's your family. We will follow your lead."

"The stronger the magic, the higher the price, and this is not something I ask of you. I intend to do this alone, and I am prepared to pay the price."

The sound of the dogs changed. Their voices became sharp, rapid, and seemed to carry to the heavens. I knew something, or someone was treed or at bay.

"I know you are trying to scare me, Miss Moll, and it is working. I don't know the price. No one ever does, but Mister Sean needs us, all of us now."

"No! You do not know the cost to you or your loved ones!" I said.

"There is more power with three," Bluebird said.

"Try and stop us." Nema said and jutted out her chin.

I touched their cheeks. "Then you are fools. Come." I turned on my heels, and headed for the barn. Bluebird walked right beside me, and I glanced back to Nema.

She too followed, perhaps as there was nowhere else to go.

Chapter Twenty-Eight

I led my sisters to the corner of the barn where Uncle built the small room for me. I stepped inside, and waited for their reaction. Bottled potions and dried herbs lined the many shelves. I painted the symbols that decorated the walls, some from the memory of mother's room, but mostly from the books she'd given me on the day we parted ways. Every word, every drawing scribed in her own hand, or the hands of our ancestors.

I insisted my uncle build the walls out of oak, that most sacred of trees, and he went along with what I'm sure he thought a foolish whim. The room was further protected by bundles of elder bush, with mistletoe in every corner.

The women first noted the triskele, the trinity knot and the spiral of life.

"Yes, all things in threes," I said.

Nema then examined those symbols I suspected she felt most connected to, Brigid's cross, and the so called Celtic cross. Bluebird stared long at the tree of life carved into the north wall. When she spotted my rendition of her Okeus, she giggled and pointed. I was not above learning new things.

They tried to take it all in with their mouths agape until I thought I allowed them enough time to acclimate.

"What is all of this, Moll? How long have you been doing this... whatever this is?" Nema asked.

"I'm sorry to only bring you here now, but I wanted to be sure you were ready, and my thoughts were of protecting you, but now the need is great," I said.

"I guess we're ready, what do we have to do?" Nema asked.

Bluebird just smiled, a perfect innocent, a child of nature, and my eyes welled with tears.

"First you need understanding. What do we know? All cultures, and all belief systems recognize a creator. From that most revered and powerful being springs many lesser beings, be they Okeus, and Ahone, Loas, haints, saints, demons or angels. They are interceders, but beings of power in their own right. Some are spirits of pure white energy."

"That's how Bluebird describes Ahone," Nema said.

"Yes, and some would say the angels are too. Others are the tricksters, Manitou, demons, but most of them reside in a grey area, they just are. They come when we beckon, but they answer in their own way. Then there are our ancestors, who try to direct these forces on our behalf, but the Other World taints their memories, and they forget much of the mortal world of men."

Nema had a faraway look in her eyes, but concentrated on every word.

Bluebird eyes still swirled about the room, and she said, "Moll is pauwau," but I didn't understand the word, and had little time.

"This is complicated, Moll." Nema said. "Please tell me you know what you're doing? This is far beyond me, and far from any Christian thought I've ever been taught."

"I'll not lie to you, Nema. I never called on these energies before, but I am very confident in my mother's teachings, and the readings she provided. Rest assured, God is God. She manifested to each of us, in every land, the face we needed to see. She shows every culture the way to know her, in the way that each could understand. Religion is the name each culture gives to the path she's shown them."

Nema pointed to the Okeus figure. "Should we be mixing the paths we've been shown then?"

"Religion only goes wrong when it becomes divisive, when we allow our arrogance to muddy the paths shown to us."

I knew it was too much to throw at them at one time. It was true that these truths were exposed to me in much the same way, the night before Uncle and I departed for the colonies, but my background was stronger. As my mother said she just needed "to pull the connecting threads together" for me, but wish as I might for time, there was none to spare.

I turned away, and stepped over to an altar built of rock from our stream, and I lit the incense.

"I'm done with my speech, ladies. The doorway is hard to see, but once found, it is not hard to open. I don't know if closing it is within our powers, and I don't know what will happen once we enter. I promise I will not hold it against you if you want to leave. In fact, that's what I would do in your place, but I ask that if you do leave, you not speak of this to anyone."

I paused with my back to my two sisters to allow them time to depart with grace. I lit the four candles: green, yellow, red and blue first, then the large center candle. I placed the sheriff's handkerchief, soiled with the man's blood, on the burning incense. I placed Uncle's picnic note under a raven's wing. When I heard no sound of movement behind me, I turned back to them.

"Shall we begin then?"

Both nodded yes, and I pulled the fisherman's knife, still stained from another's blood, from under my blouse. I slid it across the base of my palm, and squeezed my hand to allow the blood to drip onto the incense. I motioned for Nema and Bluebird to step forward, and in turn, they drew blood from their palms.

I said the foreign sounding words, and my sisters repeated them in turn. When we finished, Nema asked, "What do we do now? How do we know if it worked?"

"Now we pray." I said.

Bluebird adjusted the hair on the figure of Okeus, and Nema wrapped our hands with some herbs she recognized hanging on the wall. We squatted on the floor and prayed, each in our own way, each to our own embodiment of the Creator.

We heard a soft rumble in the direction we last heard the dogs, and a crack of thunder rocked the barn rafters sounding like a cannon shot. The lightning was close! I smiled, but Nema's fear was easy to see.

The storm appeared to be concentrated around our farm.

A screech owl trilled, and another answered from just beyond the walls of the barn. Other species of owls joined the chorus, and shivers ran down my back. I did not call them, I would never call them!

"I think it worked, or at least something happened." Nema said with a nervous laugh.

A raven began croaking out its raspy call. Over and over he announced his presence. The sound made me feel at peace, as if he signaled the end of the storm. The raven's voice changed as others gathered and joined in. The owls renewed their haunted song, and as the wind slowed outside, I heard the beating of many wings. Calls of pain from owl and raven alike.

"Why do the ravens call at night?" Bluebird asked.

"I hope they speak in answer to our prayers." I replied.

"Gaagii," Bluebird whispered. "Gaagii pauwau!"

Nema and I exchanged glances.

"What does that mean, Bluebird?" Nema asked. "I think our Algonquin is rusty."

Bluebird's mouth curled up like a child given candy, "Raven witch," she laughed pointing at me.

Chapter Twenty-Nine

A screech owl and a barn owl lay dead on the ground outside the barn, and a second screech owl dragged itself off with a stiff broken wing. Our spell cost the lives of a half dozen ravens as well. I wasn't sure what that meant.

I hoped the sudden violent storm, and the raven-owl battle were signs that all was well with Uncle, and that Zachary kept out of the way of the hunters. There was no further sound of pursuit in our woods that night, but did that mean the men called off the chase, or that it was already successful? The men did not tramp back through our homestead that night.

No under-sheriff showed up the following day to repair our door, but that was no surprise, just our tax dollars at work, or not. The Maryland and Virginia colonies were at war with the Susquehannocks, and the effort still drained the treasury, even though I'd never seen anyone of that tribe.

Nema helped me with the door repair, and we worked in silence. No subject seemed safe enough not to turn into a discussion of the night before, or to the fate of my loved ones.

The day passed with the speed of a toothache, but unlike that pain, chewing a willow twig would not help bring my men home. Many ravens kept watch with us, filling the late afternoon with their chatter.

"So you brought 'em here, can you send them away too?" Nema asked, pointing at the trees, joking I think.

"Like St. Patrick with the snakes?" I laughed. "They're always here, Nema. Maybe you're just noticing them more now?"

The ravens in the big oak by the stream took flight, and Nema looked at me and smiled. "So you say...," but then two men emerged from the woods there.

"It's Grey Deer and Two Bears!" Nema said, and ran to meet them.

They walked back to the cabin together, and Nema's relief at Grey Deer's return was obvious.

"What happened? Are Zachary and Uncle all right? Was Uncle captured? Did the mob quit the chase?" I asked without giving pause for them to answer.

"Sean get away from men. Zachary not home?"

"No, we haven't seen him, he's not here. What happened?"

"Sean run through stream so dogs not smell him. He take Two Bear's canoe to island you name Saint Clements." Two Bears explained, then spoke to Grey Deer in their language and they both laughed.

"Brother Zachary run through middle of woods so even white man can follow him. Dogs chase Zachary, so him climb top tall sycamore tree. Zachary hide face, bad men think it Sean in tree." The men again broke into laughter.

"Zachary still sit in tree. Man with strong axe, he chop on tree long time. Tree start to shake, and Zachary jump to poplar tree."

"Woods full of spirits then," Two Bears continued. "Much fire comes from the sky, man almost hit, him fall in Potomack. He no swim, sink. Rain and hail hit men, white man no like rain. Me think Manitou no like white man either, but maybe wind blow Zachary from tree? One man run from storm, him trip and shoot gun, hit skinny white man in chest. Men run everywhere, much afraid. Big white sheriff say "Enough, shoot him from the tree," so we shoot arrows at the white men instead."

"Two Bears, now they will come for you." I sighed, but the two men only laughed.

"No, sheriff's man says, "Run, run, Susquehannocks!" Not know who we are. We scare men, but not hit them. Two Bears and Grey Deer follow men back to road, and we go back to village."

Two Bears looked over my shoulder into the cabin. "Where Bluebird, her with Moll and Nema?"

"No, she left us last night after we… after the storm," I said.

"Two Bears find her," he said, and scrunched his eyebrows together.

"We will go with you," I said.

"No, Two Bears move fast. Women follow with Grey Deer. Grey Deer slow too." With that, he turned and disappeared in the trees.

Somehow Grey Deer found the trail Bluebird walked, although I couldn't say how he knew it was her tracks we followed. I could see the slightest impression in the leaves, and only then when he pointed them out. He walked with his back bowed and his eyes close to the ground, insisting Nema and I walk well to the side of her trail to not disturb any sign. He also showed us where Two Bears took up the trail, and two sets of tracks were easier to follow.

We came to a rocky patch of ground, and Grey Deer slowed.

After a few more steps, he smiled.

"Two Bears move too fast, miss this," he said pointing at some bent over dogbane branches.

We pushed our way through the tangle of fox grapes and greenbrier.

"Blood!" Grey Deer said pointing.

We hurried over to him, and at first glance, I thought Grey Deer was mistaken. Maybe a fallen holly berry in the leaves, but Grey Deer touched the small dot and held up a finger stained with red.

Grey Deer said no more, but rushed through the woods with a pace that Nema and I couldn't keep up with. Every small vine, every broken branch seemed to conspire to slow our advance until I could no longer see him and feared becoming lost in the thickets.

"Grey Deer, stop!" Nema yelled. "Where are you?"

"Here!" he answered, and I spotted him waving his arms halfway up the next hill. "Come quick!"

"Let's go, Nema," I said, but she was already two steps ahead of me.

We found Grey Deer kneeling beside Bluebird. The chest of her shirt covered with blood, but she was still breathing! I felt her neck, and the beating of her heart was strong.

"We have to get her back to the cabin," I said. "She's been shot!"

"Take to village, get her medicine," Grey Deer said.

"The cabin is closer. She needs to have the bleeding stopped. The village is two miles further, and we shouldn't move her so far."

"Village have many medicine people."

Bluebird shook her head back and forth. "Moll is gaagii pauwau, Grey Deer. Take to Moll's."

Grey Deer put his hands together as if in prayer, but blew into them making the sound of a hoot owl. He repeated this several times, so that "Two Bears will hear."

Nema and I ripped portions of our shirts to help stem Bluebird's bleeding. Her wound was high in the chest just below the collarbone. Grey Deer put together a travois type stretcher from branches and vines to drag her out. The going was fairly level, and he had no difficulty dragging the travois, but Bluebird winced at the second bump, and fell unconscious, so Nema and I took turns toting the other end.

Back at the cabin, we placed Bluebird in my bed, and examined the wound. I cut her shirt away from the wound to examine it.

"It looks clean, Nema. The ball went all the way through her." I looked where the ball entered, and something didn't look right.

"Grey Deer, we need some fresh chickweed, I noticed some growing on the shady side of Nema's cabin. Do you know plantain? White man's footprints?

"Nema, can you start a fire? Get a big pot of water boiling and put in lots of pine nettles for a tea. We need a poultice from the plantain and chickweed, so put it on top and heat it until it is mushy. Let the nettles boil."

Two bears swept into the cabin, knelt at his wife's side, and held her hand.

"Kitchi Chimalis (Brave Bluebird)," he said and brushed the hair from her eyes.

Bluebird's eye fluttered open, "Kitchi Ninge Makwa (Brave Two Bears)," she smiled.

"Bluebird cold," Two Bears said to me, and I pulled two blankets to just above her waist.

"We must clean the wound," I said, retrieving the rum from Uncle's room. "This will hurt her," I said shaking the bottle.

I mopped the seeping blood from where the ball entered, and held a candle near to help me see.

Grey Deer returned with the plants.

"Nema, I need your help, the ball passed through, but the patch is still inside her. It will make the wound fester if we don't get it out."

"What do you need me to do?" Nema asked.

"Hold open the wound with one hand and keep the blood out with the other?"

The patch was just under the skin, and I managed to remove it with tweezers on the first try.

I poured a small glass of rum. "Drink, Bluebird," I said.

Bluebird managed to get a bit of it down, and only spat out a little.

"Now the hard part. Grey Deer, Two Bears, you must hold her still. This will hurt her, but you must hold her still. Understood?"

"It will sting, Bluebird. Tell me when you are ready."

She nodded. "Ready, Moll."

The men held her at the elbows. Nema pulled open the wound, and I poured a full glass of the rum into the entrance wound. Bluebird's shriek sent a stab of pain through my ears, then she bit down on her lip cutting short the raw sound. A thin trail of blood trickled from her mouth, and again she lost consciousness.

"Good, she will feel less pain now, let's hurry." We turned her over, and did the same with the exit wound. We applied the poultice, and bandaged her wounds.

"Grey Deer, she will need many willow twigs when she wakes," I said. "Now we say our prayers."

Chapter Thirty

For the next few hours, fever gripped Bluebird, then chills, and we alternated from stripping her down and fanning her, to covering her with every blanket we could find.

I sent Grey Deer out for one addition to my supplies, some inner bark from the red or slippery elm to keep the wound partially open, and allow cleansing with the nettle tea. He was unsure of what I requested until I described the wood his tribe liked to use for starting fire with their bow-drills.

"What else Moll need?" he asked when he returned with the bark.

"Nothing for Bluebird, I think she'll be fine, as long as the wounds do not fester, but I do need something, Grey Deer."

"Zachary? Moll want Grey Deer to find?"

I smiled at his understanding. "Yes, Grey Deer, I need to know he's safe."

Grey Deer slipped his arm around Nema, and said something to her I couldn't hear, then slipped away into the night. Two Bears stayed at Bluebird's side that night, waking me whenever she so much as turned in her sleep, or whispered in her dreams. Nema and I slept on the floor beside the bed.

I woke before dawn, and touched my palm to Bluebird's face. Her skin was neither hot nor cold, a good sign. Two Bears dozed on his knees, his shoulders and chest draped over his wife's thigh. Grey Deer had yet to return. I tiptoed from the cabin. They all needed their sleep, and there was nothing better for Bluebird's recovery.

I walked to the barn as our rooster greeted the morning. In love with his own voice he was. I knelt in my "sewing room," said my prayers of thanks, and asked for Zachary's safety, and Bluebird's return to full health.

As I left, I cut off a piece of salt cured ham, and gathered the eggs for our breakfast. Nema saved the shells, and ground them very fine for her protection powder.

Back at the cabin, I found Nema and Bluebird chattering about what happened to her. Two Bears still slept.

"Catch me up, Bluebird," I said. "Who did this to you?"

"Good day, Moll. You have eggs to eat, they raven eggs?" she asked with a smile.

"No, Bluebird, they are chicken eggs, but I'm glad to see you are feeling better."

"Moll and Nema fix Bluebird good."

"I hope so, we must have a look, but first tell us what happened to you?"

She reached to touch my hair, and looked puzzled. "Wopi?" I knew how different my hair must look to her than that of her people, but her confusion concerned me.

Nema shook her head, and took Bluebird's hand. "Can you tell us what happened to you?"

"Bluebird leave Moll's house, go home. Hear many men coming, and hide in bush. Men talk, say they no catch Sean, say Susquehannocks in woods. Bluebird want to tell Two Bears about the Susquehannocks, and try to sneak away, but men see Bluebird. Say "Look, there go dirty Indian now!"

She shifted on the bed to find a better position, her face drawn up like Uncle's many years ago when he changed Zachary's diaper. I gave her a willow twig to chew for the pain.

"Bluebird run, and I hear voice, Zachary close by. Bluebird stop to find, and man's gun roar like thunder. Much smoke, like when burning the fields, and smell of bad eggs. Then hot fire hit Bluebird on shoulder."

"Zachary? He was there? Where is he?"

Bluebird shook her head, and did not meet my eyes. "Zachary come, help Bluebird. Put hand on chest and press cloth there. Then white man hit Zachary with end of gun, and drag him away. They say "leave the Indian, she's done for." Bluebird try to follow, help Zachary, but can only crawl. Men go fast on horses, they scared of the Manitou and Susquehannocks."

"Where did they take him?" I asked.

"Bluebird not know. Try go after men, but head get funny like when drink Sean's hot water, and then Bluebird sleep. Wake up when Grey Deer come."

"Let's clean your wound, and change the dressing, it needs some air to heal, and I need to think."

Two Bears woke then, and Bluebird told her story again, while Nema and I attended to her wounds. I inserted a thin tube of the inner bark from the slippery elm in the wound, and we washed it with nettle tea. Two Bears was impatient with us. Bluebird's pain prevented her from finishing her story, and she soon lost consciousness.

Nema filled him in on with the last parts of her misadventure.

"I will go free Zachary, and Sheriff must die!" He said.

"No Two Bears, we must live with these people. Justice will be done, Zachary has done no wrong. The men thought Bluebird was of the Susquehannocks. They did not know she was of your people. We are at peace, but will be no more if you do this." Nema said.

"Moll's family and Nema friends. Two Bears wait for new moon. Bluebird heal, Two Bears forget. Bluebird die, Two Bears will kill white man sheriff, and bring Zachary home."

He stepped through the door and Nema followed. I heard them speak of Bluebird for a moment, and then the sound of something hitting the porch floor boards, followed by Nema's scream.

Many thoughts raced through my mind as I reached for the rifle. Was Zachary returning hurt? Were the sheriff's men back? Did Two Bears become crazed in his grief, and harm Nema when she tried to comfort him? Nothing prepared me for the vision I beheld as I ran through the door.

As my eyes adjusted to the brightness of the day, I could see three men approaching from the road. Two Bears walked towards them, and Nema ran, already halfway there. The man in the middle was Uncle, and I was in his arms before I bothered to identify the other two.

"Good to see you too, Moll," Uncle said, as he pried my arms away.

I then allowed myself to greet his companions. I'd expected Grey Deer, but…

"Gideon? What are you doing here?" I asked.

"Moll, merciful Lord, what has happened to your hair?" Uncle asked.

"For God's sake! Men! I haven't washed it, Uncle. I've been rather busy," I answered.

"It's full of white, Moll. Look." He pulled forward a few strands that I might see.

"Mock my grey hairs, Uncle? I wonder if you were worth all of that worry, but how is it you're here? Is it safe for you to be? Have they dropped those foolish charges?" I asked, and pulled at the white in my hair.

"Look at your reflection in the silver platter from home. It's quite a sight, Moll."

"Enough, Uncle. Do not torment me."

"Very well, Moll, but my news is not good. I have only returned for some supplies, and my pipe of course. I cannot stay here now."

"Where will you go, Uncle?" I asked.

"Grey Deer will take me to their village, and I will stay out of sight, live among them for a while. Their village is practically deserted now, and many of the longhouses stand empty. There is plenty of room there for me."

"That may be best until things settle down here for you, Uncle," I said, "and if they find out? What then?"

"The Pawtuxant and Chaptico have banded together and will head west soon. Grey Deer says the Conoy may follow. I will also if need be. "

I turned my attention to Grey Deer so Uncle wouldn't see my reaction to his plan.

"Grey Deer, what of Zachary?"

"Actually, that is why I am here, Moll." Gideon spoke up. "I just met up with Sean and Grey Deer, and I came to tell you, as his…sister. The sheriff has him jailed in Saint Mary's City."

"Jailed for what?" I asked.

"They charged him with conspiring against government officials for helping Sean escape. They are holding County Court next Wednesday, and he'll be detained until then. They'll not release him on his personal recognizance."

Chapter Thirty-One

I prepared poultices in advance of court day, and gave Nema precise instructions for Bluebird's care.

"Remember, Boss Lady, I do know a little bit. Bluebird is well on the mend. I think I can handle it now," she said, and pinched her lips together.

"I'm sorry Nema, I forget myself. You are a fine healer. Anyone can learn the plants, but few have your manner with the sick."

Nema shook her head. "It is already forgotten. Take care of Zachary, all will be fine here."

"This isn't right," Uncle said. "I should be there with my nephew."

"Well sure, and why don't you come along then? Just what I need, my brother and uncle both in jail!" I said.

"I know, but I can't stand this feeling. I'm powerless to help my own flesh and blood. I thought it was only the mothers of very naughty boys whom died of worry. Promise to get word to me if you need help, and as soon as court is done!"

"I won't be calling on you for help, Uncle. When I return, I'll build a hot fire and add in some green wood and leaves. I'll send up a column of smoke they'll see clear to Virginia. Then you will know to come."

The Assembly Hall in the new State House was where the county court and the provincial, or colonial court met. Whenever in session, the people flocked to town. It was a real social occasion judging by the buggies and horses tied at the rails, and the number of people in the streets. I never guessed my first glimpse of the new building would be under such conditions.

The scent of fresh sawdust lingered in the hall, and the wooden benches shined like the silver my mother kept from the old days. Christopher, the clerk from the land office, waved when I entered. I suppose he noted my confusion, and made his way to my side.

"Your brother is the second case on the docket today. I'm surprised they are trying it here instead of in provincial court considering the charge."

"Is that good? Is the jury here?" I asked.

"There is no jury in county court, but it is more lenient I think. Of course, the judge is a relative of our new governor, and these trials are not reported to the crown, but this court cannot impose the direst punishments."

"Dire punishment, leniency? How harsh can they be to a child who has done nothing?"

"Miss Dyer, I shouldn't-"

"Moll, please call me Moll, everyone does, and thank you for your help."

"Well Moll, I assumed you knew, but death or dismemberment is the harshest punishment for the crime he is charged with, but they're off the table in this court."

The walls moved in a gentle wave around me.

"Miss Dyer, Moll, are you all right? Sit with me, court begins soon."

I heard very little of the first case, other than it concerned the theft of two chickens on a neighboring farm. The man was found guilty, and he thanked the judge for his mercy when he heard the sentence of a week in the stocks.

The judge added, "If this was a second offense, the higher court would chop off a hand, and will do so! Your family's name is one of some repute here, but we will not tolerate thievery in our fair colony!"

Mercy indeed, I thought, and then they brought in my shackled brother. His face was ashen, and his clothes dirty, but otherwise appeared healthy.

The clerk read the charges. "One Zachary Dyer, your honor, stands accused of conspiring against government officials."

"Why do you have me hearing this case, Sheriff? This should be heard by the provincial court," the judge said.

"He is a very young lad, your honor, and has never been in trouble of any kind. I thought this case best heard in the local court."

The judge agreed to hear the case, but warned he would defer it to the higher court if the case so warranted. The High Sheriff and one of his Under Sheriffs presented the evidence against Zachary. The sheriff made no mention of what my uncle was wanted for, only that Zachary helped him elude capture.

The judge then called for character testimony from anyone who wished to speak for Zachary. Gideon stepped from the benches, and described the many years he knew him and our family. He told the judge of our arrival in the colony together, and how close Beth and I were.

"Excuse me Moll, my turn," Christopher said when Gideon was done.

Christopher spoke of his respect for my uncle, and of the years they knew each other. He said Uncle Sean always spoke of how hard a worker Zachary was, and how Zachary made many friends among our Indian neighbors.

I then stepped forward.

"What relation are you to the accused?" the judge asked.

"I am, I'm his…sister."

"Well, are you or aren't you?"

"I am, your honor."

"Say your piece then."

"Your honor, I was a young woman when Zachary came to live with us. He was no more than a baby. In many ways, I feel like a mother to him. What these men say is true. Zachary is a credit to our colony, and works from dawn to dark raising tobacco to support his family and the crown. I ask that you forgive him this one transgression, and allow him to return to his duties to his family and his king."

The High Sheriff escorted me back to my seat beside Christopher. The judge slapped his wooden hammer on his desk.

"Thank you Miss Dyer, and witnesses. Zachary Dyer, please stand. I hereby sentence you to be nailed to the pillory through your ears. You will be publicly flogged and then released in the morning. Young Master Dyer, your punishment is slight. You are an asset to this colony with your labors, and you have contributed to our continued peaceful relations with the savages, but do not count on this court's mercy in the future."

I heard a man's laughter from the back of the room. James' evil laugh? I jumped from my seat.

"That punishment is slight? Are you insane? He's a boy, he's just a boy!"

The judge started beating his table again. "Order! Order! Sheriff, remove this woman from my court."

"I swear to God, I will avenge the deed you've done this day!" I screamed as the Sheriff dragged me from the courthouse. I sat confined in my cell when I heard the sound of the hammers the bastards used to drive the spikes through my dear son's ears. I paced the floor hearing the crack of the whip, and his cries of pain. I knew the moment his head jerked back, and his ears ripped away from the nails. I listened with tears of grief as the people cheered on the wielder of the whip, and through wet blurry eyes, I plotted revenge on them all.

The streets were filled with frivolity for hours when the outer door of the jail opened, and the High Sheriff entered.

"Oh what a mess you've caused for yourself."

I said nothing, but stared at him with all of the horror and hate that filled my heart.

"Look Miss Dyer, I understand your concern for your brother. I even managed to have him tried in the lower court, rather than the provincial court due to his youth. Our new governor, Thomas Notley, does not have the merciful reputation of the Calverts."

"Merciful, Sheriff? Is that really the word you want to use for having a child's ears half ripped from his head and flogged for aiding his uncle?"

"Miss Dyer, do I need remind you of what his punishment might have been? Your family's reputation served him in good stead, nor did I advise the court that Zachary's uncle is wanted for murder. I strongly advise you to hold your peace lest that be revealed, but you have problems enough of your own now. I've spoken to the judge in his chambers. I told him you were a good citizen. I also told him you are going through your woman's time. You may get off easy for your contempt of court."

"I am very contemptuous of the court, Sheriff!"

"That may well be, woman, but you'd be best advised not to let the judge know that. He will be here soon. He can hold you for weeks until the next court date. He can have your case seen by the colony court. It would behoove you to exhibit your best behavior, and apologize profusely!"

The sheriff left in a huff, and shortly after, the judge walked in. He reminded me of our rooster, head held so high I expected to see him trip over his feet.

"What do you have to say for yourself, Miss Dyer? I understand you are truly distressed about your actions this morning?"

"I am indeed, your honor. I don't know what came over me, especially after your generous display of mercy. He is my dearest brother, you see, your honor, and-"

"I am the law in this colony, Miss Dyer. Do you think you are the only one with a brother? Even little brothers must obey the laws of the crown!"

"Yes sir, I understand. But then too, well I feel so embarrassed to say it, but there's my moon cycle you see, and I-"

"Yes, yes, well..., such impudence cannot go unpunished, Miss Dyer, I have the dignity of my office to consider. I've decided, due to the circumstances, to avail you of my mercy. Consider yourself blessed to find me in such a giving mood. You will be placed in the stocks until your brother's release, or you may await trial confined to the jail. I will spare you the whip, and you can take your brother home when this is done."

"Yes your honor, and bless you," I said with a bow as I imagined the hissing sound of his stomach's gas released by a sharp blade.

Chapter Thirty-Two

Zachary's head was down as we approached the stocks, and they shackled me facing away from him. The stocks held my ankles in a seated position with my legs extended. I could still twist around to see him, and I knew I'd be able to hear his voice. The pillory afforded Zachary no such comfort. He was forced to stand with his neck and hands secured to the structure. When I heard his soft moans announce his waking, I asked him about his condition, and his voice was soft, yet strong when he answered.

"I'm fine, Moll, but you just had to say something, didn't you? At least we didn't get noosed."

"Yes, they take a dim view of a woman speaking her mind."

"What of Bluebird? Did you find her? She was shot."

I filled him in on Bluebird's condition, and told him that the pass through wound was healing nicely. He knew of Uncle Sean's escape, having played a vital part in it, but we couldn't discuss it. I couldn't tell him of Uncle's visit, and his plan to take up with the Conoy. We were in the midst of too many curious ears listening for any word of Sean Dyer, but they wouldn't waste their gossip on an Indian like Bluebird.

Our helpless condition engendered much merriment among the townsfolk, and the younger boys and older women were the worst of the lot. Whatever rotten fruit they could find, they hurled in our direction. I avoided most of it, but Zachary could not move his head, and proved an easy target. One yellow haired boy hoisted a dead rat in my eyes and I slapped it away. He then shoved it against my face, and I smelled the rot of it, but Zachary fared far worse. The stinking fruit smacking his face and shoulders was little compared to the feces some upstanding citizen tossed his way. Relief came in the form of the setting sun. The townspeople wasted no time retiring to their homes to prepare their repast, praying to their Lord for his mercies, and forgetting us for the night.

My legs felt like immoveable lengths of rock, and I doubted my ability to stand once released. The little needles of pain from inactivity passed long ago. Now there was a lack of feeling, as if my legs were no longer connected to my body.

Zachary groaned in anguish through much of the night. He stretched his legs, wiggled his hands, and twisted his head back and forth, trying to retain some feeling there. I took some comfort in knowing he slept often, as he did not respond to my many questions regarding his welfare. He did, however, speak often in his slumbers. I heard little of what he said, but he spoke as if another replied to his words. His voice changed when he spoke the part of the other conversationalist. I turned several times thinking he was being harassed by a returning village hypocrites, but only dreams tormented Zachary in the night.

I kept vigil on the town, and on Zachary. The houses I watched for signs of life, signs our torment would begin anew, and I watched Zachary for signs of distress. There was nothing I could do to help him, or either of us, but I kept sleep at bay in case a kind word might ease the passage of the night for him.

Despite the miserable day and night, the sun still rose in the east at the start of the new day. As the first beams of light streaked across the Chesapeake Bay, Zachary grunted awake.

"Zachary, are you in much pain?" I asked.

"I'll be fine, Moll. My back hurts from the whip, and my neck, oh God! I think I slept some, and twisted my neck in knots. Lucky I didn't yank my head off in this thing. You?" he asked.

"Wonderful, I'm assuming we will be released today at least," I said.

"Not soon enough," Zachary said, and paused. "Did you see the man who was here last night? He seemed familiar, but I can't remember where I know him from. Did you recognize him?"

"I heard you talking in your sleep, but I never saw anyone. I believe this town is afraid of the dark."

"But there was someone here. I spoke with him! He stayed with me the better part of the night telling me old stories," Zachary said.

What sort of stories?"

"He talked about the old country, Ireland. He knew a lot about our homeland, and something about a family of Druids we were related to? Is Druid an Irish surname?"

"No, it's not. It's a group of people from long ago…"

"Moll, you've promised to tell me about our family, and our bloodline since I was a bantling. Why our mother didn't want me, and why she and Father sent us here. You need to tell me of the place we came from."

"I will, I do promise."

"You always promise, but tell me nothing. The man told me it's good for a person to know something of his past, and that you had much to tell me."

"I was awake all night, Zachary. No one else was here, you were dreaming."

"Seemed real enough to me," he said.

"Ah, here comes our savior, the dear sheriff."

"Good day, Miss and Master Dyer. I trust you slept comfortably?" the sheriff asked.

We didn't respond.

"Yes, sorry, that was not very considerate of me. I tend to joke during stressful situations, often poor jokes I confess." The sheriff released Zachary's pillory lock, and he swayed on his feet, but leaned against the platform. He then released my stocks in turn. I rubbed my legs and feet to get feeling back in them.

"I'll spare you both the normal speech about not committing further offences against the crown and colony," the sheriff said. "I know this is a trying time for your family. I trust you won't have any problems with the good citizenry, but if anyone treats you unfairly, or without respect because of this, you let me know, hear?"

"Thank you, Sheriff," I replied, "but I think we'll be avoiding this town of yours for a while." I turned to leave.

"Miss Dyer, have you given any thought to what you are going to do now?"

"Do about what, Sheriff?" I asked.

"Well, ma'am, as you know, we still haven't captured your uncle, but whether we do or not, the implications for you are the same. You are without a man to work your farm, and keep up your holdings. I could run out and check on you on occasion, if you'd like? I have some time on my hands since my dear wife passed."

"Thank you for pointing that out Sheriff, and for your generous offer, but I'm sure Zachary, Nema and I will manage just fine."

Zachary and I walked through town to our carriage, in a hurry to return to the farm. Several of the townsfolk saw us and waved as if nothing happened. We walked on without acknowledging them.

We were both full of questions on the ride home, and spent the time filling each other in on the events of the past few days. Sitting proved to be uncomfortable for Zachary, and fresh blood still seeped through his shirt. We stopped at Saint Mary's River, and I washed his wounds. He flinched when the brackish water touched him.

"Sorry, brother. I should have warned you. The salt in the water stings, but it helps your wounds heal faster."

Zachary laughed. "It is nothing to what we already went through."

"It is terrible what they did to you, but it's past now and I'm proud of you. You were very brave," I said.

"That's what the man last night said too. He said it is in my blood- strength, resolve and power. What do you think of that?"

"Dreams are funny things, Zachary. Do they portend the future, or are our minds throwing out garbage it no longer needs?" I asked.

"I don't know, but the dream helped. It made me feel stronger, so I guess that's enough for now. I almost forgot, and you'll think me touched, but the man, even if he was a dream, asked me to tell you something."

I coughed and spit out the sip of water I drank from the canteen. An icy shiver jolted down my back. Someone stepping on my grave, my mother would say.

"What did James have to say to me?" I choked out.

"Who?"

"Oh, James is an old fashioned word for a stranger. Haven't you heard that before? So, what did this dream man have to say to me?"

"Let me see if I can remember exactly what he said. It was something like "One to start, two is done, one to go." That make any sense to you? I guess it was a really strange dream," Zachary said, and laughed.

With the words echoing in my head, I finished washing his wounds. We resumed our trip home in silence. The horse seemed to sense the urgency, and made exceptional time to the cabin. As anticipated, Nema took great care of our patient while I was gone, and Bluebird was sitting on the porch when we arrived.

"Why are you up and walking, Bluebird? Does Nema think you are strong enough?" I asked.

"Don't be mad at Nema, Moll. Bluebird is strong, and go home soon," then she yelled to the cabin. "Nema! Moll and Zachary are home."

Zachary led the horse toward the barn, and I called him back. His wounds from the whip needed more attention than the horse did. Nema met him at the cabin door, and seeing the blood seeping from his back, removed his shirt and dressed his cuts.

I gathered green wood, and added it to the fire to create a smoke signal for Uncle to see, knowing he was sick with worry.

Chapter Thirty-Three

"What happened to the two of you? I expected to see the smoke yesterday!" Uncle said entering the cabin. The rays of the setting sun were beginning to filter through the trees, the day nearly done.

"Good day to you too," I said. "Things did not go quite as well as planned." I described the torture Zachary endured, and how my words placed me in the stocks as well. Uncle looked out of the window at the distant horizon as I said my piece.

"Zachary did nothing to be treated in such a way, that judge is an arsworm! He helped me, but all they could really accuse him of was climbing a damn tree." Uncle turned to Zachary. "I'm sorry, I would not knowingly put you in danger. I did not foresee your suffering on my account."

"It's done, Uncle, and I do not blame you. The welfare of a man's family is far more important than a bit of discomfort. You and Moll have taught me that, but I won't forget what they did to me." Uncle stood and shook Zachary's hand.

"Nor will I forget what you did for me." They stared at one another for an uncomfortable silence. It was as if they didn't know how to escape the moment, frozen like leaves in the winter's ice. Nema, Bluebird and I exchanged glances, and smiled. Men are such poor custodians of the heart, its language is foreign to them.

"It was your news to tell, Uncle, but after much questioning, I told Zachary of your plans. He deserved to be answered," I said.

"Plans? Ahh, more of an escape hatch I think. The Conoy offered me sanctuary at their village for as long as they remain here. I doubt that will be long given the current political climate, and the strained relations with our native neighbors."

"That sounds wise, Uncle,." Zachary said. "I promise we will still see much of each other."

"Good, but don't make me the excuse when it's really a certain young maiden who draws you away from home." Uncle smiled.

"Yes, Chenoa and I have a lot in common, and Bluebird and Two Bears are always welcoming. What of you and Sarah? Will she go with you?" Zachary asked.

"No, I'll not make that request of her, it is too much. I don't even want her to know my whereabouts. When she asks, when anyone asks, neither of you know where I've gone. The pain of a broken heart will pass for her much faster than a lifetime lived as an outcast, a pariah."

Two Bears and Grey Deer arrived, and I examined Bluebird's wound and changed the dressing. The leakage was minimal, and Nema and I agreed she was fit to return home if she travelled slowly, and had proper care from her people. Uncle and Two Bears soon left to return to the Indian village with Zachary. He wanted to see where his uncle would now live, but like Uncle, I suspected it was a young woman he most wanted to see.

Nema and I cooked a hasty dinner of beans, corn and fresh rabbit. She and Grey Deer kept glancing at each other, and at the door while we ate. When we were done our meal, Nema stood to clear the dishes.

"Go home, Nema, I'll take care of that," I said. "You need to spend some time with Grey Deer."

"I don't want to leave you alone, Moll. You've been through a lot."

"I'll be here in the morning, until then, go home," I said.

I settled in, looking forward to a night of peace and quiet, and a comfortable bed. It's peculiar how sounds in the night seem different when one is alone. Little noises that would normally go unnoticed, now alerted me to some immediate, imagined danger. Foolish really, but still I slept little, and it was with some relief I heard the cackling of our arrogant rooster announcing the day.

I gathered some eggs, and prepared two for my breakfast, and then sought solace in my sewing room. Many changes were in store for us, and I needed reassurance all would be well.

I said a few prayers, and cast for protection for my family and friends when I heard a high pitched whine, followed by a sharp knocking at the door. I pretended I wasn't there. I waited, quiet as a mouse, until I knew who it was coming to call at my secret place. There was another knock at the door.

"Good day, Moll," Two Bears said.

I pulled open the door, and there he stood with a white ball of fur in his arms.

"What's this?" I asked as the puppy lifted its head.

"It's a puppy, Moll."

"I can see that, Two Bears. I'm not a dolt-head. Where did he come from? I've never seen a dog so white."

"Bluebird send puppy for Moll. He a present to thank Moll."

"I didn't expect…you don't need to thank me, we are friends," I answered, but the little pup was striking.

Two Bears stretched out his arms, and I took the bright eyed puppy from him, and scratched behind his furry ears.

"I guess we could use a farm dog around here. He might at least keep the foxes from eating all of our cacklers," I said.

The little pup lifted his ears as if he understood the conversation. He barked in his little puppy voice, and licked my face. Quite a charmer he was going to be. I'd have to think of a name as original as he was.

Being near animals, and the natural world, always made me feel closer to the creator. The best sermons from the black coats in the fanciest churches were no match for a peaceful walk in the woodlands. The church intended those places to draw the faithful into a higher plane, into a closer relationship with the Almighty. I thought more souls would be saved with a simple plank altar set up on a river bank. There is no greater measure of God's love than that seen through the lens of her creation.

In the following weeks, even months, I saw little of Zachary, and even less of Uncle Sean. Nema was busy catching up with her own household, and chores on the farm were at a lull for the season. Blue Bird and her tribe spent most of every day hunting and drying food for their migration north. They anticipated the move to occur before the following summer, and I worried about its effect on Zachary. I feared he might follow Bluebird's daughter, and I hoped their relationship was not that serious, but I dreaded having the conversation with him.

The little dog proved to be a worthy gift. I named him Waba, the word the Conoy used for "white." It wasn't exactly original, but it did sound properly exotic, and it fit his origin. Due to his disproportionate and massive paws, I knew he would attain a great size once he grew into them. Every day his appearance looked more and more like a wolf. I suspected he was the result of crossbreeding between a wild dog, and one of the native's dogs, but he was gentle to me, and to anyone I welcomed to the cabin. He played havoc on the moles and young rabbits around our farm, however. I tried to break him of the rabbits, but it appeared his taste for them was as strong as my own. At least he wasn't an egg sucker, and seemed protective of the birds, although he was not yet of a size to do much more than complain should a predator come calling.

Waba enjoyed relaxing in my sewing room while I studied, prayed and prepared, or perhaps he just sensed its importance to me. The hours there filled a missing space since my family and friends were no longer a part of my daily life. Mother's books were dog-eared now from constant perusal, even the leather covering on the long winded Malleus Maleficarum wore thin.

I worked around the cabin, and flitted about the farm performing such chores as I noticed needed doing. I tried to make the days pass by being busy as a hen with one chick, as my mother often said. Another of her famous sayings came to mind. "It's always calm before the storm."

Chapter Thirty-Four

One warm morning in early March, I rode to Mr. Hammond's farm to inquire about the availability of any extra tobacco seedlings for the spring, but I found him reluctant.

"Well, Miss Dyer, I have a lot of money in those seeds, and your holdings have grown larger. I don't think I'll have enough to support your entire planting. Some other small planters offered to pay for my extras as well."

"I'd not ask you to cut into your profits, Mr. Hammond. Indeed, if you'd give me a chance to purchase them off of you, I'd appreciate the consideration," I said.

"Well ma'am, I've sort of promised this fellow the plants. How do you figure on getting your crop in? Sean ain't been seen for a spell, has he?"

"No sir, but I suspect Zachary, Nema and I can get the crop in. We will do what we have to do, isn't that right, Mr. Hammond?"

"I know you have a strong back, and are as hard a worker as they come, but tobacco farming ain't for the ladies, Miss Dyer. Maybe you should think on selling?"

I felt the heat bloom on my face at his remarks, and at his cool reception. "Mr. Hammond, it was hard for me to come here asking. On the basis of our long friendship and your past generosity, I suspect I should be on my way. Thank you for your time." I turned back toward the hitching post.

"Now wait a minute, Miss Dyer, don't be going off all halfcocked like that. Forgive my lack of hospitality. Tell you what I do have, and that's a whole mess of seed from last year. Plant them a little heavier, and they'll do fine.

I've got a few yards of old cotton sheeting for covering the tobacco beds too, if you're of a mind to start your own?"

I felt like an ingrate, and silently cursed my hotheadedness as I answered. "Thank you, Mr. Hammond. I truly appreciate that, and will take you up on your generous offer. What would the seed and cloth cost me?" I asked.

"Ma'am, I reckon you got enough on your shoulders. You just get that crop in, and prove everybody wrong, bunch a busy bodies around here anyway. I don't take kindly to folks who go around sticking their sickles in another man's harvest."

"Mr. Hammond, again the Dyers find themselves in your debt," I said.

"John, breakfast is ready," Mrs. Hammond yelled from inside the house.

"Tell you what then," Mr. Hammond said, "pay me back by having breakfast with me and the wife? She grows weary of only having men folk around, and just hearing man talk, you know?"

Nothing tastes as fine as a meal you didn't have to prepare yourself, and Mrs. Hammond's table provided a fulsome quality and quantity. Ham, sausage, eggs, bacon, grits, and fresh baked bread with homemade jelly filled every available spot on the table before us.

The Hammonds bowed their heads in thanks, and I did likewise. I could hear my mother's reproach in my ear as I dished myself a plateful, just as if she was whispering beside me. "Moll, a young lady does not eat heavily, what will the young gents think?"

Mrs. Hammond however, only smiled. "It's good to see a young person with such a healthy appetite."

"I believe you've about wasted away to nothing, Miss Dyer, mostly skin and bones," Mr. Hammond said. "You eating anything at all over at your cabin?"

"Now John, quit flirting with our guest. I'm sure she gets tired of cooking just for herself, but Moll, you are welcome here anytime. I never get any company since those ungrateful men have been adrift hereabouts."

"What men?" I asked.

"Nothing for you to worry over, Miss," Mr. Hammond said. "Just politics, some local freemen not happy with their lot in life. It won't amount to nothing."

"Some of them think they got a raw deal because the planters haven't kept up their end, having no land to give them. With unclaimed land getting scarcer, it isn't so easy to come by," Mrs. Hammond said.

"What are they doing?"

"Nothing Miss Dyer, don't let my lovely wife get you all worked up. Had the same problem a few years back and it got some ugly, that's all. All they're doing is talking, but it has some folks all lathered up, but if you do notice anything peculiar out your way, you let me know, hear?"

I helped Mrs. Hammond with the clean-up, and we spoke for some time of simpler things. She told me stories of her old friends, and I thought of Zachary, Bluebird and Uncle, and decided to visit the village. I seldom did so, and I missed them! Mrs. Hammond seemed reluctant to let me go. She made me promise to come back soon for a visit, and I closed the door with the promise still on my lips.

As I unhitched Waba and my horse from the post, I heard a familiar voice.

"Hello, Miss Dyer, how have you been?"

"Peter! Good day. It has been awhile. Mr. Hammond keeping you busy?"

Peter filled me in on his days spent mending fences, and hauling hay to the few head of cattle the Hammonds ran on the place, while working to improve his own twenty five acres.

"Twenty five? I thought they provided fifty acres at the end of an indenture?" I asked.

"As did I, but it seems the colony fathers did not plan very well. Twenty five is all they'd grant me," Peter said.

"Can you raise enough to sell, and provide for yourselves on twenty five acres?" I asked.

"It won't be easy. I'll need more land from somewhere, somehow. My wife is expecting our first child in the summer. I just hope it don't eat much."

"Peter, that's grand news!" I hugged him, but he stiffened at my touch. "Sarah, does she fare well?" I asked with reluctance.

"Guess you didn't hear then?" he asked.

"Hear what?"

"Sarah up and left a few months back. Took a boat up to Anne Arundel Town, and said she wouldn't be back, that there was nothing for her here. She had a year left on her indenture, but Mr. Hammond seeing how hurt she was on account of your uncle, forgave the debt. Pretty good deal for her. I was surprised, he's been so close fisted of late. You'd think he didn't have a bit of chink in his pocket."

I made no mention of Mr. Hammond's generosity to me, but instead asked if he'd heard from Sarah since she left.

"Only a letter to say she was there, and safe. You know, I never figured Sean Dyer to be the kind of man who would do such a thing to a fine woman like Sarah. I guess you never really know what's inside a fellow's heart." Peter said.

"Peter, I don't know what's become of my Uncle, but you know the situation he was in. He never meant to hurt Sarah."

"Moll, don't lie to my face. I know where he is, and so do you," Peter said. "What part are you forgetting? That Two Bears and me are friends, or that Indians don't understand the scheming and lying of white men?"

"I'm sorry. Uncle thought it best not to tell Sarah. He didn't want her to be forced to a decision, and ruin her life. Sean is still your friend, and he loved Sarah," I said.

"She loved him, and the bastard broke her heart. Seems he got over it fast enough though, having taken up with Bluebird's cousin already. I reckon when the candles are out, all cats are grey, huh? As for me, I no longer count any friends among the Dyers."

"I'm truly sorry you feel that way, Peter. I always reckoned you a friend, and I know Uncle is sorry about all that happened too, especially the part about Sarah."

"Don't waste your fiddle-faddle on me. I ain't telling the High Sheriff nothing I know. I'll hate to see Two Bears leave, but it will mean I'm well shed of Mr. Sean Dyer. Maybe you ought to think on selling that farm of yours? I doubt a lone woman and a boy can farm a place that big, nor protect it."

"There are few Susquehannocks left in the colony, Peter. I doubt we'll have any more troubles from them."

His eyes narrowed, and I could swear they darkened.

"Wasn't talking about them." He stalked away toward his cabin with no further word. Waba growled at his back.

Chapter Thirty-Five

The Conoy village changed little since the last time I was there, except there were fewer inhabitants. Some of the longhouses stood in need of repair, which was unusual. Many were empty, and all soon would be. It was a beehive of activity though, as the woman set up drying racks, and chewed on raw leather to soften it for clothes. Some of the children ground corn with mortar and pestle. Others stood on the bank of the river pulling their fishing nets in. The only men I noticed were the very old; I guessed the others were hunting. Everyone greeted me warmly, and one of the smallest children recognized me and ran off to tell Bluebird.

I didn't spot Sean or Zachary, but looking in the direction the boy ran, I spied Bluebird cutting deer meat in thin slices to dry.

"Good day, Bluebird," I said.

"Good day, Moll. Look at Waba, so big!" she said with a wide grin, and he wagged his tail in delight. Bluebird wiped her hands on her shirt and gave me a hug.

"Your people are so busy preparing to move, and I dread seeing that day come."

"Yes, we leave soon. Moll should come with us. Moll can teach Bluebird the ways of the Gaagii pauwau?"

"I cannot, my sister. I have a farm here we worked hard to profit from. My only family here is Zachary and Sean, and Sean is leaving too. I have to make good on the place before I get too old," I said.

"Moll, Zachary and Sean all come?"

I shook my head. "Maybe Bluebird should stay here with me?"

She shook her head sadly, and pointed to where her daughter, Chenoa, sat weaving a pack basket for their journey. "Bluebird go with Two Bears and Chenoa."

I hugged my friend again. The little children squealed in sudden delight.

"The men return," Bluebird said.

They marched through the village with pride carrying several large bucks on poles. I saw Zachary and Uncle toward the end of the pack, and ran to meet them. They too carried game in the form of a half dozen rabbits.

"Moll, what do you make of this?" A very scruffy Uncle Sean asked. "They don't trust us to pursue men's game, and we have to thump rabbits with the older boys!"

"Waba, no!" I said, as he licked his lips smelling their prizes. "Sit!"

"He's well trained, Moll. Looks like he could eat you out of house and home though!" Uncle laughed.

"He catches much of what he eats," Zachary answered, "but he always comes home."

"Yes, he's much better trained than my brother." I said with a pout.

"I know, Moll, but I'll do better. I promise. You'll be needing me more around the farm soon."

"We will have our hands full come planting season, and there's tobacco beds to get in as well this year."

"What of John Hammond? Will he have enough to spare for you?" Uncle asked. I told him of my visit with the Hammonds, and his offer of seed.

"Uncle, Peter knows you're here. He said he wouldn't report it, but I thought you should know."

"No doubt Peter is as disappointed in me as Sarah is," he said with a shake of his head.

I did not tell Uncle of Sarah's heartbreak, or of her move to Anne Arundel Town. I knew the hurt he felt over the pain he'd caused, having caused such pain myself. Personal agony is easier to overcome than seeing the pain you've inflicted on a loved one's face. He didn't need to know.

"Hello Bluebird. Did you tell Moll about Chenoa's vision?" Zachary asked.

"Moll not see Chenoa yet, Bluebird take her now. You talk with Sean and Zachary later, Moll?"

She took me by the hand and led me to where her daughter sat weaving a cattail reed basket for their journey.

"Good day, Moll," Chenoa said.

"Good day, Chenoa."

"Moll come with our people upriver?" She asked.

"I cannot."

She looked sad, maybe for me, and maybe for what my answer might mean for her and Zachary.

"Moll is a good friend to my parents. They will not forget."

"Nor will I forget them."

"I have never been to where Moll lives."

"I know, Chenoa, but you are welcome there any time. I might get to see my brother more than twice a week then." I smiled.

"It is a house made of many trees where the ravens fly?"

I laughed. "I see Bluebird told you."

"Told me what, Moll?" She looked at Bluebird, and both women shrugged their shoulders.

"Never mind, why do you ask about my house?" I asked.

"I dreamed of your home, Moll. In my dream, I am walking at night in a strange woods, and I am not sure of the way home. I see a house, and I think it must be yours, the house by the stream with many logs.

It is a very dark night with no stars, and a moon hidden by clouds. I am lost and afraid, and I feel something is not good there. Ravens call, although it is night time. I feel cold, like icicles, creep up my back. An owl answers the ravens, and drops from his tree near me. Owls do not hurt our people, Moll, but this is a dream, and owls are not good in dreams. He dives towards me, so close I hear his feathers sing. I jump away, trip over a rock, and feel its talons slice my chest. Ravens are loud, and sound angry, but more owls answer.

The birds make a terrible sound in the trees. Leaves and branches fall, and something hits my shoulders. I snatch at it, and feel fur and warm blood. I pulled the rabbit hide off of me, and threw it away. My knees are shaking, but I run as fast as I can, like the wind! I feel so foolish! I am running away from a dead rabbit! Then the soft whistle of wings are behind me. Owls fly faster than I can run. They are about to catch me, and they call my name "Chenoa! Chee-noooo-ahhhh!" The ravens squawk, and many follow me through the trees screaming. Again I trip and roll down a small hill. I am very clumsy in my dreams. The woods become still, and the birds stare at me, waiting, waiting for something?

I see a small trail in front of me, but something stands there, hidden in the shadows. "Who are you?" I ask.

The bushes shake, and a handsome white man limps out, and smiles with many white teeth. I am afraid. This is not a good man, or maybe not a man but a Manitou?

"Good evening, Chenoa," he said. "It is a nice night for a walk, I love meeting girls on their late night walks. Are you lost?" My fear prevented my answer.

"This is not a good place for you." He pointed toward your house of trees.

"What do you want?" I asked.

"We want the same thing, Chenoa. How much do you love your Zachary? She will stop you, the woman in that house. Maybe we can help each other, but for now, follow this trail. It will lead you home. We will talk again soon." The man smiles at me again, and in the darkness, his pretty white teeth now look pointy and sharp. The man laughs, not a happy laugh, and the birds go crazy.

I run down the trail until I can run no more, but all is still. I stopped, listening to the woods. No birds were following, and there were no footsteps behind me, so I turned to check my back trail.

Two sets of glowing green eyes stare at me from steps away, close enough to pounce! I scream for help, and I fall to my knees in fear. The creatures' snarl sounds almost human. The leaves rustle beneath their feet as they leap. One creature knocks me to the ground as the other lands straddling me, its hot wet breath is in my ear! I scream again! This is when Zachary wakes me shaking and very afraid."

"That's a frightening nightmare, Chenoa, but it wasn't real. It was just a dream," I said.

"Show Moll, Chenoa," Bluebird said.

Chenoa dropped her eyes, and opened her shirt. The top of her chest was bandaged, and she pulled the cloth away. There were two fresh claw marks across her shoulder and down her left breast.

"The owl's marks are real. Mother said I must warn her friend too."

The hairs rose on my neck. I did not know Chenoa well, but I was familiar with her dreams. Bluebird believed they were visions, warnings from the other world. Would Chenoa contrive this story to get what she wanted from me? Did she think she was in love with Zachary? Was she so determined for him to follow her north? Could the scratches on her chest have been inflicted by her own hand?

"What did this man look like?" I asked.

"Many white men look the same to Chenoa, but this man handsome like Zachary, but older with a long scar on his face."

Chapter Thirty-Six

Uncle and Zachary escorted Waba and I to the longhouse they shared with Two Bears, Bluebird and Chenoa. Grey Deer and another family shared the next longhouse down, along with Nema during her frequent visits.

The frame of the longhouse consisted of spaced saplings, with one end embedded in the ground, and the other ends bent over and lashed together to form an arch. Tightly woven reeds, and sheaths of bark completed the roof.

It felt warm and comfortable inside. A fire burned in the center of the dwelling, and a small section of the roof remained open directly overhead to allow the smoke to escape. The burning wood left a pleasant scent, but little smoke remained inside. Wide knee high benches covered in furs served as beds.

"Moll stay with us tonight?" Bluebird asked.

"Only a visit, my friend. I should get back before nightfall," I said.

"Bad storm comes, Moll." Two Bears pointed outside at the trees. The wind blew in a new direction, turning up the leaves. It was midday, and the sky looked as dark as at dusk.

"Has anyone seen Nema and Grey Deer? I've asked around camp, but nobody's seen either of them since the morning hunt started."

Two Bears said something to Bluebird I couldn't understand, and laughed.

"Two Bears said Grey Deer is a grown man, and if he doesn't know when to come in from the storm, Nema will tell him," Zachary translated.

"Poor Grey Deer," Uncle said. "I never knew Nema's tongue had so much clack. You cannot imagine the verbal thrashing she gives Grey Deer whenever they discuss where to make their home. It seems she's not much inclined to move."

I smiled, but my heart sank in my chest. I assumed that, like me, Nema's personal investment into her life here was too great to leave behind. I didn't know moving was even a consideration for her. I felt stupid, but it perturbed me she never mentioned it to me. She was a free woman, but we were friends, and I counted on her heavily.

Bluebird added another deer hide to one of the benches, and patted it down. "Moll sleep here tonight."

"I really should go…" The wind gusted, and shook the framework of the longhouse. Mothers yelled for their children to come inside, and sheets of rain followed. Waba ran inside, sopping wet and shook water on all of us.

"Waba, go sit in the corner, you stink of wet fur," I said. He walked across the longhouse with his head down, and his tail between his legs. Everyone laughed at his antics.

"I think maybe I'll stay a while after all. It sounds really nasty out there."

A young woman ran into the shelter, as soaking wet as Waba. I thought her to be one of Chenoa's friends as they looked to be the same age. She ran to Uncle and threw her arms around him.

"I stay with Sean tonight," she said.

"Uncle, who is your new friend?" I asked, as he unwrapped the girl's arms. His face turned the color of steamed crabs.

"Moll, umm… this is my friend White Swan. Swan, meet my niece Moll."

Like many of our native neighbors, White Swan used a shortened English translation of her name. Unlike most of her sisters, especially in the company of whites, she wore the traditional style of mantle draped from one shoulder, leaving her left breast exposed.

The young woman extended her hand.

"Good day, Moll. Sean speak of you many times," she said. She hugged me, a full face to face hug with both arms engaged. My mouth fell open, and I stepped back.

"Good day. I heard my Uncle had a new little friend, but I didn't believe him to be so weak," I said.

"Not weak, Sean is big strong man. Swan is proud to be his woman." She giggled.

"Well Uncle, you wasted little time recovering from your heartache," I said.

"I've started a new life, Moll. Did you expect me to live like a black coat forever?" Uncle asked and crossed his arms.

"Forever? No, but a few months or so might be appropriate," I said.

"Just be happy for me, Moll. Swan is a good woman," he said.

"Oh, indeed I am happy. I'm sure Sarah would be happy for you as well," I answered.

"Don't be impertinent, Moll, and leave Sarah out of it. You know I couldn't bring her with me," Uncle said.

"Apparently not, and I can tell how upset you are," I said.

"Perhaps you should keep your oars in your own damn boat?" Uncle asked, puffing out his chest.

Zachary and Uncle exchanged a wordless glance, a male conspiracy of mutual secrets? Two Bears and Bluebird dropped their eyes to the ground as if to disappear, but Swan just stood grinning.

"We should eat. Two Bears is hungry."

Little light reached the inside of our shelter, so Bluebird started skinning the brace of rabbits near the fire. I asked to help with dinner, and she pointed to cattail roots on one of the benches. Swan pulled a string of dried squash from the rafters. By the time I had the roots peeled, Bluebird had the rabbits spitted on the fire. I'd never boiled water using the native's method with hot rocks. One advantage provided by the whites was metal pots, and I smiled with relief when Bluebird pulled one from under a bench.

A boom broke the silence, and the ground shook in answer.

"Was that thunder?" Zachary asked.

"In March? Doubtful," Uncle said, but another roar proved him wrong. The sound of the rain changed, and Zachary walked to the doorway.

"It's hailing," Zachary said, "and I think there's snow mixing in. I'm glad you stayed, Moll." Chenoa stepped to his side, and he put his arm around her. Their eyes moved back and forth between the storm outside and each other.

A jolt of icy fear clenched in my belly, and I walked over to Bluebird and nodded in the direction of Zachary and Chenoa.

"Bluebird, no secrets? Are you sure Chenoa is Two Bear's child? There has been no other?" I asked in a whisper.

Bluebird looked confused, but smiled. "No other man for Bluebird, Moll. Two Bears first man, last man, only man," she said, and dropped her gaze to the ground.

"Thank you," I said, and hugged her.

The wind blew and whistled through every gap in the longhouse, making the fire swirl. When a hot ember flew up, Two Bears and Uncle stacked more rocks around the fire pit to protect it.

"Don't get dirt on rabbit," Bluebird warned.

Waba began whining in the corner, fearful of his first storm, but Bluebird treated him with the offal from the rabbits. She made a new best friend, and Waba followed at her heels as she moved about the longhouse. He lost interest when no more rabbit entrails came his way, and settled back in his spot in the corner to sleep.

Over dinner, we talked about the tribe's migration north. Two Bears described the new land, the mountain valleys, and the animals living there. He said the deer were smaller, but the squirrels larger, and bears more numerous. Rafts of ducks and geese covered the Potomack where it became a swift clear river a man could wade across.

The storm continued to vent its anger outside. Snow was steady, and a few flurries, pushed by the storm's breath, drifted into the longhouse.

"I hope Nema and Grey Deer got to their shelter before this storm hit," I said.

"How far to Nema's house?" Swan asked.

"Walking, about the time it takes for the sun to move one hand's width to get to her cabin, but Moll means to their longhouse," Uncle said.

"No, they are not here. Grey Deer say they go to Nema and Moll's farm after the hunt," Swan said.

"What? Are you sure?" I asked.

"Yes, I see them by river when the men came back. Nema say she must go home, that you are there alone. Grey Deer say plenty time before storm, but must walk fast."

"The storm hit soon after, they didn't have time to get home," I said. "Nema didn't know I was here."

Chapter Thirty-Seven

A cold wetness in my ear jolted me awake. I jumped upright, and Waba licked his chops, and smiled his canine grin informing me it was time to rise, or that he was lonely. I stared through the door at the new and unfamiliar landscape. Several inches of snow fell through the night, coating the world in white and showing no sign of slowing. Waba pranced about at my side and whined. I scratched him behind the ears.

"It will be fine, Waba," I said.

The fire burned down to embers, and the house grew cold. I threw the remaining small pieces of wood on the coals, and blew on them until they flickered into flame.

I looked around the longhouse, trying not to wake anyone. Bluebird remained in her bed, but Two Bears' spot was empty. Zachary and Chenoa had the decency to sleep apart, even if they did pull their benches close together. Uncle and Swan displayed no such modesty, both naked and entwined in each other's arms. I doubted anyone slept well with the bear-like moans and pig grunts issuing from their bed throughout the night.

"Good day, Moll," Two Bears said and stepped inside. Snow stuck to his legs as high as his knees. He brushed it off, and dumped the armload of wood near the fire.

"That's perfect, Two Bears. Thank you. At least the wind died down, but it's still cold."

"Snow stop soon, then Two Bears find Grey Deer and Nema," he said, but his prediction was false. The snow continued well into the night.

It reminded me of being shipboard when the winds stop, the sails fall limp and no progress is made. We talked, played games, and did what minimal indoor chores that needed doing. We kept the fire going, of course, but mostly we divided our time between staring at the walls, looking out at the weather, and eating. We ate so often, and so much, I feared their food preparations might not survive the storm. Sitting around doing nothing creates a good appetite, and I imagined it was the same in all of the longhouses. Sit, watch, eat, and repeat.

Chenoa showed me how to weave a basket. I admired the one she created, and wanted to make one for my own cabin. She proved herself a good teacher, and before night fell, my basket was complete, shoulder sling and all.

"Thank you, Chenoa," I said. "This will serve me well."

"Thanks to you, Moll," she replied, and pointed toward Zachary.

My face flushed, and I bit back an annoyed retort, but it wasn't the time, and I was a guest in their home. I was not comfortable with how close the two of them were. I liked Chenoa, but they were so young, and her tribe planned to leave! Did she really believe I would allow him to go with her? Uncle was as close to a father as Zachary had, and he was certainly not proving himself a worthy model of Christian manhood.

Sleep did not come easy with these thoughts corrupting my mind. I knew Zachary was attracted to Chenoa, and to the native way of life. What boy wouldn't wish for such freedom, in a world unblemished since first touched by the Creator's hand?

A second night spent on the benches did little to improve my outlook. I woke blinking my eyes from the brightness of the sun filtering through the smoke hole. Waba slept at my side, and I stepped out to get the full impact of the sun on my face.

The snow came to mid-thigh nearest the house. I hoped the drifts on the woodland trails wouldn't be as deep, but I needed to go soon to check on Nema and Grey Deer. I brushed off some firewood, and toted it back to the shelter. Two Bears and Zachary were pulling on boots and lacing snowshoes.

"Are you getting ready to look for them?" I asked.

"Yes, Two Bears and Zachary go. Moll stay here."

"I certainly will not, Two Bears. I can keep up with you," I said.

"Moll is tall woman, but snow is deep."

"Can't we take the horses?" I asked.

"With uncertain footing, and the ice layered under snow, they could break a leg," Uncle said stirring from his slumbers.

"Zachary, is there another pair of snowshoes?"

He walked to Chenoa's bunk and pulled out a pair from beneath. "Chenoa made these last week. She said we'd need another pair soon."

"She is wise, Zachary, perhaps we should call on her for our future weather predictions?"

"The weather is too fickle a beast for that," Uncle said. "Two Bears, you take good care of my nephew here, but I don't think you should try the trip yet, Moll."

"Don't start, it is already decided," I said.

Two Bears laughed. "Sean keep village safe. Two Bears keep Moll and Zachary safe. Back tonight or tomorrow."

Bluebird packed food for the trip, and gave us each a hug before we left the longhouse. Waba ran up behind me ready for a new adventure.

"Stay Waba. Bluebird, I'll be back for him in a day or two."

Waba would not take no for an answer and ran out ahead of us. The thin layer of ice covering the snow crushed easily under my weight, but Waba had four feet, and less weight. He pranced across the top of the snow, his paws leaving only small indents to mark his passage.

"Looks like you're coming along too, boy," Zachary said.

Chenoa ran to Zachary, and wrapped her arms around him. "Be careful, Waba Kitchi." I heard her whisper. "I dreamed of Grey Deer, and many owls."

Again with the owls, I thought, but the tendrils of fear from Chenoa's dream still crept into my thoughts. I decided not to dwell on it, and I forced my mind to focus on other, more pleasant outings.

I remembered roaming the green rolling hills of home, and gathering herbs for Mother's cures. We hunted for mullein with its large fuzzy rabbit ear leaves for brother's asthma, and stinging nettle root for father's gout. We were blessed with no other cares in the world. We never harbored a doubt of finding what we sought. I locked my mind on the images playing through my mind, and hastened to keep up with the men on our journey home.

The snowshoes made it possible to make fair time in the snow, but learning to walk in them was learning to walk all over again. The timing of our steps, the exaggerated up and down motion of our legs, wearied all of us.

The trail was not the same trail I followed so many times in the past. The snow distorted everything, and even the trees took on a ghastly, otherworldly appearance. The white world smelled clean and fresh, and so bright, but it was also heavy, bog-like and secretive. After three hours of walking, we were but half way home, and Two Bears suggested we break for food and water.

"We have far to go. Must keep up strength for more to come."

We consumed the dried blueberries, acorn meal bread, and dried meat in short order, and pronounced ourselves ready to travel.

Shortly before dusk, we found ourselves in the cabin clearing, but if I didn't see it standing before us, I would question where I was. The cabin, encased in the snow, looked smaller and less significant than I knew it to be.

Two Bears pointed to something small and black buried in the snow, and tugged at it. What began as a few black feathers, grew into an entire raven. Two Bears turned the bird this way and that, inspecting it. He pointed out the frozen blood on the bird's neck, and its eyes. They were plucked from its head.

"Raven get lost with heavy snow, smash in tree." He shrugged his shoulders and tossed the bird back to the snow.

I saw the door of my cabin standing open, and ran toward it.

"Wait, Moll!" Zachary yelled behind me.

I reached the door, again broken from its hinges. Snow had drifted inside and half of the floor was covered by a foot of the white stuff. I shook my head, so many of our possessions were blown to the floor, and ruined.

"Don't worry, Moll, I'll shovel it out, make it as good as new," Zachary said, but I was already outside and headed for Nema's cabin, fearful of what I might, or might not, find there. A flattened trail in the snow snaked between her cabin and mine. Was it carved by the wind? Packed down by animals? If done by men, they'd not worn snowshoes. The lack of any tracks meant it was made before the snow stopped.

Nema's door was closed, but opened slightly at my knock.

"Nema, are you here? Grey Deer?" I yelled.

I heard no answer, but I did hear something, a sound as soft as the steps of a mouse.

"We're coming in, Nema," I said, and pushed my way inside. Two Bears and Zachary followed close behind me, unprepared for what we saw.

Chapter Thirty-Eight

I noticed the pictures, chairs, and other light items tossed about the room. A single shaft of sunlight reflected on shards of glass on the floor by a broken window on the side wall. The snow accumulated in the floor in front of it, and I guessed the wind caused the disarray.

The fireplace coals were long dead, and the air in the cabin seemed even colder than that outside. Long, thin icicles reached down from the inside of the broken window frame, grasping at the air. Winter's hand of death, I thought, shook my head to clear it, and stepped into the darkness leading to the bedroom. A soft lump caught my foot, and only ramming my shoulder into the far wall prevented me from planting my face on the floor.

"Moll!" Zachary shouted, and I turned to see the cause of my stumble.

Side by side, entwined in one another's arms, Grey Deer and Nema were unmoving, as still as death. They were bloodied in many places. A horrible screech rent the stillness of the cabin, my own scream. When the echo ended, there was a murmur of sound. I dropped to the floor at Nema's side. Did her lips move?

I placed my face near hers, and felt the barest whisper of breath. Her heart tapped with no more force than the ticking of a clock.

"Nema? Can you hear me? What has happened?" I asked, and she mouthed words I couldn't hear.

"Zachary, look to Grey Deer. Is he breathing? Check his wrist, can you feel his heart beat?" I asked.

I opened the remnants of Nema's shredded clothes to determine the location and extent of her injuries.

Numerous wounds crisscrossed her chest, legs and arms. They were gashes, but inflicted by…? I could not tell.

Blood loss seemed heavy, but her wounds were shallow. I began to wash the wounds to better see and treat them. "Dear Mother, this is beyond my skills," I prayed aloud. "Help me to know the right things to do!"

I ran back to my cabin, hoping I had enough herbs on hand, and that I could remember! I gathered what I could, and returned to find Zachary still bent over Grey Deer. Nema continued mouthing unheard words. Two Bears stood watching, appearing lost.

"I think he's gone, Moll," Zachary said.

"I'll be right there, Zachary. I need something from the room in the barn. It is a book, brown leather and written by hand. There's a string of dried beet slices there too. The key to the room is beside my bed, do not tarry!" I said.

"Two Bears, we need the fireplace lit. Can you get it going? There's dry wood by the back door," I said.

I turned my attention to Grey Deer. I checked his heartbeat, his breath. I prayed for some indication of life, but Zachary was right, Grey Deer was no longer with us.

I turned toward the fireplace as an unwanted tear streaked down my cheek. Two Bears watched me as he started the fire.

"Two Bears…" I said with a catch in my voice.

"I know." He bowed his head. The flame flickered and grew.

Zachary raced back into the house with the book, and the dried beets. "What is that room in the barn? I never saw anything like that," he said in a rush.

"Zachary, the little garden patch you worked up for me? I have a small bed of kale in there at the farthest end. They've barely sprouted, but will have to do. You'll need to dig them from the snow." I put the beets in water over the fire to soften them.

Most of Nema's cuts proved superficial, unlike Grey Deer's. Her wounds were intended to torture, his to maim or kill, and both of them showed the marks of a beating. Along with the cuts were many raised welts and bruises. I covered Nema with blankets until the room warmed up.

"Nema, who did this to you?" I asked.

"Men…Pe…" and then something too soft to hear.

"It's fine, Nema, rest and get warm. I'll be here."

I didn't know the extent of her internal injuries, but the Conoy used wild ramps for cleansing the body in the spring, and I knew of a patch near our stream, if it could be found under the snow. Nema fidgeted and pushed off one of her blankets.

"Are you too warm, Nema?" I asked. Her head slid from side to side.

"Grey…Grey D… D?" she asked, shivering.

I shrugged my shoulders, and pretended not to understand. She didn't need to hear the answer, not yet. I turned away from her, and threw another piece of wood on the fire, then retrieved a needle and thread from my room. I poured a glass of Uncle's rum, and returned to Nema.

"Two Bears, I may need your help. Nema, this is going to hurt," I said.

I wished Mother spent more time teaching me to sew, but I did my best, especially on the two cuts running side by side on her face from the corner of her eye to the edge of her lips. Nema was not a vain woman, but I knew such scars on her face would prevent other, deeper scars from healing. It is a perverse mind that inflicts pain on another, but only a black souled fiend could have intentionally disfigured Nema's beauty. My best work would not conceal the work of his blade.

What was it that Mother used to prevent scarring? I dropped my head, and cut short a sob. Why couldn't I remember? Please Mother, you said you'll always be with me. I need you. Distressed and confused, I conjured my mother's face in my mind's eye for comfort. She smiled at me, as she always did. It was hard to picture her without a smile. Mother stood at the back door of our Kinsale home. She reached out, snapped off a branch with multiple tiny white flowers and held it out to me. Remember Moll? Elderflower extract, how could I forget? I was not surprised it was one of the vials Mother packed for me.

Chapter Thirty-Nine

Two Bears stayed the night, rising with me every time Nema moaned in her sleep. She was the same as family to him, to all of us. She and Grey Deer were not priest-linked, but they were the same as man and wife nonetheless. Zachary, too, slept in the floor near Nema's bed, but was up and down all night feeding the fire. The cabin warmed, as did Nema, although her teeth still chattered.

Nema slept well through the night, and into the next morning. While we ate our midday meal, we heard her stirring.

"Moll? Grey Deer?"

The three of us went to her side.

"How are you feeling, Nema?" I asked.

"Sore, Moll, tired," She answered.

"Just rest then. Are you thirsty? Can we get you anything?" I asked.

"Moll, where are those men? Are they gone?" Nema whispered, and I saw a grimace of pain on her face.

"They are gone, Nema," I said.

"They were evil men. They…," she sobbed.

"Not now, Nema, tell us when you are up to it," I said.

"No, now. I didn't know them, the men. When the storm slowed, we heard a banging noise in your house. Grey Deer looked out the window, and a man stood at our door. He knocked, and asked if we were the Dyer family.

"Grey Deer opened the door to let the man come in from the cold, but…. Where did the others come from? No, Grey Deer! No, watch out, there's a …." Nema stuttered.

"What did they want, Nema? Why did they do this to you?" I asked.

"Miss Grace came and said bastard freeman, … fifty acres to avenge, not Peter, Grey Deer on head, rights…, I feel foggy, Miss Moll." her speech slurred, slapped at figures that weren't there, and soon after, she slept.

"Free men, fifty acres, and revenge? Is that what you heard too?" Zachary asked.

"Yes, and something about Peter?" I was worried about her state of confusion. It would be evening before we had any answers.

Zachary found a few ramp bulbs, and I boiled them out, thinking it too soon for Nema to eat solid food. The sun was strong enough to melt some of the snow, and chase the lingering chill from the cabin. Two Bears covered the broken window with blankets to hold in the warmth, but then none of the sun's light reached inside to help brighten our mood. I read from Mother's book to assure myself I was doing everything possible for head and internal injuries. We were not a talkative trio, or quartet, as even Waba acted sullen. He stared straight ahead, curled in a ball at the foot of Nema's bed, only lifting his ears when spoken to.

While Nema slept, I left to inspect the damage to my cabin, and to root through the dried herbs for anything else of value. The men promised to come for me should she wake, or if it seemed she was in pain.

The damages I saw there were not the result of the elements. In my earlier haste, the chairs and tables appeared blown about, but I now saw the legs broken from chairs and used in the fire, as were many of my hard earned herbs and valued books. Papers tossed and ripped in pieces, our tin dinner plates mangled on the floor.

I went into my room. Someone carved two pictures of exaggerated male genitals on the logs of my walls. "For you, Moll" was written on a piece of paper, and tacked beside them.

"How nice of you bastards to consider my needs!" I shouted to the walls.

All of our beds, thrown to the floor, were now soaked from the melting snow, but the worst loss? My Mother's last letter to me, ripped in half and blurred from the dampness. I sat in the floor, cursing the men responsible.

When my anger was in check, I put on a neutral face, and walked back to Nema's. She was awake, and sipping from a cup Zachary held for her.

"Why didn't you..?"

"She just woke up, Moll. We were coming for you, but she was parched," Zachary said.

"How are you feeling, Nema?" I asked.

"Better now. Where is Grey Deer?"

"Zachary, go check on Grey Deer in the other room," I said.

He was quick enough to understand what I wanted, but Two Bears looked at me as if I was touched in the head.

"What happened here, Nema? Who did this to you?" I asked.

She shook her head. "I told you about the four men getting in the cabin?" she asked. I nodded yes.

"They were looking for the Dyer family. I told them I didn't know where any of you were, and I was worried about you, but they did not believe me. Grey Deer was on the floor after they hit him, and they threw me down beside him.

"I told them to get the hell out of my house, but they kicked me and ripped my clothes. I think they were going to..." Nema glanced at Zachary and stopped. Her breath was rapid, her face covered in sweat.

"Who were they?" I asked again.

She took a deep breathe. "I don't know who they were. They were complaining about their treatment by the landowners, by the colony fathers, and that they didn't get what they were promised. When I thought they were going to… you know, Peter came in and told them to stop."

Two Bears jumped from his seat, but waited for more.

"Peter was with them?" I asked.

"He was here, he told them I wasn't one of the well-born Dyers. He said I worked hard for my land, earned it with elbow grease, same as they had. Peter told them they came for you and Sean, and to burn the tobacco in your barn, but the men didn't listen to him. They said they weren't arsonists, and Peter should fight his own battles. He hit the man on top of me with a chair, and there was a fight, but there were too many of them. Then one of them pulled a knife, and things got blurry. I don't remember much after, except pain. The next thing I remember was the three of you coming to save me." Nema said.

"Oh, Nema, I am so sorry. I wish I came home sooner. Maybe this wouldn't have happened," I said, and cradled her head.

"Maybe it would be worse, Miss Moll."

"You're going to be fine, Nema. We'll take the best care of you. You are family," I said, and she smiled.

"How did you fare in the storm?" she asked. "Zachary looks well, is he looking after Grey Deer?"

"We are fine, Nema, and you have enough to worry about, just get well for now," I answered.

"And Sean, he is also well?" she asked.

"Uncle will always be Uncle. He's found a woman to play with it seems, a very young one too," I said, hoping to distract her from uglier things.

"White Swan is a good girl, not smart, but good. They both need comfort," Nema said, and my face colored.

"What suffering could that woman child need comfort from?" I shook my head. "I'm sorry, Nema, we can talk about this when you are better," I said, ashamed of my outburst.

"White Swan lost a husband and a newborn boy to smallpox, Miss Moll. Sean lost his life and his family, just like you," she said. A jolt of pain appeared to be written on her face.

"You must rest now, Nema. We will talk more tomorrow," I said.

Chapter Forty

When Nema fell asleep, it was all we could do to keep Two Bears from running off to murder Peter. Zachary and I assured him white man's justice would be done, but it was only his love for us and Nema that kept him there. An entire regiment of lobster coated soldiers could not physically contain the raw rage blazing in his eyes.

No, these horrific deeds would not go unpunished, but Peter? How could he sink to such a depth? How could his anger burn so hot? His unwarranted betrayal stung us all!

It was impossible to travel to Saint Mary's City with the snow piled high on the rough road. Newtowne was conceivable, but no constabulary resided there, not to protect a dozen homes and the new general store. Until the snow cleared, we were on our own. Was the mob of crazed men still lurking nearby, waiting to strike again?

"Zachary, make sure the rifles are loaded. If they come back, we need to be prepared," I said.

"I think they are long gone, Moll. We saw no fresh tracks when coming in, and Two Bears has reconnoitered some too. The rifles are loaded, ready for whatever comes, but if I get a hold of one of them, they'll never see Saint Mary's City," Zachary said.

"I know how you feel, Zachary, but the Lord is their judge, and until they get a chance to meet their maker, it will fall to the law of the colony. I won't have you standing before that court again."

"Maybe I can hurry that meeting along for them some then." He said. "They can't be right in the head anyway, Moll. Nema said they were adamant about not being arsonists, yet had no qualms torturing Nema, and killing Grey Deer? What sense does that make?" Zachary asked.

"Grey Deer?" Nema wailed from her bed. I hushed Zachary with my lips.

"Nema, how are you?" I asked, but she had already returned to her tortured dreams, only awake enough to pull Zachary's words into her dream.

"I agree, Zachary, they are touched in the head, and that makes them even more dangerous," I said.

"We aren't the lawmakers of this colony, you honored your commitments at the end of Nema's indenture, and we received our headrights legitimately. How can they blame us for any of their troubles?" Zachary asked. I thought of the fifty acres less than honestly procured at his birth.

"The timing of Peter's indenture was not good, and he's chosen us to be his scapegoats. The men are angry and lashing out, and we are easy targets with most of our friends leaving soon."

"I thought Peter was a decent, level headed man, but this was pure evil." Zachary said.

"He said the same thing of Uncle. Peter blames him for his sister's broken heart. She moved away, you know, to Anne Arundel Town. It wasn't you, or even Nema and Grey Deer they wanted. It was Uncle and I they were after."

"Peter was a friend." Two Bears gritted his teeth, and shook his head in a vicious back and forth movement.

"They had no right to do this to our family, Moll. I don't care what they were bilked out of. They must pay," Zachary said, and stifled his sob as men are wont to do.

I hugged him close, and scratched the back of his head the way he liked when he was a baby. "I know, Zachary, I know."

When I woke the next morning, the cabin was dark, and quiet. The others didn't stir. Two Bears slept by

Nema's bed, but Zachary must have found a softer spot to rest. Sleeping on the floor grows wearisome. I snuck out to my sewing room, hoping to find another vial of elderflower oil, but with little hope of doing so. Still, I knew a brief respite there would break the monotony, and ease my tension. Waba lifted one ear as I opened the front door, and rushed past me, all but knocking me down.

The outside walls of the barn formed the south wall of my sewing room, and shrinkage of the drying wood created minute cracks I'd been intending to caulk. As I approached, I saw a flicker of candle light through them.

"Heel!" I whispered to Waba, and he jumped to my side. Were the men back to finish what they started? Should I go back for Two Bears? No, there might be more of them, and he could better protect Nema and Zachary where he was. I knew Waba would do his all to protect me, but I wished I had one of the rifles for good measure!

I reached for the door to my room, and threw it open in a rush. Waba leapt inside snarling his displeasure.

"Oh, good morning, Moll," Zachary said, crimson faced.

"What are you doing here, Zachary? You know this is my private room."

"I know, but I just wanted another look." He held up the book he'd been reading, the one of mother's. "Do you believe any of this?" he asked with a twinkle in his eye, and biting back a smirk.

"There is a lot of passed down knowledge there. Do not mock it. It's a part of your heritage I thought to share with you soon, but I see now you aren't ready!" I pointed to the door.

Zachary dropped his head. "I am sorry, but I really want to know more. I am so tired of all the secrets!" he said, as we walked back out through the barn.

Halfway back to Nema's cabin, a cry of anguish pierced our ears, and the ever present ravens screamed.

Waba ran for the house barking with Zachary and I close behind him.

Nema's bed was empty, and Two Bears was gone! My eyes circled the room for them, nothing.

"Nema? Two Bears?" I yelled.

I turned toward the other bedroom as another wail ripped through my ears and heart, the bedroom where we laid out poor Grey Deer.

Two Bears stood by the bed tugging at Nema's arm. Her body stretched across Grey Deer, shaking in grief. Her sobs echoed through the room.

I sat on the side of the bed, rubbing her shoulders with one hand, and brushing at her hair with the other. Zachary turned away, and sat in the kitchen with his head cradled in his arms on the table.

We could not pull Nema away from her beloved, and I was at a loss what to do when she fell asleep in his cold arms. Two Bears thought it wise to leave her there, and thought it might help her grieve to be alone with him. I covered them with the blanket and we left the bedroom.

"Tomorrow I will ride to St. Mary's City and get the sheriff," Zachary said.

"The snow is too deep, Zachary. Another couple of days should melt it enough."

"No, Moll, the sheriff needs to get out here now. Nema needs to see that the men who did this will pay, and the trail is getting colder. There may be some signs or tracks to follow before the snow is gone," Zachary said.

"If you leave tomorrow, it is at least a two day trip. If you wait two days, it's a half of a day travel. What would you gain? Two Bears wants to get back to his village, and tell his people what has happened. They too must have their time to grieve."

"I can take one of the horses, and pack light, no need for a cart or carriage. I can be there in a day, or day and a half at the most. The sheriff and I can be heading back in two days' time, if not sooner," Zachary said.

I looked at Two Bears. "The killers could come back. What do you think?" I asked, hoping for support.

"No sign of men near cabin. Two Bears light smoky fire, and some men from village come. Two Bears stay, help Nema and Moll until Zachary return."

Trapped by their male logic, I felt like a lone rabbit chased by a hawk into the jaws of a fox. I knew no good would come of it, but no argument would sway the stubborn men, and some of what they said made sense. I knew my main objection was Zachary traveling alone on that long hard trail.

I packed warm clothes, and plenty of food rations for his trip.

"Moll, you'll weigh the poor horse down in the snow with all of that!" Zachary said, and removed some of the extra clothes.

"You don't know what you will need," I said. "Better to be prepared!" Then he was mounting his horse as I waved goodbye.

"Zachary be fine," Two Bears said. "Watch for Nema to wake. Two Bears start fire."

"Nema will be fine now, if only her heart will heal," I said with little conviction.

Chapter Forty-One

It was a long night in the cabin. Two Bears didn't say much in the best of times, and these were not the best of times.

Nema wasn't fine. I woke to her renewed sobs through the night, but the morning found her quiet. I hoped the sleep would help her regain strength for the awful days ahead.

"Moll?" I heard her whisper. I hurried to her side to comfort her.

"I'm here, Nema." I knelt at her bedside.

"Grey Deer is dead, Moll. You should have told me."

"I know, but I was worried about you."

"Guess the love spell you and Bluebird cast really worked? And to think I was pining away for another. Grey Deer was a good man."

"He was a good man, Nema, you were happy together. I pray my family can find such happiness in love."

Nema's eyes grew large, and she coughed. A fine spray of spittle and blood struck my cheek and spotted the front of her blouse. Blood!

"I must tell you what Bluebird told me, a secret," Nema said.

"It can wait, Nema. I need to look at you," I said.

"No, it can't wait, little time. Bluebird said she only ever loved Two Bear's."

"I know. She told me, she has known no other man since her wedding night," I assured her.

"Yes, then Bluebird told you?" she asked.

I smiled and pushed her hair from her eyes. "I really do need to have a look at you, Nema. We can talk about Bluebird's love life later."

"Not about Bluebird, it's Chenoa. The letter…"

"Chenoa?" I stared at her without understanding, but she lost focus.

Another trickle of blood oozed from the corner of her mouth, and I tried to hush her, but she struggled to speak.

"That is enough for now, you must rest Nema," I said. I covered her in a blanket, and left the room to the echoes of her sobbing. I knew she needed sleep above all things, but it hurt me to ignore her as she softly called my name.

I listened by the door, and Grey Deer was the name she now called, repeating it over and over again. When the sounds of her pain subsided, I looked in on her, and found her sleeping. I tiptoed back to the table and pulled open Mother's book. The blood from Nema's mouth meant the beating damaged her inside, and I knew of no plants in the book to help her. Prayer was the strongest medicine I had to use.

Near dusk, two men from Two Bears village arrived, bows and clubs in hand, expecting the worst, young men poised for a fight. Their faces looked familiar, but I did not know them by name or family.

Two Bears did not offer an introduction, and I assumed he explained what happened in his own language. The young men greeted each sentence with excitement and a violent shake of their clubs. Two Bears pointed to Grey Deer, and then to the path the men used to come to the cabin. It seemed Two Bears was sending them away, and they were not happy. After a heated debate, and more yelling by the young men, Two Bears raised his voice, and pounded his chest. The two dropped their eyes to the cabin floor.

"They will return Grey Deer to the village in the morning," Two Bears said.

I cooked enough to feed the three men, and we all found spots to rest our heads. I dreamt of my mother, and her admonition to do no harm, but a sudden commotion interrupted my dream.

Two Bears and the young men were again engaged in a shouting match. I noticed a chair tossed on its side, and Grey Deer tied to a travois on the floor. Nema still slept.

"What is going on here? You will wake Nema!"

"Young men scared. Many owls and ravens sing here, and they run home like women." Two Bears spat out in English.

"Let them go then," I said. "They are of no use to us if they are forced to stay."

Two Bears nodded at the men, and pointed to the door. The two men tried to explain themselves, but he waved a hand at them in dismissal, and turned away. They spoke some more in their language, sounding contrite, but Two Bears ignored them as if they weren't there. They grabbed up the travois, and hurried from the door.

"What did they say, Two Bears?" I asked.

"Boys say they are great warriors, fear no man or animal, but will not fight the Manitou."

"Let's hope it doesn't come to that."

"After Zachary comes back, we all go to village? Nema be ready?"

"No, I don't think we can move her. I am afraid for her, Two Bears. She is hurt inside."

I checked on Nema, and somehow she slept through the noise. I suggested to Two Bears we do the same, but the quiet did not last long enough to allow us our dreams. A long screeching moan pushed me from the bed, and Two Bears and I collided passing through Nema's door. She sobbed, a deep twisting gasp of pain that wrenched a piece of my soul. We went to her side.

"Miss Moll?" she asked.

"I'm here, Nema. What can I get for you?"

She shook her head, and a tear streaked down her face.

"I left a letter for you in sewing room… remember," she said, and coughed. Her eyes closed, and her mouth fell open releasing another trickle of blood. Thick and red, I thought of mother's black pudding, before the pig blood and liver congealed. I gagged to avoid adding my own secretions to the mess on the bed, and ran from the room, returning with a wet cloth. I knew of nothing else to do for her in her time of need.

Two Bears held her hand as I began to cool her face with the cloth.

"Nema? Can you hear me?" I asked.

"Miss Moll, my sister Moll." She smiled.

"We are going to make you strong again, Nema," I said, fearing the lie.

Her expression changed from a momentary joy to a wrenching agony. At last a deep pain-free calm settled over her, smoothing her features into angelic beauty.

"Nema, be strong, hold on," I said, and shook her gently.

Two Bears shook his head, and covered my hand with his.

"Nema is gone," he said. The cabin floor shifted, and the room darkened, as I felt myself fall from the bed.

Chapter Forty-Two

I heard voices as if from far away, or through the hull of a ship. I forced my eyes open to face the day. I was still on the floor in Nema's room, but several blankets were tucked under me for comfort. Two Bears, I thought. The gesture warmed my spirit even as the memory of my friend's death sliced through my heart.

I recognized Zachary's voice and another's speaking with Two Bears, and I pulled myself from the floor. A sob racked my body, and I struggled to catch my breath seeing Nema there. I allowed myself a few sobs, as I draped my body over hers in a final farewell.

I pulled away, wiped my eyes, and returned to the living. The High Sheriff stood just inside the door of the cabin with Zachary and Two Bears.

"Good day, Sheriff," I said. "Zachary, you did even better than we expected. Any problems on the road?"

"It was cold, and the road was either frozen or bogged down in mud, but passable. I think the bigger problem is here." Zachary's mouth pulled into a straight line as he faced the Sheriff.

"Oh?" I asked.

"Misses Dyer, Two Bears here tells me that your slave woman passed?"

"Nema is…was a free woman, and my friend, Sheriff, and yes, she's gone. Peter and his mob attacked her and Grey Deer. It happened during the storm while we were at Two Bear's village. They are both dead, murdered," I said.

"Peter, you say? The one who works over at Hammond's place? Who else witnessed this, Miss Dyer?" he asked.

"Witnessed?   The witnesses are the victims, Sheriff."

"Was anything left behind to implicate any of these men?" the sheriff asked.

"We have Nema's word, her description of her attackers, and her cold body on the bed. How's that for implications?" I asked.

The sheriff shook his head from side to side. He opened his mouth to speak, thought better of it, and then tried again. "Ma'am, I understand what you are saying, and forgive me, my condolences for your loss, but this is all something you were told by another. Since the mess up in Massachusetts a few years back, you know, with all them witches? Well, when you are told something by somebody else, that's called hearsay evidence. We can't use it in a capital offense trial any more. It has to come straight from the horses' mouth, so to speak."

"Then who can speak for the dead? They cannot speak for themselves," I said.

"Yes ma'am, but I cannot arrest anyone based on hearsay, even if from a dead citizen. Do you understand?"

"Yes. I think I do. I understand because Nema was once a slave, and Grey Deer was an Indian, you won't see to it that justice is done!" I said.

"No ma'am, I am not saying that at all. I'll poke around here a bit if you don't mind. Maybe the men left some evidence behind. Have any of you found anything out of the ordinary? Anything that didn't belong here I mean?"

"Do as you will Sheriff, and no, we haven't noticed anything like that," I said in disgust.

The sheriff bowed his head and spoke toward his feet. "I'm sorry ma'am. I will do whatever I can to get the men who did this. I promise you that. I'll question Peter when I leave here, and I'll make inquiries on the neighboring farms. Someone maybe saw something we can use to get these men."

"Two people are dead, and the best you can do is a few inquiries on the neighboring farms?" Zachary asked.

"Hold on, young Master Dyer, I will not..." Two Bears pushed the sheriff aside on his way through the door. The sheriff's face flushed.

"Let me be clear," the sheriff said. "I feel for your loss, but if anything happens to this Peter fellow, or there's any interference from the two of you, or your rough friend out there, I'll know who to throw in the bail dock. This will be handled by the laws of the colony and the crown. Is that understood?"

Zachary and I nodded.

"By all means, do your inquiries and find your implications, Sheriff. We will be outside," I said.

Two Bears sat staring at the cold rocks of the fire pit, and we started a small fire to warm ourselves. We advised him of the Sheriff's warning, and secured his promise to wait, but he assured us he would not wait forever.

Before the flames grew enough to provide any warmth, the sheriff left the cabin without speaking, climbed on his horse, and left the farm. Two Bears grunted, and stood.

"We must bury our friend," he said.

The ground was hard, but we found soft ground beside Nema's garden and thought she would like it there. She could hear the gurgling of our stream surrounded by the flowers she nurtured in life.

I did my part with the digging, and even helped place Nema in her grave, but I dropped my shovel and fell to my knees when the men began to cover her. When it was done, Zachary looked to me, and I shook my head, so he spoke from the heart for all of us:

"Heavenly Father, we ask that you accept the soul of your child, Nema. She was a good and faithful servant to you, and always a friend to our family. Her life was a struggle, but she faced all challenges without complaint. She is already sorely missed by all who knew her, but we wait to meet her again in your glory. She will never stray far from our hearts. Hold her in your loving arms, and bestow upon her all the blessings of paradise. In your name, we pray."

We bowed our heads and made our own private pleas to our Lord. Zachary lifted a small patch of dead Black-eyed susans with his shovel, and worked them into the center of the mound.

"Will they come back in the spring, Moll?" he asked.

For many weeks, my heart felt as dry and brittle as the flowers, my spirit buried in the dirt with Nema. On the second night of our mourning, Uncle arrived. He knew of Nema's death, but paled when told the circumstances.

"Nema was a good friend. It is hard to imagine a world without her. Her spirit was as strong as her hands," Uncle said.

I provided Uncle with blankets as he intended to sleep in the woods beyond the cleared field, and return to the native encampment in the morning. I bid the men good night, and tried to rest, but thoughts of Nema and what I might have done to save her would not release me. The men tried to keep their voices low, but their words carried in the stillness of the night.

"Tomorrow I will go with you and Two Bears," Zachary said.

"No nephew, Moll needs you here," Uncle said.

"Those men will not come back, not with the sheriff making inquiries," Zachary said with scorn. "They went back to the holes they crawled out of."

"It's not the men that Moll needs protection from. We went through a lot together, and I never saw her so melancholy. She needs a reason to carry on, and a hope for the future. I cannot stay, but it is you who owns her heart. Your future is the hope she needs," Uncle said.

My eyes misted when Zachary said I was as close to a mother as he knew, and I slept.

Chapter Forty-Three

The early spring was a wet and muddy time in the colony. The tobacco beds sprouted well after the moisture from the late snow, but the soggy ground was so rotten, it caused a delay in planting. Zachary and I hoed in the yellowed drowning seedlings with concern for the harvest.

May through early June, not a drop of rain, nor even a dribble of dew fell on our crop. The corn leaves folded over, and the tobacco looked more brown than green. Our heavy clay soil began to crack like porcelain plates. We hauled buckets of water from the stream, but it was a delay of the inevitable, rather than a solution. Waba panted in the shade and watched us work. I imagine he thought us addle-headed.

One evening, I emptied my bucket in the last hill of plants, and wiped the sweat from my eyes. Looking up I saw Uncle, Two Bears, Bluebird and Chenoa approaching. I yelled for Zachary as I ran to greet them.

"What a wonderful surprise," I said, embracing Uncle.

"The day finally comes, Moll," Uncle said with a frown.

"The day?" I asked, but derived my answer from the darkness of my uncle's face.

"The move? Already?" I asked.

"Yes. I hate leaving you and all we worked for, but it's not a moment too soon for me. The under-sheriffs visit the village every week now, looking for me. I suppose someone pointed them in our direction. I spend more time hiding in the woods than I do in the village," Uncle said.

"Then it is good. I will be happy for you, Uncle," I said.

"Moll come too," Bluebird said.

I turned to see Zachary and Chenoa engaged in their own conversation, ignoring their elders…

"I cannot leave what we built here, Bluebird. I hope to make it a thriving farm, something Zachary takes pride in, and earns him respect. Nema's death showed me we have little time here. Father taught me to fight for our family's prosperity, and happiness. Life must have meaning, and Zachary deserves it," I said.

"Have you asked Zachary what he wants?" Uncle glanced at the two young people.

White hot lightning bolts leapt from my eyes at my uncle, but I only said "Come, let's find something to eat." Zachary was young, and did not know the cost of poor decisions. If he could stand on his own, not beholden to others, my life had merit.

Two Bears smiled and pulled a dozen deer steaks wrapped in grape leaves from his pack.

"Let's cook them over the fire pit, like the old days," Uncle said.

We talked about the hard but happy times we shared in our early days in the colony, in the early days of our friendship. We were very young, and content, even though we had nothing. Two Bears and Bluebird spoke of future trading with the merchants in town, and promised to stop to see us on every occasion. I trusted their sincerity, but doubted its actuality. It was a short reunion, and in the morning, our visitors packed up to leave. I embraced them each in turn.

I wondered if I would see my uncle again in this life. The law might forget his name in a few years, but we were older, and our remaining days were not guaranteed. I held him for a long while. I didn't want my friends to see my body shaking with sobs. Uncle understood, and held me until they subsided.

Zachary and Chenoa were the last to pull apart. I heard his promise to visit soon, and her promise to wait for that day.

Our long summer began as Uncle and our friends rode away from the farm. The weather remained unchanged, and I blessed the memory of Nema and Bluebird's protection spell with every bucket of water we drew from the stream.

The heat and the drought drew a heavy toll on us. One hot afternoon, I sipped the cool water from my bucket, then poured a cup over my head. Zachary was not in sight, so I unbuttoned and sprinkled water on my chest. I knelt in the shade and said a prayer of thanks. I noticed the underbrush shaking near our stream, and my mind leapt to the days of Gideon's folly. Then the winds began to swirl, and thunder rumbled in the distance. Zachary ran to me excited as the first drops fell.

In the life giving rain we danced like fools. We ran for the cabin with our clothes sopping wet. As we closed the door behind us, a ray of sun streaked through our window, the rain already done. What little moisture nature provided burned off before the sun set. Every day convinced me more of the futility of our efforts, yet every day we drew water from the stream for the plants. The loss of a year's tobacco would be painful, and the corn we needed to get through the winter.

Zachary completed his chores every day and went to bed with the sun. My best attempts at humor elicited a brief smile from him at best. His mood mirrored mine, and I prayed for a long soaking rain to lighten our spirits and hearts.

"I don't know why we bother, Moll. We are fighting a losing battle. There is no hope for a decent crop this year," Zachary said, picking at his dinner.

"All is not lost," I said. "Farming is not easy, but it will provide for you and your family. Our land is fertile, and it will make you a wealthy man someday."

"Me? This isn't about me. I don't give a damn except to help you," he said. Zachary shot up from the table, rattling the dishes when he shoved in his chair, and went to bed.

One morning as we pulled the only growing things on our farm, the weeds, he said, "Moll, do you ever wonder about how Uncle and our friends are doing?"

"I do. I hope the season up north goes better than ours."

"I miss them, they were family. Chenoa was…well, all of them, were our only friends here," he said.

"Is that why you cry in your dreams at night?" I asked.

"Do you ever think of following them?" He asked.

I had not. My dreams for Zachary, and our family's prospects did not include a new struggle in the wilderness at the end of my years, but I misjudged Zachary's level of devotion to Chenoa. I assumed his dream for the future was the same as mine. I recalled a promise I made to myself years ago: I'd not force my child to share my dreams. I knew now what must be done.

"Is that what you want to do, Zachary?" I asked.

He looked at the barren clouds, the shriveled trees, and back to his feet, anywhere but at me. "Would you consider going?"

"After this season, and seeing how you miss our friends? I would, perhaps in the spring, but I must stay and get what we can from the crop."

I saw Zachary counting the months in his head, and snatched away the tear welling up in my eye.

"I think Christopher and Gideon would help sell our farm then. Spring brings hope, and the farm would not bring much at the end of the season," I said.

"Yes, Gideon and Christopher are proven friends."

"At least they aren't enemies, sometimes that's all we can hope for. I suppose it would be a waste of time for us both to linger here until then," I said.

"This is a lot of farm to handle. I won't leave you alone." He bit his lower lip.

"I will be fine, and that's is what you should do. I will spend a lot of time at the Hammonds. You know they always welcome me there. I may even pass the winter with them, but I'll be prepared nonetheless. The tobacco will not make much, but I'll not leave it for another to profit from. Tomorrow I'm punching holes in those damn buckets."

"No Moll, you can't do this alone. I don't think…"

"You sound like your uncle, and I proved him wrong. You are a good boy, but I can manage fine without you, and what I do need your help with, you balk at it! Think like an adult, Zachary! We don't know where the village is, you must find it, and no wagon road leads to their door. There is no place for us to stay, and I want our own longhouse built before the spring. I won't be underfoot in someone else's home, or dependent on our friends' generosity. I am depending on you, you aren't a child any more. We must put in winter stores here before you leave, and I need your help."

"Of course, Moll, but…"

"I need two deer to dry cure. Go for them in the morning. The does still have young, so you only take bucks. I want two with some meat on their bones too, no button bucks! Lay me in a supply of firewood, and then I can handle the farm on my own."

Zachary was a hard worker, always was, but for the next two weeks he worked as a man possessed. Two deer hung in the barn before the sun set the following day, and every evening he worked on my winter's heat supply. I could handle the farm, but I dreaded losing Zachary for so long. I allowed the wood pile to grow to a height I wouldn't burn in two years before I said enough.

On our last morning together, Zachary secured my promise to ride out the winter with the Hammonds. I yelled as he rode from sight, "Find the village before winter, and come back for me in the spring."

"I will be here, and I won't let you down, Moll."

When the sound of his horse's hooves faded, I was as physically alone as I often felt to be in my heart. I made light of the chores left to be done, but Zachary's happiness and safety were assured. Uncle was right. Zachary needed to be free to find his own happiness.

I didn't lie to Zachary. Perhaps I would follow my friends come spring, but I feared a bleak future for my Indian friends. I knew well the insatiable appetite of Englishmen. Perhaps my family would be better served if I labored on alone, turned our farm into a thriving concern? Many long hard months stretched out ahead of me. Plenty of time to decide what would be best for our family's future, and the generations unborn.

Chapter Forty-Four

I approached the Hammond's plantation around midday. His tobacco had not fared well. Not a tinge of green favored their growth, and never had I witnessed his farm so devoid of activity. No laborers worked the fields, and no horses grazed in the meadow. I hoped the cattle huddled together somewhere in the shade as they were also unseen.

I tied off my animals, and John met me as I walked toward his door.

"Good day, Miss Dyer. What can I do for you today?"

"Good day, Mr. Hammond. I hoped to pay a visit with you and your Misses today."

"My wife has taken ill, Miss Dyer. I am sure you are well aware of the fever that struck the colony, along with the worst drought ever known."

"I have heard nothing of the sickness. May I look in on her? I know a little of such things."

"I'm sure you do, Miss Dyer, but we will do fine without your ministrations. We are a God fearing Christian family."

My brows knit together at this strange response. "Of course you are, but…"

"No illness has befallen your family, Miss? It appears the Dyers are the only ones in the colony not so cursed."

"No, we are blessed by a strong constitution I suppose."

"Peter tells me your stream, alone of all the fresh water around Newtowne, is still bloated with water."

"Ah, Peter… well, it appears we are doubly blessed, John, even in these hard times."

"Blaspheme!" he said.

My eyes flew open in surprise. "What? What do you mean by that, John?"

"Miss Dyer, the colony's grievances against you are legion. I am not one to listen to idle talk and such, but I have on good faith that the Dyers cheated to gain headrights, and many hard working men paid the price. Your uncle is a murderer and worse to my mind, an abuser of a woman's trust. You, and your so-called brother aided in his escape from justice I believe?"

"Mister Hammond, we paid our debt and then some to this colony. Seeing Zachary beaten and disfigured was far worse than any punishment that could have been meted out to me. What more is it that you would demand of us?"

"Is that the reason for the drought, and the sickness? You perceive your righteous and lawful punishment as an inequity?"

"As a child I enjoyed riddles, Hammond, but I am no longer a child," I said.

"Years ago, Peter told me about Gideon's wife's death, and I chose to consider it the ravings of a grief stricken man. There are tales of strange happenings near your farm."

"Strange happenings? Indeed, the murder of my two friends by your man Peter was strange indeed." I tried to calm myself, to take deep breaths, to unclench my fists… but could not.

"The sheriff told me of your appalling accusations. He treated Peter like a common criminal, and questioned him for hours. Peter is a hard-working man. Every coin in his purse he's earned by his own labors. Kill someone? Who do you expect to believe such drivel?" Hammond's face was flushed, and his jugular vein throbbed.

"He committed murder, and he will pay the price!" I said.

"Neither Peter nor his friends frolic naked in the moonlight. He does not pervert children's minds dancing in the rain and casting spells. A strange rain only touching the Dyer farm, I might add. His land is not plagued by Satan's evil black birds. God struck down your friends in divine retribution. Did you think practicing witchcraft and cavorting with pagan savages would go unpunished? Your curses not avenged?" His skin colored like the sky before a thunderstorm. Waba strained at the leash and growled from deep in his chest.

"It is your beliefs and superstitions that curse you, Hammond."

"Leave my property, Miss Dyer. There is a law against witches in our land to protect God fearing people."

"I doubt your fear of God holds you in good stead where you are going," I replied.

Hammond did not answer, but with trembling hand, pointed to the road leading away from his farm. I threw my arms towards the heavens, and then pulled my elbows to my side. I danced a little jig and threw my head about in a circle, shouting gibberish. "Henchen bentar. Freen sakium, freis sacrum. Cu Chulainn, Dispater, Druidae, curse John Hammond and his spawn for all eternity."

I thrust my fists at him, and laughed as if I wasn't right in the head. He raced for his door. His retreat reminiscent of when Zachary disturbed a ground bees' nest. I was dizzy from spinning in circles, and choking from the effort to contain further laughter, but I managed to mount my horse.

My wild laughter was a weird accompaniment to the tears blurring my vision. The trail ahead appeared as if in a red fog. My hands trembled from the blistering heat of anger, but more than that, I considered John Hammond, and his wife, two of our truest friends in the colony. How vile was this day!

A hundred yards from Hammond's door, Waba froze and my horse reared. Peter stepped from the roadside ditch. The gun in his hands pointed towards my head.

"Get off of our property, you lying witch," he waved the gun in small circles.

"Surely even a dim witted killer such as yourself can see I currently travel in the direction of departure? Perhaps you should save your coin, Peter, and purchase a compass, or maybe a smidgen of decency?" I asked, mustering my sweetest voice.

Peter's face flamed, and he spat on the ground and turned his back to me. "Witch! The whole colony will know you for what you are!" He stalked away.

I felt ripped apart by John Hammond's hate, and by Peter's gall. Luckily my horse knew her way home. Ever faithful Waba ran alongside us, and despite the pair of rabbits darting across our path, never left my side.

"I do have one friend left," I told him.

I spent my days in the fields, and my nights trying not to think of those in the colony who conspired against me, trying not to think even of those I loved. Memories were spiteful things, and too often visited without invocation. When I felt weakest, the piercing roots of the past poisoned my heart, and nagging tendrils of regret crept through my veins.

In early fall, I began harvesting the minimal fruits of our labors. The scorched waist high tobacco yielded little weight, but was far better than the norm for the surrounding farms. Many planters left the seared brown leaves in the field to rot, deeming them not worth the effort to cut and cure. Our patch of corn provided half sized ears with kernels to match, but it was enough to sustain the chickens and I through the cold months ahead.

Food and warmth were the least of my worries.

Chapter Forty-Five

The days turned cooler, and with the drought plagued tobacco now curing in the barn, teeth chattering rain visited with regularity, more so than sleep. There was little work to do in such weather, and only more time to think.

I felt proud seeing the diminutive tobacco plants hanging in the barn, but I dreaded the long days and nights to come. Too much idle time to think is a blight. My thoughts and dreams were of my family on both sides of the ocean, and of my scarce remaining friends. My dreams were seldom pleasant.

I dreamt of my mother and father, Uncle and Zachary, Bluebird and Two Bears, and even the murderous Peter, but oddly, Nema's memory did not plague my sleep? I thought dreams grew from our daytime wonderings, and Nema too often stirred my thoughts. I puzzled over this one evening and questioned whether Nema was angry with me. Lack of sleep inspires mad thoughts, but in the early morning hours, too early even for the rooster, she found me.

Her apparition floated above my bed, cloaked in the whitest glow.

"Nema, is that you?" I asked.

"Moll, I thought you'd forgotten me."

"I have not, and I never will."

"What became of the men who took my life and that of my beloved? Do they still roam free?"

"They do, Nema. The sheriff angers me with his inaction."

Nema paused as if in thought. "They will pay in time. Did you read my note?"

"Your note, Nema?"

"You don't remember, Moll? Look in your sewing room."

Nema's image swirled away as the morning fog would, as did my dream. There was something she said about a note to me. My grief hid it from me.

I lit a candle to ensure no other spirits frequented the cabin, and as the sky began to push back the night, I ran from the cabin to my sewing room. I threw open the door, and looked around quickly, so many books, so many places to hide a piece of paper! What struck her as so important for Nema to come back from the grave to remind me?

I began pulling the books from the shelves and leafing through them. Bluebird, didn't Nema say the note was about her? What did she tell Nema of such significance? I thought of Bluebird, my last friend to leave, and I felt very alone. Where was the small figure of Okeus? It wasn't in its place on the altar! There, on the bottom shelf it stood, almost hidden by a bundle of dried mullein. I picked it up to replace it on the altar, and a slip of paper fell from underneath. I recognized Nema's writing, and sat to read my friend's last words to me.

Miss Moll,

I hope this finds you safe! Snow has begun to fall, and we are very worried. I pray you found adequate shelter elsewhere. Grey Deer said a bad storm was coming, and thinking you were at the cabin, we left the village so you needn't face it on your own.

I have a very strange feeling about this storm, afraid of what it brings. Strange visions fill my dreams, and I fear I may not see you again. I know how foolish this sounds, and when the storm passes, I will retrieve this note so you won't know how childish I am, but there is something I need to write down to tell you, just in case.

A few weeks ago, Bluebird and I were making mindless girl's chatter, but when the talk turned to men, she became very serious. She said on the night she married Two Bears, he became a different man. He was rough, coarse, and he even spoke in the voice of another man! She feared she chose her mate unwisely.

Bluebird said Two Bears never acted like that before or since. In the morning he was kind and loving again, as if nothing happened. She soon became with child, with Chenoa. Ever since, Two Bears has been gentle with her, a wonderful husband and lover, but still she fears he might change back, become that other man again. She asked if Grey Deer ever acted that way with me.

Knowing you as I do, you are thinking "Poor Bluebird," and what you might say to reassure her, and I did my best to do so. I told her Grey Deer was never like that, but Two Bears was nervous, or perhaps his mind was touched for a spell. I told her it happened so long ago, and that it shouldn't concern her any longer. I said Two Bears is a fine and honorable man. She seemed comforted, but I am chattering on too long. The wind grows outside, and this isn't about Bluebird or Two Bears. It's about Chenoa.

This morning, Two Bears helped us lash new reeds on the roof of our longhouse in preparation for the storm, and when he reached over his head, I saw the marks! The three parallel scars just like Zachary has, and I had! Do you understand? I pushed the thought aside, and figured it was my imagination, but I couldn't take the chance! Before I could think of a polite manner to ask to examine his underarms, we had to rush to beat the storm back to you. It is likely of no concern, but I should have wrestled him to the ground then and there to see for myself! If for any reason I don't weather this storm, Moll, look under his armpits, concealed by the hair there! It may be more important than you know.

I did not tell you all of Miss Grace's story. She thought these demons want more than just a handhold into our world. She said a child born of two Cambions conceived in love would issue a new age, perhaps even the end of times! Please be careful and take no chances!

I hope this note is never read, but if it is, I want to thank you, Moll, for my freedom, and the knowledge you shared, but your love was the greatest gift of all.

Your Sister Always, Nema

At the beginning of Nema's letter, I felt like an intruder on another's private life without the right or permission, but I read every word without shame. By the end I was in dread terror for my son and my family, perhaps our world.

If both Zachary and Chenoa wore the marks… what had I done? I tricked him into leaving, and surely pushed him into her arms! Zachary and Chenoa could be possessed by demons at will, such was the curse of Cambions, but living a simple life among the natives might hide and protect them until I could find a cure, some deal. If what Nema's Miss Grace said was true, it was far worse for any child born of their union! He would be taken, damned, tortured, tormented, and twisted into a foul, filthy creature without soul, a scourge to his kind, never knowing happiness, never tasting love, cursed to never know paradise! Once corrupted, he would bring a living hell to earth.

Our family and all its future generations stood poised on this cliff, ready to fall into the pit below, pushed to the brink and destroyed by my hand. This could not be the way our family ended! No, please Dear God, not this evil of my making!

"Mother, I need my strength! Guide my hands?" I shouted to the heavens, but to no answer.

Chapter Forty-Six

I packed provisions: food, water, blankets and clothes in preparation for the journey to the native encampment. If I prevented Zachary and Chenoa from consummating their love, all would not be lost. There was no other to aid me, but my foolish and prideful independence led us here, I could only hope it could pull us through it.

I fed Waba before I saddled Matilda, the mare. Waba sat with head bowed and his tail tucked under him, with such clarity he read my heart. Was this a quality once possessed by humans, and since atrophied from disuse?

It was nearing midday before we left the farm, and only travelled as far as the old native village. I planned to take my rest in one of the deserted longhouses, and begin anew at first light. Instead, we found white settlers there, adopting the abandoned village and houses as their own.

Some of the villagers looked familiar, but no one approached or tried to stop us. The women, of which there were few, yanked the children into the buildings as we walked past.

"Waba is friendly, he won't hurt you," I said as I dismounted. I examined each longhouse, and the inhabitants continued to avert their eyes, or turn their backs at our approach. One young boy looked familiar, and I tried to recall from where.

"Good day," I said, and he smiled with a mouthful of grey teeth. Then I remembered him, and the rat he dangled in my face as I sat shackled in the stocks. I stuck my tongue out at him, and he ran away.

"Witch!" he yelled in retreat.

"What did you call me?" I asked.

"A witch," answered a slovenly matron sticking her head out from a longhouse. Waba bared his teeth in displeasure. Red blurred the edge of my vision and I rushed at her, slapping her face hard enough to drop her fat backside to the dirt. She sat rubbing her cheek, and an elderly man stepped to her aid.

"I believe you are Miss Moll Dyer?" he asked.

"I am, and who are you, the leader of this most hospitable group?" I asked.

"My name is not important, but we are prepared to pay you alms." he said.

"Alms? For what?" I asked.

"We want no trouble here. We know about the plague on the colonists of Newtowne and clear south to Saint Mary's. We want no parts of your vendetta against them. We have done you no harm, but we cannot harbor a witch. We will pay you to pass over our town." he said.

"Your town? What if I refuse?" I asked. The man withdrew into a longhouse and returned to toss a bag of coins at my feet. Several smaller bags followed, tossed by unseen hands from inside the longhouses.

"What do you know of the Indians who lived here? Do any of you know the location of their new settlement?" I asked.

"No, and good riddance to the heathens." The fat woman replied from her seat on the ground.

"Come Waba, heel. Wipe the dust of this town from your paws," I said.

We slept in the woods outside of the village. Packed and ready, we left camp in the morning with stars still sparkling overhead. I knew the tribe followed the Potomac north, and I yearned to gallop headlong in that direction.

Fearful of missing sign of a large movement of people, or anyone who might recall their passage through, I fought myself for restraint. I compromised by planning to cut short the route around the two fingers of the Wicomico, and mushing through the swamps at its headwaters.

When the sun reached its zenith, we crossed the major stream feeding Chaptico Bay, still low from the summer's drought, and I continue to ride. I hoped to make nightfall near Allen's Run, and attempt the labyrinth of Zekiah swamp the following morning.

The few locals we met on the deer path of a road seemed no friendlier than the squatters at the old native village. They did not throw insults at us, but neither did they throw coins. Rather, they ignored our passage.

I picked a campsite on a dry hillock of land at sunset. Zekiah swamp appeared an inhospitable place, covered in twisted vines and hordes of voracious mosquitos that a week of morning frosts did nothing to dispel. The air reeked of rotted vegetation and all manner of life that met its fate within the marsh's wet embrace. Peering through the thick, tangled brush, the stained water of the stream flowed through the trees and cypress knees bubbling with gaseous secretions. The sickening sweet smell clung to my nose as I led Waba back to our fire.

"Tomorrow will be a test of our resolve, Waba. We will need our rest." I said, but the night was test enough. Sleep came easily, but with many disruptions. Annoying high pitched whines assailed my ears as the toothsome winged pests contended for a spot on my skin. I swatted at them, and covered my head with blankets, but somehow they found their way in.

Moments of sleep followed by hours of blood sucking torment distressed my spirit. Thoughts of my desperate errand, and the fate of my loved ones, wove spider webs of despair. When I dreamt, I dreamt of Beth. Brief snippets of incomplete dreams: Beth falling from the ship, Beth trying to nurse her still-born child. Beth crawling over the side of my bed, seaweed entwined in her hair. Beth warning me to turn back, to avoid the swamp and go home.

I woke with Waba licking the bloody splattered insects from my face. Shivering in the cold morning air, I folded the frost crusted blankets. Wispy fingers of fog hung over the wetland as Waba and I shared a meal of cold jerky and hickory nuts. "We have a long hard day ahead of us, Waba." He seemed unimpressed, and we entered the marsh.

Chapter Forty-Seven

The stream skulked forward in a crisscrossing pattern of inlets and outlets, and I tossed in a handful of leaves to determine the current's course. I dismounted when the underbrush thickened, blocking my view of the sun.

The old mare was more hindrance than help in the swampland, and balled in complaint as we pushed through the muck. Waba was light enough to walk over the swampy spots, and small enough to swim through the shallow muddy waters. I bulled my way through, using the strength of my hands to extract my boots from the gummy sludge with every step. The ground released me with a sucking sound, and the nauseating odor of decay.

After several hours in I admitted, if only to Waba, that we were lost. I looked for higher ground to get my bearings as a light snow began to fall, and I spotted an ancient oak. The ground was checkered brown and white by the time we reached it. Through a century of growth, the tree's roots held the soil secure from the water's encroachment to create a small dry island.

Waba flopped on the ground as I tied Matilda. We were soaked, chilled to the bone, and needed a fire to dry out.

"You're more mud than fur, Waba," I said. "I probably look just as bad, but I hope I smell better."

I went back to the horse to retrieve my pack, but the pack was gone! I pulled off the soggy blankets, and threw down a bag of dripping clothes. I went through it all, and went through it all again. The pack was not to be found, broken loose somewhere in the swamp, and with it my healer's bag, fire kit and our food! Waba and I would be reduced to scavenging or face starvation.

The night did not sneak in on the bog, but in the blink of an eye slapped us into darkness, leaving only the snow's soft glow lighting our surroundings. The stars deserted us behind the wall of clouds, and my stomach growled in response to our predicament.

I hoped a morning climb in the oak's branches might provide an insight to our location, and a route out of the marsh. Waba and I curled up together, but old Matilda the mare seemed immune to the cold.

A high pitched squeal echoed through the trees, and Waba barked in warning. I listened and after a short pause, the sound of the woman's scream repeated, and Waba dashed into the night. My ears followed his progress from the splashes of water until he moved beyond my hearing.

I circled the oak, attentive in every direction, but heard nothing. "Waba!" I yelled. "Here Waba!"

Waba's distant battle cry floated to my ears, and I strained to isolate its source. It was no woman, but some fearsome sounding animal that screamed in answer, and I ran toward it as Waba squealed in pain. I yelled again for Waba, but with no response, I continued on what I hoped to be the same direction.

I sank to my chest in the water and mud, and dragged myself from the hole. Waba whined again, sounding closer this time, but weaker. My clothes froze, as did my hair and the tears on my cheeks. The hard ache of my toes changed to a dull tingly numbness. The ground shifted beneath me, and I glanced down hearing a whimper.

My foot rested in matted fur, and I fell to my knees hugging Waba! One of his ears was sliced in three pieces, the top part dangled over his left eye. Such wounds bleed profusely, and the fur of his face dripped blood. I rubbed his side in the dark, and he whined. My hand came away stained with blood, and I discovered the deep gash exposing his ribs.

"Waba, why would you go up against a mountain lion? You are one silly, lucky dog," I said. "Another inch and it would have gutted you. We'll patch you up as best we can, boy."

With hands drawn up into frozen claws, I ripped wet lengths of petticoat from beneath my dress, bound his chest wounds, and wrapped my arms around him for warmth.

Light snow continued to fall as we shivered in the cold. I tried to stay awake to keep an eye on Waba, but caught myself dropping into short exhausted naps. He cried out often, and I wondered if dogs dream? If so, my little one faced nightmares.

I drifted off, then jerked upright. Could it still be night? It seemed like hours since the mountain lion attack. Did we sleep through the day?

I sat up and felt the inside of Waba's thigh, and he felt cool to my touch. At least the shivering stopped, and my teeth no longer chattered. I felt his slowed pulse and unwrapped his bandage, then fell asleep. When I next woke, my face was puffy and swollen as if stung by a nest of bees. Waba's pulse dropped to a level I strained to detect. My movements were slow and clumsy. My body did not want to answer my mind's demands. Did my heart slow as well? The sun needed to rise soon!

I awoke to warmth. We would live, I thought, we were saved! My eyes refused to open, but I did not question the heat of the sun on my skin. I reached for Waba and felt his fur between my fingers, but I couldn't close my hand. He was so cold, but it was so hot today, too hot... why was it so hot? I fumbled with my blouse and shrugged it from my shoulders, but felt no relief. I pulled at my dress, but my hands hadn't warmed enough to respond to my commands.

The exertions took a toll on my strength, and I fell into a deep peaceful sleep, troubled only by the voices from my past.

"Why didn't you turn back, Moll?" Beth asked in the darkness. "Why didn't you heed my warning?"

"I have to help Zachary, Beth. You know that, my family... "

"This path leads to death, Moll," Beth said.

"It doesn't matter, this path leads to Zachary!" I said.

"Today Chenoa became Zachary's wife, Moll." It was now my mother's voice that answered. "We all must die. Do not do so in vain."

"No Mother, that can't be true!" I said.

"You are very close to us now, Moll," Nema said. "This is no place for you, not yet!"

"Close? I would go with you then, there is nothing left for me here," I said.

"It's not yet your time, sweet child," Mother said. "Your family needs you, and you cannot do this alone."

"No, I have failed everyone. I was not strong enough! It is done, all is lost," I said, wiping my brow.

"You must take care of yourself, Moll." Mother said. "You are my little girl. You must leave this accursed swamp."

"But I've lost my way! I need to find Zachary!" They did not answer. "Mother! Nema! Beth! Answer me!"

The woods were silent.

Something tugged at my blouse and I slapped it away. My body lifted above the ground and flew, then floated to rest on hard dry ground.

I heard Waba whine from far away. "Where are you, boy?" I asked.

"I'll get Waba too," Zachary answered.

"Zachary? How did you find us?" I asked.

"Rest now, Moll. Get warm and then we'll talk." A man said, not Zachary?

We were moving. My body bounced as our chariot floated toward the clouds.

Chapter Forty-Eight

My face warmed, and I saw the reddish halo of the sun behind my closed eyelids. I opened them, but I couldn't see! I tried to wipe them, but something held my arms. I twisted as my body slammed down on the ground. "What was that?" I asked.

"Sorry Moll, I didn't see the hole," A man's voice said.

Was it a horse's hooves I heard? I turned my head to the sound, and my head popped out from multiple layers of blankets. My body perspired, yet I shivered. My gums ached from the constant teeth chattering. I was bundled up on a wooden wagon. A man sat in front of me, his hands at the horse's reins. Waba's head rested on my thigh, and my horse, Matilda trotted behind our cart. I tried to sit up to tell the man to turn around, didn't he know the village was the other way? But my head swam, and my vision blurred. I laid back down to rest, just for a moment...

For hours, or perhaps days, we travelled. The man refused to answer my questions, or even acknowledge them. I thought of Mrs. Boyles' son in Kinsale. What was his name? Charles? When I was a young girl, I saw him fishing a feeder stream off of the River Bandon. I walked up behind him and asked how he fared. Repeatedly I made the effort to engage him in conversation until I became agitated at his rude silence. Who did he think he was to ignore me, the king of England? I stepped to his side to give him a dressing down, but he turned and seemed surprised to see me. He favored me with the widest, warmest smile.

"Good day," I said. "How is the fishing here?"

He shook his head, and pointed at his ears. Embarrassment colored my face, and I was at a loss for words. I patted his shoulder and wished him luck, then turned to hurry home. Perhaps the driver of the wagon was also deaf, and could not hear my words? I shouldn't be rude.

"Who are you? Where is Zachary?" I asked, but the wagon rolled on as darkness fell.

I never knew such fatigue, such confusion. Day was as night, and night was as day. There was no wagon here, no man. Where was Waba? Was I touched in the head?

I sat up and looked around at the familiar confines of my room. How did I come to be here? How long did I sleep? Was it all a dream? Where was my dress?

I flipped my legs over the side of the bed and slid my feet to the floor. I was unsteady, as if learning to walk for the first time. My head swirled like a man drinking heavy spirits, but my mouth felt full of dust, and I needed water. I made a step toward the kitchen, then another. For a moment, I held on to my bedroom door for support. A vigorous fire burned in the fireplace, and I spied a pitcher on the table. I took another step, but red and black fingers crept into the edges of my vision. I reached back for the door, and it slipped from my fingers as I fell to the floor. Waba barked, then darkness.

"Moll? Can you hear me?"

I opened my eyes. "Gideon? Why are you here?"

"I've been with you for a while. It's good to hear your voice, talking sense that is."

"Where is Zachary?" I asked.

Gideon shook his head. "Sorry, only me…and Waba. You kept calling for Zachary in your delirium."

"Delirium? I have to find him. How long have I been here?" I asked.

"It's been days since I found you in the swamp, and you aren't yet even strong enough to stand. Zachary can wait. What's so important for you to go on such a fool's errand?" "There's no time," I said, sitting up. "I have to find out…," I stopped as the blanket dropped and cool air rushed over my naked breasts.

Gideon averted his eyes and pulled up the blanket. "I'm sorry, Moll. You were so hot, like your skin was on fire. I've been drawing cold water from the stream to cool you off. I didn't know what else to do."

"You did the right thing," I said crimson faced. "I was just…surprised."

Gideon shook his head and smiled, also blushing.

"How did you find me? Why were you even looking for me?" Gideon took his time answering, then shook his head.

"I was just lucky, Moll. We both were," he said.

"There's not that much luck in the world, Gideon Coombs! Tell the truth, and shame the devil," I said.

"No, you will think me a fool."

"I would be a fool to doubt whatever brought you to my rescue," I said.

"Very well then, Beth told me… in a dream. She showed me where you were, and said you were in the briars deep and needed my help. Satisfied? Is that crazy enough for you?"

"Not crazy, Gideon. It is obvious that your dream was true, and if so, mine was as well, and it's already too late," I said.

"What do you mean?" he asked.

"Tomorrow I must go to town for supplies.,

Chapter Forty-Nine

Gideon balked at my plan to travel to town, and warned of the epidemic sickness there, but I tolerated no discussion. I could manage the four miles to Newtowne proper. The small general store there sold all I needed. Gideon made a grand show of reluctant approval when I agreed to his company. In truth, I dreaded even the short journey on horseback, and though I would not have asked, I silently rejoiced when Gideon hitched up his wagon for me.

People scurried around Newtowne's streets like ants around a disturbed anthill. It seemed to be a celebration of some sort.

"I'm going to find out what is going on. I'll be right back," Gideon said.

I spotted Christopher from the land office, and walked his way. His knowledge of colony gossip was second to none. He acted pleased to see me, but knew nothing of the location of the native's village. Like many others, he spoke of the many branches that the Potomack followed to the northwest, and the futility of attempting to discern its main branch.

"Who is to say our old neighbors did not follow one of the many forks to their new home?" He asked.

"Then you heard nothing from them since they left?" I asked.

"You might ask the vendors. The young natives come here to trade flour, salt and such for their furs."

"Why are all these people here today?" I asked.

"The governor has an interest in the area, more expansion for the colony. He is touring the area, but speaking for the land office, I believe his intent is to survey small lots around the head of Britton's Bay. It won't be long before this village of yours grows into a proper town," Christopher said.

"Wonderful, more people," I thanked him for his time, and we said our goodbyes. A heavy hand fell on my shoulder and twisted me about as I moved to cross to the general store.

"Miss Dyer, may I ask what brings you to town on this frigid day?"

"It is chillish, Sheriff, but I wasn't aware a free woman needed to explain her comings and goings?" I twisted away from the tight grip of his hand.

"No, but I won't have any trouble here either, especially today. Many are against you in this town, Miss Dyer. They blame you for the drought of the summer, and the cursed sickness that plagues the colony. There is talk of witchcraft," the sheriff said.

"I don't concern myself with such foolish gossip, Sheriff. Have I committed some crime?"

"It is my duty to keep the peace, Miss. Today the governor is touring our town, hoping to provide some relief to our citizens. I want no trouble, and I am concerned for your safety as well."

"Supplies, Sheriff, I am here for supplies," I said. "After I acquire what I need, I will gladly move on." I turned away, weary of his company.

"A wedding gift for your brother, perhaps Miss?" he asked. I spun around.

"What did you say?"

"I apologize, Miss. None of my business of course. Good day to you then."

"Wait Sheriff, please. What do you know of Zachary?" I asked.

"Only what the young Indian lad told Samuel, you know, the general store fellow? Well, the boy came in to trade for salt. There's none in the river where they are, of course, only fresh water," the sheriff said.

"Yes, yes, but what did he say of Zachary?" I asked.

"That he took a wife, of course, didn't you know…?"

The sheriff continued to babble, words I did not hear. An anger born of desperation swallowed my soul, and I dropped to my knees in the street, and slammed my fists against the ground. God, my dream was true then! Tears soaked my cheeks as the horror sank in. "Miss Dyer, get up quickly, please. It's the governor." The sheriff pulled at my elbows.

The carriage slowed as the sheriff pulled me from the street. "Good day, Sheriff, is there trouble here?" Said a voice inside the carriage.

"Dear God, it's true. We're cursed to hell!" I wept, defeated.

"No trouble, Lord Blackistone, the lady here slipped on the ice," the sheriff answered.

"Good day then," and the driver slapped the reins to depart.

The streets stood still as death, and all eyes were upon me, but I stood alone in my fog of despair.

"Miss Dyer, are you all right? Have you eaten today? Can you make it to the ordinary? The proprietor has some fat oysters, or so I am told. Mr. Coombs, will you assist me, sir?" the sheriff asked.

Chapter Fifty

Gideon pronounced me healed, and went on his way, leaving Waba as my only companion. He wasn't much of a conversationalist, but if he grew tired of my laments, he didn't show it. He wagged his tail when I fed him, morning and night. He spent the rest of the day curled up on the floor beside my bed.

The snow painted the world outside of my window a blinding white. Icicles hung from the edge of the roof. The boards of the cabin creaked in frozen protest. Bitter, bone rattling cold arrived with December, but there were few chores to do, and no reason to do them.

"Mother, I need you! I know that now!" I pleaded to the ceiling.

There was no one to blame for my situation. I carved my own destiny. Any self-pity, or accusing fingers pointed at perceived injustices only testified to my weakness. My failures destroyed my friends, and forfeited my family's souls. My hubris in calling on powers I did not understand brought the demons into our lives. My arrogant vision of returning my family to wealth and glory put them in harm's way. Pride is the true root of all evil, placing ourselves before others.

I ate when I remembered to, but I didn't know hunger. Waba's appetite did not waver. At least I was a good friend to him. Sleep was unwelcome, and it devolved into nightmares whenever I dropped my guard. Wakefulness was little better, as idle time allowed the mind to wander, and my mind only crawled through the dark shadowy places, places better left unseen.

"Mother, I need you." Madness waited for me. It was patient in its resolve, ever patient. What a blessing it would be to shed the rigors of reason, to lose my fears? Embrace them with joyous abandon! Insanity slithered near me always, whispering sweet lies in my ear and promising the paradise of redemption, escape.

What held me here? What hope remained? I tried to recall the quote my mother often repeated to me as a child: where there is life, there is hope?

My father shared my dream for our family's future. He never gave up, he fought the good fight, as the bible says. His entire life, despite many set-backs, despite the naysayers, he battled on. I could do no less.

I bathed from a bucket, and ate more jerky than I needed. Waba danced around the cabin, either relieved by my forced mood, or happy for the shared jerky. My stomach growled and fussed, unaccustomed to the hard labors of digestion.

I heard a horse outside.

"Moll? It's Gideon." He rapped at the door. "Moll!"

"I'm coming! I'm coming, Gideon, good gracious, is it that cold outside?"

Gideon rushed inside as I opened the door.

"Moll, what happened between you and Peter?" he asked.

"What? Are the two of you friends? What did he tell you?"

"No, we aren't friends. Peter became a changed man after they cheated on his headrights. He's always angry, and violent. I haven't spoken with him in a while, but he's made you the talk of the colony. He tells anyone who listens that you caused the drought, brought on the sickness, hell, he has them blaming you for everything from bee stings, and sour ale to stillborn pigs!" Gideon said.

"He's telling them I am a witch," I said.

"Yes, Moll, that's it exactly, and it's my fault. I told him what I thought about you, when I was grieving. I…"

"I don't care what they think, Gideon, don't worry about it. Peter was part of the gang who killed Nema and Grey Deer. That makes him a murderer too," I said.

"You don't understand, Moll. They are coming for you."

"Who?"

"The men! Peter's gang, and his new friend from England, a scar faced guy with a limp, about our age, but other men from town too, even the governor has said he will turn his back while they seek their revenge. He says you cast a spell over him when he stopped his carriage in town. His children, Abigail and Betty, took deathly ill upon returning home."

"So James is coming to call," I said to myself.

"Who?"

"When Gideon? How much time do I have?"

"They are coming tonight to run you off. The governor says with no proof of wrong doing, they can't bring you to trial. He told the men they can only chase you away!" Gideon said.

"Kill me, more like," I said. "Thank you Gideon, now go home. I'll not have them catching you here with me."

"Are we even now, Moll?"

"Even? Even for what?"

"For how I treated you, after all you did for Beth? I turned on you. Do you forgive me?"

"No, we aren't even, old friend, I owe you now," I said, and kissed his forehead by way of farewell.

Before Gideon was out of sight, I ran to the barn, and packed up what I needed from my sewing room. It was a few hours before nightfall, so I bowed to the altar, lit candles, and said the prayers to cast a love spell.

"Now I hope we are even, Gideon," I said. "Bless you for your kindness at the end."

I will place this journal on my altar, knowing Zachary will be sure to find it there. I pray he forgives me for the lies of his birth. I will not ask for forgiveness of my failures, or for authoring our family's damnation. Such pure forgiveness cold only come from the divine. If I could make it so, the price would be mine alone to pay. The sound of the men draws near, and I can see the light from the torches flicker through the trees. My time has come.

Zachary, I will be with you always, and I will smile at the sound of your name. I love you, my SON!

Moll Dyer, 12/22/1697

Chapter Fifty-One

Zachary Dyer's postscript:

To fulfill my mother's final request I sit, heavy of heart and dull of wit, to scribble the end of her tale. She felt the story important for our family's future, and I will begin this as she did:

My name is Zachary Dyer, SON of Moll Dyer, and of a father unknown to me, and for that I have no regret! If you read my mother's discourse, you already know more of our family than did I.

I have no means to assure you of the veracity of these happenings of December 22nd in the year of our Lord 1697. Indeed, I ask for your indulgence, as I was much wearied from travel, but I swear on the name of my mother, no hard drink passed my lips that day. I will inscribe here all that I witnessed with my own eyes and ears on that fearful night.

I returned to St. Mary's before my promised time of spring. Chenoa's dreams, Two Bear's thirst for vengeance, and my own concern for Moll hastened my return.

The fire's glare alerted me to the assault on our cabin well before my horse shied from the acrid smell of smoke. I forced him forward, and beheld the terrible sight. Our home in flames while a dozen cowardly and scruffy men milled about at the edge of the clearing. My thoughts centered on Moll, and I tied off my horse, and ran to our creek in the hope she escaped the inferno.

I discovered one small footprint in the mud at the stream's edge. Moll followed Sean's escape route of long ago. I raced along the stream's twists and turns, (amazed it held water after this driest of summers) until I spied a glowing light in the distance. The strange voices I heard sped my progress, and I stumbled through the dark woods.

The light of the moon filtered through thick cloud cover, and barely illuminated Moll. She stood bent over a large flat boulder topped with burning candles and objects I could not identify. Waba crouched at her side. I waited to evaluate the danger, and determine the sources of the other voices I'd heard.

"Forefathers, saints and sinners, peasants and lords, I call upon you now in my hour of need. Come forward and drive away my enemies. Grant me my freedom, and relief from their persecution," Moll said as if in a prayer. She pulled a knife from her sleeve, and before I could respond, blood dripped from her hand into a smoldering bowl.

"See that I am of your blood and call upon your intervention. Heed my call!" she shouted.

A man and a woman stepped from the underbrush, or so I assume. With my own eyes, I can only attest that one moment Moll was alone, and in the next the two stood before her. Waba growled, but dropped to the ground when the man glared at him. He whined, and his body trembled. He appeared unable to move.

I took a step forward, and the man jerked his head toward me, and held up his closed fist. I yelled, but my throat constricted, and no sound escaped my lips.

"There is no part for you to play here tonight, Zachary. Others already interfered to prevent the men from following you, but it will entertain us to allow you to watch," the man said.

"Leave Zachary be!" Moll shouted.

"Would I harm my own son? I am not the parent who disowned him! Zachary, I kept up with you throughout the years. I've wanted to meet you, but Moll always stood in my way, but we will have many chances to chatter later," the man smiled, and again waved his hand toward me.

I tried to run to Moll's aid, but my muscles betrayed me, I could move nothing save my eyes, a conscious, impotent statue of a man.

"We've been waiting for you to call on us again," the woman said to Moll.

"I never called for you, Ladonna, not this time, nor any other! Why do you place yourself in my business?" Moll asked.

"Your mother opened the door to your family, but you are the one who sought forces to bend to your will, for deeds against your own kind. Of course we came to your rescue, and it appears we are the only ones who did so, does it not? Are there others who've heeded your call? We are your guardian demons after all. Is it your wish that we dispose of your attackers?" the man laughed.

"They persecuted us, but I seek no retribution against them, they are only sheep cursed with ignorance. I came to escape them, and I swallowed my pride to ask for the help of my ancestors, not of you!"

The man gazed to his left and right, then behind. He shrugged his shoulders and grinned. "I don't see them, but it matters not. Ancestors, demons, it's all the same when you seek personal profit or harm to others, and here we are."

"Again, I wish them no harm, but despair fills my heart. I offer a barter. Demons love deals, is it not so?"

"What can you offer that shines brighter than what we have already earned?" Syrupy drool dangled from the man's lips.

"By your own admission, I have only called you. I have not set you to task."

"A mere technicality, you called for us, we are here. Indeed, your summons alone bent us to your will," he pointed back toward the cabin. "Without our help, you will die. We did promise you your miserable life."

"Release your hold on Zachary, and I willingly trade my soul for his and his son's."

"We have no need of Zachary now. There has never been a need to claim him as was my right. He mated freely with the Cambion girl. We are not ungrateful for your help, mind you, but what you are asking is to trade your soul for our unborn king?" The man threw back his head in laughter.

"I know you want me, Laris. I see it in your eyes, the glee when you describe the tortures you plan for me."

"Tempting, but it is not enough, the die is cast. You made the summons, forfeit your command or make it known."

Moll lifted her eyes, and sobs racked her body. "Mother, oh mother, I need you. Why have you deserted me?" The baying of the hounds sounded closer, moving towards us now.

"It is getting late, and we do have another appointment," Ladonna said, admiring the top of her fingernails.

Moll dropped her head to the rock, and I strained to hear her words.

"End this now, you defeated me, and took everything from me: my friends, my mother, my son, and now his son too. All of us felt the poisonous sting of your world. Take my life now if you will, and I will barter for my soul with your queen."

"How very human, Moll, to imagine there is yet hope." The man's grin split his face, but it was a smile without mirth, the face of a boy pulling the wings from a butterfly.

The two demons raised their arms toward the full moon, and small cyclones of dark smoke rose from their fingertips, and gained in size as the demons muttered in an unintelligible language.

Three balls of white light formed high in the heavens, and a triple bolt of lightning streaked to the earth, the impact knocking the demons from their feet. Columns of blue light rose from the points of impact. The central pillar assumed a vaguely female shape, then thickened into a beautiful, luminous woman.

"Cathleen Dyer, you are not welcome here," Laris said. "She called upon us, and we answered her call. Your debt is yet unpaid, and she will be ours. I claim my grandson!"

"Mother?" Moll asked.

"Did you conjure these creatures for aid, Moll?" the specter asked.

"I called for you many times, Mother. Why have you only come now?" Moll asked.

"I could not come, my beautiful child, your soul was too dark, and your pride too strong. You had to reach these depths to acknowledge your need for our help." the woman said.

"There was nothing left, and I could not stand alone. I failed the family, the children. I failed everyone."

"Strength cannot stand alone! We only fail when hope dies, even these filthy demons know that, but we were always with you!" The spirit woman turned back to the man. "Laris, you have done enough harm to my family. We will not allow you to do more."

"She called us, Cathleen, you have no power against us!" Ladonna said.

"I didn't address you, demon bitch, but we will see." I could swear I saw flickers of fire flash from Cathleen's eyes as she waved her palms towards the other beams of light, and their human form was also revealed.

"Nema, Beth!" Moll said.

"Sister," said Nema.

"Anam Cara," said the other, and they smiled.

The three women shouted to the heavens "Senoi, Sasenoi, Semangloph, your intercession protects our children from the foul spawn of Lilith. Come now to our aid." Distant thunder rumbled, shaking the ground beneath my feet.

"Apostles of Erin, look now to your children. Patrick, our patron saint, you brought the Lord's word to our shores. Bigid, patron of babies, spiritual mother and heart of us all, in the name of our Father, hear our plea!"

A heavy mist, laced with ribbons of white light, swirled around Laris and Ladonna, distorting their images. Lightning struck the large oak at their backs, splitting it at its fork. Tongues of flame leaked through the fissures of its bark.

The demons crawled to their feet, and shouted "Lilith, demonstrate your power, your glory. This woman and her progeny are yours to claim."

The mist fizzled away from the demons. Sparks popped from their fingers. They clenched their fists, then thrust their open hands forward. Tendrils of red flame shot out from the demons' fingertips, and whipped toward Moll's friends. The vines of fire crackled with energy and united to strike my grandmother's essence. She fell to the ground at Moll's feet. Black smoke curled from her breast.

"Mother!" Moll screamed.

"Sisters!" Grandmother coughed, and black ethereal blood trickled from the corners of her mouth.

The ghosts of the two called Nema and Beth joined hands, and they reached for the hands of their fallen sister.

Grandmother's image drew a deep breath, perhaps from habit, for what need of air has a spirit? With care, she gathered her feet beneath her, and placed one knee on Moll's rock to maintain her balance. She lifted her voice to the heavens.

"We implore the spirits of our ancestors, a persecuted people, a people of sorrows, and acquainted with pain. A millennia of inequity cries out for your vengeance! Seamus, Liam and Anna, hear now our prayer. Conor, Fianna and Regan, attend to the call of your blood!" the three spirits said.

Miniature stars of light fell like snow and circled the combatants. The glow brightened to illuminate the unearthly arena. The demons sank to their knees, and a dusky voice echoed from beneath the earth.

"They are mine by covenant, made before your kind crawled from the slime. Cease your insipid interference!" The voice hissed. Black smoke infused with orange sparks seeped up from the soil and a female shape emerged. Her face was carved from fire, and fingers of flame licked at her hands and shoulders.

The entity threw her fists to her sides. Moll's friends fell back as if struck by an unseen hand. The small stars dimmed to the brightness of candles. They orbited Cathleen's head with a whispering sound. They stopped as one and circled above her head like a crown. My grandmother's ghost crawled to Moll's side.

"We can do no more. The spirits say it is now up to you to end this, only you can save the souls of our progeny," she said.

"Save? I would do anything, but don't you understand? Zachary is marked by this beast. He took Chenoa, a Cambion, as his wife! My grandchild will be Lilith's toy. It is lost, I have destroyed all I love, and opened the gates of hell!"

"Demons lie! They use a thread of truth and weave in a skein of lies. It becomes their truth. There is a way, but the ancestors say the price is yours to pay if you do so willingly."

"Yes, Cathleen, do tell her all about it," Ladonna said. "Don't leave out the part about her loving mother condemning her family for eternity!"

"I opened a door, a door best left closed, but I didn't know the price. I would take this misery from you, but my reparation is yet unpaid, and fully rendered only now, by having to watch yours," Grandmother said, and hung her head.

"What is the price, Mother?"

Grandmother dropped her eyes. "We never know the full price, do we Moll? I know the price will be high, and there will be pain. There will be so much pain, my darling baby girl." A shiny silver tear slipped from her cerebral eyes.

"What is the reward?" Moll's body trembled.

"The soul of your grandchild, and I pray your soul too, eventually. Zachary will be left in peace. The curse will be broken."

"They can yet be saved?" Moll asked, and smiled.

"If the sacrifice is made."

Laris stepped towards Moll's rock, and bent down to her. "Suffering beyond comprehension, pain unknown by man, this I promise! Send them away!" A forked tongue snaked from his lips, and wiggled across his smiling face, and a drop of brown drool fell to Moll's cheek. It sizzled on her flesh, and she wiped it away in agonized disgust.

"The world will be at his feet. Isn't that what your heart truly desires?" Ladonna asked in a seductive voice. Flashes of red light crackled from within the smoke where the queen entity resided.

"I only want my children to be happy, safe. What do I have to do?" Moll asked without pause.

My grandmother's spirit rose, and embraced her daughter. Her form became vapor like, as Beth and Nema joined in the embrace and the four were as one.

In a moment, they separated and Moll stood to her full height. She raised her arms over her head. Blood stained tears flowed in rivulets of terror. She fell to one knee on the rock altar, and I heard the thump of the rock and the crack of her knee from where I stood. She slammed her palm to the rock's surface.

"For Zachary and his child unborn, for my family, and for our world, my life, my soul. Let it be done!" She pulled a fisherman's knife from her dress, and with both hands plunged it deep into her chest. Pulses of blood covered the rock. It hummed and glowed with flashes of blue energy. My scream went unheard.

Lightning flashed in a circle around us. The wind grew to gale strength. Moll's mouth opened in a silent scream. Her arms quivered loosely at her sides.

The two demons and their queen squealed, and the earth cracked open at their feet, and sucked them downward. Please help her, dear Lord, I thought, and the use of my knees returned. I fell forward in prayer, but I was unable to take my eyes away.

Moll's head jerked backwards as if by unseen hands, and I heard a distinct crack. A final scream of horrific pain ripped from her throat, filling the woods with the sound of her unholy anguish. As the echoes abated, Moll also ceased to be. A pulse of white steam surged from her mouth, nose, and eyes. Her white essence was yanked in a mocking circle around her friends, and with a whooshing sound, it followed the demons into the abyss.

The vision of the spirits were gone, but I heard a voice in my mind, my grandmother's voice. "I regret not having known you, my son, but accept this gift for your unborn child." I felt a warm tingle caress my palm and a slight weight in my hand. I glanced down, and realized I was able to move, to speak.

"What will become of Moll?" I asked.

"We will pray for your mother, for such she was. She only sought to keep you from pain. Her suffering will not be eternal, not for one who has sacrificed all for others." I felt a sudden emptiness of spirit, and looked up.

"Grandmother? Are you still here?" I asked, but the woods stood deathly still. I heard the hounds far away, but moving away from me.

I sat beside the rock with Moll, with my mother. I saw the indentations made by her knees and hand in the giant rock, both as distinct as prints in soft clay. I cried unashamedly then, as a child might cry.

When the sun's rays reached the clearing, I wrapped my arms around her and hugged her to me for the last time. I noticed the necklace she always wore, made of horn with carvings of a raven and a crooked arrow. I removed it gently from around her neck, and placed it around my own as a remembrance of her. Her body was unyielding, already frozen from the night air. The knife was gone, as was the blood. Nothing remained to mark her suffering, as I rested my head on her breast.

"I never knew you as my mother, Moll, but a kinder, braver one no boy ever knew." I said aloud. I found Waba's discarded leash in the pocket of Moll's dress. With effort, I managed to drag him away.

The sound of a young boy calling for a lost cow reached my ears, and Waba and I snuck away through the underbrush. In fear over what I had witnessed, and concerned for my safety from the colonists, I left Moll there alone. I imitated the mooing of a cow and waited to ensure the young lad found her.

Chapter Fifty-Two

I left some coin in an envelope at the sheriff's door to ensure Moll was not placed in a pauper's grave. I stood behind a tree during the ceremony, but the funeral was attended by few. No one knew her for the hero she was.

The cabin was a pile of burnt lumber and ashes, and I searched Moll's sewing room for mementos of her. I packed up the herbs, books, and found the pages I now write in, the story she always promised me.

Before leaving Newtowne, I sold the farm and all of our holdings. Christopher and Gideon were eager to help, and they obtained a fair price for us. From what they knew of the new owners, it appeared they were a hard working lot. I can only hope they appreciate the sweat and blood we spilled on those fertile fields.

When I returned to our village, I informed Uncle and Moll's friends of her death, but not the manner of it. I left out everything I saw during that horrid night. I described only the scene at the cabin, and finding Moll frozen. I told Sean of Sarah's return to Hammond's farm. He appeared pleased, relieved of guilt, and even happier to hear of her engagement to Gideon Coombs.

Peter was unable to attend the wedding. One of the organizers of the freemen's days of terror came forward. He withdrew his participation in their mission upon discovering the manner of men enlisted by Peter's hate. His guilt at discovery of the happenings at Moll's cabin drove him to turn on the conspirators. Peter and four other men were brought to justice. The five of them hanged on the first Saturday of May. Nema and Grey Deer were avenged at last.

Chenoa presented me with the grandest news of all. She was with child, and expected him in the early spring. Yes, she convinced me the child was a boy. She saw it in a dream, and of the dream's veracity I had no doubt!

Zachary Moll Dyer (also known as White Deer) greeted his own new world on March 17th, Saint Patrick's Day. Born perfect in every way, save for three scratch marks on the inside of his thigh.

I regret to report that Waba died only months after his mistress. I do not doubt he died of a broken heart. Moll was his mother too.

Years later, I returned to Newtowne. I rode to town dressed in the manner of white men, in the suit Moll had sewn for me in the months before her death. There was a time I needed to roll the pants over at the waist to hold them up. Now I had to squeeze them together to button, but the seams held, every stitch was sewn with love.

Word had come to me that Christopher sold the scraggly leaves Moll gathered from our last year of tobacco, and he held the funds for my return.

I heard Moll's name often spoken around Newtowne. They claim she haunts their community. Parents correct misbehaving children with the admonition that Moll Dyer will get them. Locals claim to have spotted a white clouded, spectral figure in the night floating up and down our stream. This spirit is said to be followed by a faithful white dog.

It saddens me. I do not doubt that her spirit roams this new land, and I am pleased her name is remembered, but the song of her heart is forgotten. None of them know the sacrifice she made for us all!

Life, love, and family- what else is there? Our only responsibility is to do what we think right. We cannot claim sovereignty for anything beyond that. That is what Moll did. I often think of this as my mind travels across the years and the miles to gaze into her loving eyes.

The books Moll left behind that were written in her mother's hands? I double wrapped them in oilcloth, and sealed them away. Uncle cobbled a small box to store them in safely until such time as my family requires their knowledge, a day I pray never comes again.

In the end, perhaps we all got what we wanted. Sean retained his freedom, a freedom unknown in these modern times. Nema rejoined her true love, Grey Deer. I am confident they reside together in paradise. As for me, I found love and family, both through the family history that Moll gifted me with, as well as with my new family among the natives of this land. Moll? Her family's happiness was her own, and our contentment drove all she did. In the end, she discovered she could draw on the strength of others who loved her!

We never gained wealth, not in the usual meaning at least, but we found our heart's desire. Moll's sacrifice would never be in vain. I often feel her standing behind me, her face lit in a smile, at least that's what I tell myself to get through the long winter nights.

I am yet unsure of the testimony of my own eyes and ears in regard to the night of my mother's death. I might easily convince myself it was a dream, but for the solid heft and feel of the very real gift presented to me by my grandmother. My son will wear it always. A thin copper bracelet deeply engraved with the names Senoi, Sasenoi, and Semangloph.

The End

About David W. Thompson

The author is a rare native of Southern Maryland, and grew up with the tales of Moll Dyer. The horrors inflicted upon her, in a colony founded on religious freedom and tolerance, have haunted him since earliest childhood. After his family and cheesecake, reading was his first love, and writing became a natural extension of this "out of body" experience. When he isn't writing, he enjoys time with his family and grandchildren, kayaking (flat water mostly please), fishing, hiking, hunting, wine making, and pursuing his other "creative passion"- woodcarving.

Social Media Links

Facebook:
https://www.facebook.com/davidw.thompson.12382

Facebook:
https://www.facebook.com/AuthorOfParanormal/

Facebook:
https://www.facebook.com/groups/1497191007012726/

Twitter: https://twitter.com/Thompson_DavidW

Acknowledgements

Special thanks to so many St. Mary's County, Md. families. They've shared their own family's tales and oral traditions about the life and times of Moll Dyer. Your stories have been inspiring.